YALGAAR

The 1659 Event That
Changed Hindustan's
Destiny

ARNOLD BOLEMAN

INDIA · SINGAPORE · MALAYSIA

Notion Press Media Pvt Ltd

No. 50, Chettiyar Agaram Main Road,
Vanagaram, Chennai, Tamil Nadu – 600 095

First Published by Notion Press 2021
Copyright © Amit Bole 2021
All Rights Reserved.

ISBN 978-1-63940-315-8

Yalgaar

16th century Farsi word for attack

'The Mohammedan Conquest of India is probably the bloodiest story in history. It is a discouraging tale, for its evident moral is that civilization is a precarious thing, whose delicate complex of order and liberty, culture and peace may at any time be overthrown by barbarians invading from without or multiplying within.'

— *Will Durant*

Contents

Chapter 1

Village Pali, 1659

The scream rent the cloudless blue sky.

Even birdsong had fallen silent under the hammer blow of the Deccan sun. Both men were stripped down to their threadbare cotton *dhotars*, worn tight around the thighs. The thin material was soaked through with the sweat of their exertions. The cloth had once been white, but years of ceaseless wear in the mineral-rich earth had stained the garments a perpetual ochre. The plow stopped in mid furrow from slowly breaking up the cruel, red earth.

Hiroji let go of the plow handle, and reflexively threw himself to the side to throw off a potential bowman's aim. These things were baked into muscle memory from years of combat.

Ramaji dived reflexively in the other direction, and in four long strides reached the embankment of the tiny field. He scooped up the spears and his *khadag* sword and tossed one spear to Hiroji even as they both hurdled the low thorn bushes that bordered the field.

Sensing release, Sarja thankfully lumbered away into the shade of a huge mango tree that formed one corner of the plot. He dipped his nose gratefully into the water running through the moat beneath, oblivious to the drama that was playing out around him.

"Hiroji, steady..."

Not yet twenty, Hiroji, was already the veteran of a hundred fights. He had learned to fight almost as soon as he had learned to work the plough. He stood five feet eight inches tall and weighed a hundred and fifty pounds, all of which was bone, muscle and determination. Working the obstinate soil in the hopes of rain, and the ceaseless weapons practice had built up the large muscles of his upper body. He could lift a boulder equal to his own weight over his head and throw it a distance of a few man-lengths. Or he could methodically and ceaselessly wield two *danpattas*, the gauntleted flexible double-edged sword of the Marathi warriors, one in each hand, for as long as needed, creating a meat grinder ten feet wide, through which nothing could pass through alive.

Panting with the sudden dash and the adrenaline, the two men slid to a stop behind a thicket of copper pod trees and looked at their little hut which lay at a little over a few hundred feet across neatly tended fields.

'Where the fuck, did they come from?'

The three men were Abyssinian *habshis*, as was evident from their ebony skin and short, wiry hair. Two held down a young girl of barely sixteen, while the third was rocking between her spread legs. The one in front of her was bleeding from a cut to the neck that had drenched the front of his shirt. A short, curved dagger nicknamed the 'scorpion' or *bichwa* lay to one side. Even at this distance, they could see the blade was tinged with blood. The second man knelt on her right wrist keeping it immobile while the third held her onto her left arm.

'Hiroji!' cautioned the father, putting a restraining hand on the other man's arm.

It took probably a second to take this all in, and the next couple of seconds for father and son to plan their attack.

The girl had been out gathering firewood and had been ambushed. Even in these circumstances, she was fighting with all she had, struggling to get free, cursing and spitting on the men around her.

Charging the men was out of the question. There was a short, recurved bow hung from each pommel on the four horses that the men had ground-hitched to a low cactus a few feet from them. One man could have been charged but charging three bowmen from a hundred feet was inviting certain death.

Ramaji pointed to a fold in the ground that curved away to the right following a natural crack in the earth's crust. It ended in a thick copse of wild *jaswand* shrubbery about thirty feet from where the girl lay. The girl was Savitri, Hiroji's wife. The *habshis* had relaxed their caution thinking the area unprotected, so the father son duo picked up the pace. Even so, by the time they had worked their way to the thicket, the first man had finished and had moved to her left side.

Exactly two minutes had passed since Ramaji had thrown aside the handle of the plow.

The two men had worked together ever since Hiroji was old enough to wield a blade, and no words were necessary. The girl's struggles were slowly but surely ebbing away as the horror of the act sunk in. Ramaji pointed to the man who was taking his place in front of the girl and touched his chest briefly. With that signal, the two men burst out of the thicket in a blur of dark, sinewy muscle. By the time the party realized the new presence, the two men had covered half the distance with four long strides and were fifteen feet away. Self-absorption gave way to shock, followed by terror on the three sweating faces grouped around the girl.

The Marathi spear, or *bhaala* was a simple weapon. While the cavalry spear was over seven feet long, the infantry variant was five feet of a seasoned *sagwan* wood staff tipped with a fluted iron point. For close quarters fighting, the move was to stab, retract, and move away, all in one smooth motion. The best places to stab were usually the neck or the face, or the lower abdomen, or kidneys, where a couple of inches of iron could put an opponent out of action. A skilled operator could level five men in under half a minute. The cavalry routine led any assault, whether on infantry or enemy cavalry by making each spear count in the first contact itself. Another variant that had come into use by the infantry was a *vita*. A slender coir rope of about twenty feet was coiled around the haft of the spear. When the spear was thrown, the rope played out and was then used to retract the weapon back to the soldier to be used again. And again.

However, none of these options were possible without risking a stray hit on the girl.

Hiroji used the momentum of his rush, to launch himself at the man kneeled to Savitri's right, aiming the spear head at a point two inches below, and roughly an inch in front of the man's right armpit. In one smooth motion, he felt the satisfying crunch of the tip entering between the two ribs, and traveling directly onwards, destroying his right lung and bursting his heart before lodging against the ribs on the left side. The man was instantly dead, and Hiroji's momentum cannoned him into the spent man who had recently taken post at her left side.

Ramaji, meanwhile with great economy of movement, had timed his lunge perfectly, to take out the man recently at Savitri's front. His man had been looking forward and Ramaji's spear took the man in his ear and crunched in, before Ramaji allowed his forward motion to wrench the man's head around and take him beyond and two feet away from the third Siddi, who had been knocked off his feet by Hiroji's tackle.

Savitri's gasps suddenly took on an urgency, but the danger was not past. If there were four horses, where was the fourth man? Ramaji's spear was stuck in the head of the first man, and in a much-practiced move, he transferred his sword to his right hand.

Only about five seconds had passed since the men burst from cover, and the blood was hot and heavy behind Hiroji's eyes. His muscles were jumping and twitching with the rush of adrenaline. The third *habshi* had already drawn his wickedly-curved *jambiya* dagger, perhaps to threaten the girl, and he kicked back away from Hiroji's cannonball lunge. The physical prowess of his tribe was legendary, and Hiroji rolled away to stay out of the range of the eight-inch blade the man brandished. The man crouched with the dagger held out in his right hand, the tip tracing small tight circles. His left forearm was covered with a thick leather guard, held out to ward off a strike. Hiroji put one calloused foot on the stomach of his impaled victim, and pulled out his spear, accompanied by a breaking of bone and eruption of blood, and approached the man from the side opposite to Ramaji. The *habshi's* eyes bulged with terror. The irises of his eyes were yellow white with a fine tracery of red veins and stood out starkly in his ebony face. There was a deep gash on his neck that had just missed his jugular, but the cotton shirt underneath his leather jerkin was soaked through with blood. His huge chest rose and fell with his labored breathing as the three turned and counter turned to seek an opening. Realizing that an eight-inch dagger was no match for two men who had dispatched two of his comrades in a heartbeat, the *habshi* finally hawked and spat something yellow and slimy at his feet and threw down his dagger.

His wound had begun to congeal. The front of shirt was open, and the dark skin of his chest was covered with tight black peppercorn curls. The light in his eyes became cunning as he sought how best to save his life.

'Do you know who I serve?' gasping, through labored breaths..

'Where is your fourth man?' rasped Ramaji, chest heaving more with battle lust than exertion. *'Fath Khan'*. Fath Khan was the ruler of the imposing fort of Janjira, set on an island a few hundred feet off the coast from Murud and about twenty-five miles away from the men's village. He was a *Siddi* warlord, and self-styled king of the Abyssinian natives who had marauded along the western coast for generations. The *Siddis* were Muslims who had answered the clarion call to Islam broadcast by the Muslim rulers of Hindustan. The land had become a magnet for Turks, Arabs, Uzbeks, Pathans, Abyssinian or for that matter, Muslims of any shade to seek fame and fortune through Sultan-sponsored rape and pillage.

Fath Khan's ancestors had taken the island of Janjira by treachery a few hundred years ago. Since time immemorial, the rock had always been ruled by clans of *koli* fisherfolk. Over hundreds of years, people had built simple wooden fortifications; nobody knew exactly when. Since then, generations had defended successive attacks by the Arabs and the *Siddis* marauding across the seas from Arabia and Africa. The smooth, vertical sides and vicious currents around the island played an equal part in the defense.

The Hindu flag of the *koli* fishermen was replaced by the crescent. The *Siddis* then converted the island to a fort, by building walls six feet thick of black basalt, on the periphery of the already steep rocks to a height of almost sixty feet from sea level making it near impregnable. A small township came up in the depression created in the center of the island that had resulted from the mining of the rock. They purchased cannons from the English and Dutch trading companies, and now controlled all shipping along the Western coast. Any vessel plying the shallow waters had to buy a certificate of passage or risk forfeiture of vessel and cargo.

They aligned with whichever power suited their immediate needs, be it the Mughals to the north, or the Portuguese to the south, in the shifting sands of politics. What was constant was the tribute they offered to the Sultans in the form of grain, gold, and baskets of Hindu heads. Their banner was a red silk rectangle with the crescent and star in the lower right corner.

Surprised at still being alive, the man's confidence was returning.

'Let me go. I'll grant you your lives... We never expected the old hag to put up a fight. She ambushed our fourth man...' he panted through shallow breaths, warily watching the two men.

Hearing these words, Ramaji went still. In the next instant an explosive grunt, and his blade cleaved through the man's leggings an inch below his left knee and almost completely severed the leg, till all that was left was the tendon. The man's expression changed from a creeping tentative relief, to surprise, shock, and agony. The meaty *thunk* of the stroke was quickly overtaken by the man's almost animal shriek. The blood sprayed out of the stump in time with each pulse of his heart as he buckled and fell on his behind.

Ramaji's heaving chest and stomach were covered with the ruby wash spraying out of the stump with thick drops clinging to the line of hair that arrowed down his stomach. Ignoring the man's cries of pain and outrage, he took one step to the left and repeated the same procedure with the man's right leg. The *habshi* was now propped up, only on his hands, watching the systematic ruin of his body. Without missing a beat, Ramaji effected a lateral blow and took off the man's left hand, neatly at the forearm. Cratered on his side by now, and watching his lifeblood pump out with each heartbeat, the man malevolently mouthed curses, with spittle showering out with each epithet.

'Motherfuckers, idol worshippers… *kafirs*…'

Ramaji calmly walked around the man's back, all the while followed by his baleful right eye, his turban having slipped over his left, and carefully, and ceremoniously raised his sword again. The man with a superhuman effort tucked his palm under his back, but Ramaji deflected the blade in mid swing, and angled the cut to take off his arm a few inches below the shoulder.

Hiroji suddenly realized that Ramaji had dealt the man the Marathi sentence for rape. *Chaudanda* had been established by the small, nascent Hindu kingdom of Shivaji Bhosle, roughly to the south of their territory. He had set the precedent almost fourteen years back.

The headman or *patil* of a village in his small kingdom had behaved inappropriately towards a defenseless widow in the village of Ranjhe. When the man was captured and brought trussed, in front of Shivaji, the lad was just fifteen years of age. Babaji Bhikaji Gujar had first blustered and then pleaded for mercy. When his offence was proven by witnesses, Shivaji had ordered all four limbs to be axed off.

However, when the man's cousin had stepped up bravely and asked whether the king had thought through who would care for the paraplegic after his sentence, Shivaji had also bestowed an annuity to take care of the criminal, and publicly admired the man's courage in speaking up. The people had been quick to realize what they were seeing was something out of the ordinary. Something was unfolding that they had not seen in three hundred years of Islamic torment.

Squatting by the ruin of the man, Ramaji proceeded to wipe his blade clean on the front of the man's leggings.

'You'll be skinned alive for this?' sputtered the *habshi* with only about a minute or two left to live. Ramaji smiled thinly without interrupting his cleaning and nodded in mock sympathy.

The killing lust was on Hiroji, and he picked up the fallen *jambiya* and slid the first inch between the man's teeth, levering his mouth open. He had very white teeth. He twisted the blade, breaking off a few teeth, reached in with his two rough fingers, grasped his tongue, yanking it out, and neatly hacked off the first three inches. Stepping back, he threw the bloody piece in his lap. 'Now you can plead our case to Fath Khan when you meet him in hell'.

'And this is for my Savitri'. With that, he held the blade up in front of his now wavering eyes, slipped the tip below his chin searching for the soft flesh underneath, and drove upward in one smooth movement, driving the blade through the roof of his mouth into his brain. Hiroji looked intently into his eyes till they glazed over, and… the killing haze was gone as quickly as it had come.

Then Hiroji turned to Savitri. She was struggling to cover herself with the remnants of her threadbare *sari*. He gently cradled her head in his lap and brushed her hair out of her eyes. Savitri was always fastidious about her personal appearance despite hardship and poverty. It was only then that he saw the wound in her side. The loamy soil underneath her was black with her blood.

'No! For God's sake, no!' He tore off a piece of her sari and pushed it against the open lips of the wound.

'I will get help, just hold on,' looking to Ramaji, beseeching him for help. He had some basic battlefield medical skills, most soldiers did, but they both knew this was beyond their capability – perhaps even beyond the reach of the village doctor *vaidya*.

Savitri's eyelids were fluttering now, and her breath was gasping out through her tortured body.

'It is for the best, Hiroji… I could never live with this shame…' she gasped.

'There is no shame Savitri...' he said stroking her forehead.

But mixed with the pain on his young wife's face was also anger.

She spat the words at him. 'And what use is your strength if you cannot protect the women in this land? Are you blind? Have you lost all pride as men that you serve these foreign swine? Leave me now... let me sit at *Draupadi's* table in the hereafter... promise me!' came in whispers from her broken mouth.

'I promise... darling, but please, save your breath while I seek help...'

She smiled then, a small, tired smile, and with that her breath rattled, and she closed her eyes once and for all.

***

There was no time to grieve. Hiroji picked up the lifeless form of Savitri and hurried after his father towards their little hut.

The simple thatched door lay off its hinges, and the inside looked like a whirlwind had erupted and strewn the meager belongings all over the place. The hut was a single room, with an earthen fireplace in the corner where the women cooked the meals. Vitha, Ramaji's wife, and Hiroji's mother lay sprawled next to the beginnings of the simple meal that she had probably been engaged in. Her neck had a deep gash, but the fourth man lay about five feet from her with the curved beak of her ten inch *koytaa* sticking out of the side of his head. She had used that heavy curved blade to crack open coconuts all her life. This time around the blade had claimed a bloodier harvest. The fourth man had obviously not expected the older woman to fight back and must have been looking away, when her blow had sliced off his ear, before cleaving into the side of his head, slicing down to the vertebrae of his neck. It was a ghastly wound and had probably killed the man almost instantly.

Both women had fought to the very bitter end. Ramaji on seeing Vitha dropped his sword and sank to his knees, holding the lifeless hand of his wife. It was the first and last time in Hiroji's life that he saw his father break down and sob like a small child.

Chapter 2

Village Kari – fortified Jedhe estate

Kanhoji Jedhe was a worried man. He was responsible for the lives of over three thousand fighting men, and he worried that he had just signed over their death warrants with the Sultan Adil Shah; at least that's what his wife of thirty years kept reminding him at every opportunity. She alone had the temerity to upbraid him though, that was always in private.

At well over forty years of age, he was slowing down. He had lived by the sword ever since he had avenged the murder of his parents at the age of eleven. His own uncles had tried to take his birthright away. His nurse had sacrificed her own tiny son, by replacing him in the crib, when the murderer's launched an attack at the dead of night. His father had died with his sword in his hand, defending the family *waadaa* or fortified estate from this treachery, while their faithful retainer, Dev Mahala had spirited away the infant Kanhoji to safety.

Their family had been the *deshmukhs* or headmen, entitled to the revenue of a few villages in this remote part of the Hirdas Maaval area. His village was perched on the shoulders of the Sahyadri mountain range, surrounded by dense evergreen forest. Only the tribesmen knew the hidden paths through the dense thorny thickets and rocky defiles. The few passes, that allowed travelers to cross the mountain range, were natural ambush sites for his hardy hill warriors.

The evening meals were done. It had been a simple repast. *Bhaakri*, unleavened millet bread eaten with a vegetable gravy. Raw sliced onion and dry coconut garlic red chili mix *thechaa* on the side, followed by two tumblers of buttermilk. Kanhoji sat on the broad teak platform suspended from the roof by thick brass links, idly using his right leg to rock the swing gently back and forth. In his right hand he used a brass pincer to slice the cured betel nut for his post-dinner betel leaf *vida*. He smeared lime on the tender leaf, with the rough pad of his index finger, and added the betel nut shavings, expertly wrapping the leaf into a fragrant parcel. As he tucked the parcel into his cheek, a sigh escaped him. Life was hard, but stable. What was this madness that had gotten into him at this advanced age?

'*Baba*, what ails you?' That would be Baji, his eldest, and most favorite son. In a sense, he was the one who most resembled him. He had the same height, and breadth across the shoulders. Ever since he was a child, Baji had insisted on riding his own horse, and had taken to the saddle naturally. Unlike the horses of the Mughal north, the horses of the Deccan were a smaller, but hardier breed. They were as sure-footed as goats on the mountainous terrain and could not be beaten for sheer stamina and bloody mindedness. In short, the animals were amazingly like the men, and women, who rode them.

Baji climbed the three stone steps to the level of the main house and sat near his father's feet at the foot of the swing. He wore a simple cotton tunic and leggings. The thick wrists and the way the tunic bulged at the arms and across his chest attested to hours of daily practice with the sword, *patta*, and spear, in addition to regular wrestling practice in the communal *akhaada or* wrestling pit, used by the village men.

Kanhoji ruffled his son's hair and grinned at him. There were very few people in front of whom he relaxed his normal stony face, and Baji was one of them. Seeing the naked admiration in his son's eyes filled the father's heart with love.

'The lad always had vision..' They both knew who was being referred to. After almost thirty years of lending his sword arm to some Sultan or another, as well as the three thousand *shiledar* cavalry he led, Kanhoji had embarked in an entirely new direction. Kanhoji employed only *shiledar*. Men who owned their own horses and weapons who were paid a monthly salary.

Shivaji Bhosle was the second son of the great Shahaji, a warrior, administrator, scholar and war strategist. In addition to his personal bravery, it was said that Shahaji could speak seven Hindustani languages besides several dialects. He had caught the attention of Malik Ambar, vizier of the Nizam Shah, and quickly rose up the ranks to be Malik's right-hand man. His personal bravery in battle and keen battle sense had been rewarded by a landholding *jagir* yielding nearly two million *hon* yearly. The art of guerilla warfare spawned by Malik had been perfected by Shahaji Bhosle.

Circumstances had led to Shahaji establishing a second base in Bengaluru, several thousand miles away from his jagir at Junnar. He ruled like a veritable king there, with his own colors, flags, and seal, though under the vassalage of the Adil Shahi Sultanate. He had shrewdly distributed his family by sending his first wife Jijabai and his second son Shivaji to govern their landholding in Pune, far away from the Sultanate capital of Bijapur. He kept his first-born son Sambhaji with him at Bengaluru and groomed him himself. Sambhaji was Jijabai's oldest living child and elder brother to Shivaji who the young boy adored and admired. He had subtly decided the question of inheritance as well in this fashion. Sambhaji was tu   ng out to be the spitting image of Shahaji, in all the manly qualiti   e father exhibited. Shahaji lso had other wives and another son Vyankoji from his wife Tukabai as well as bastards from local concubines.

With Jijabai and Shivaji however, he had with acute foresight sent a quartet of competent ministers and administrators. It was a de-facto cabinet in waiting for when Shivaji would strike for independence. Shyamraj Nilkanth Ranzhekar as chancellor, Balkrishna Hanumante as accounts general, Sonaji Pant as secretary and Raghunath Ballal Korde as paymaster. These four were rounded off by Dadaji Kondev Gochivde, the commandant of the fort of Kondana, who was the boy's tutor and mentor.

There was something different about the boy. Like all other boys of the time, he had been schooled early in the use of the *patta*, sword, spear, jambiya and other assorted arms. From a very early age, he excelled in archery. Wrestling, riding and generally tramping around the Sahyadri mountains had built strength, stamina, and a keen self-reliance. His mother's views had entered his soul and resulted in a robust democratic outlook. Though successor to a *vatan* landholding, Shivaji's band of companions ranged across the social rainbow of the region, comprising kunbi, kayastha prabhu, brahmin, ramoshi, mahar, bhandari, koli, and several other tribes that made up the social mosaic of the region. His tutor Dadaji Kondev also, no doubt, had a large part to play in the boy's egalitarian outlook. In addition to the ancient Sanskrit syntax and grammar, science, and logic, Shivaji was also thrilled with the adventures from the ancient *Ramayana* and *Mahabharata* epics.

But what had hooked Kanhoji was the boy's demeanor and sense of destiny. He had rallied people to his flag under the war cry of *Hindvi Swarajya!* A Hindu independence from the foreign rulers!

'Father, tell me once again how Shivaji-*raje* enlisted your help in this struggle!' entreated Baji, already referring to Shivaji as king. He had heard the story a hundred times before, but never tired of its retelling.

Kanhoji humored him as much as to shore his own feelings. His gaze went to a distant place as he remembered and recounted the events of that dark night many years ago.

'It was midnight at the old Shiv temple at the foot of fort Shivneri. You know the one. The road there is through thick jungle, infested with panthers, leopards and bears. That area used to house a notorious set of dacoits, but the old Brahmin Kondev cleared them out soon enough,' mused Kanhoji.

He paused to spit out a red betel-juice stream into a brass spittoon kept by the side before continuing. His gaze had automatically turned inwards, and Baji thrilled to the familiar, yet awe-inspiring story.

'I had been invited to the Shiv temple alone at the stroke of midnight. Not knowing what to expect, I carried a hidden *bichva* dagger in addition to my sword and jambiya.'

'I left my horse tethered at the approach to the overgrown path leading to the temple with my personal guard and proceeded alone as instructed. The moon had just risen, and the world was all black and silver. I loosened my sword in its scabbard, and walked on, careful about snakes or other wild creatures underfoot. The night was alive with sounds and I could faintly hear the hysterical babbling of a tribe of hyenas, signaling the remains of a fresh kill in the area.'

'A cloud passed over the moon, and I stopped to let my eyes adjust to the sudden darkness. My sixth sense warned me I was not alone. Barely had my sight returned than I noticed two *Ramoshis* had materialized out of the trees on either side of the path. I have thrilled to face a thousand Pathans and ridden into their charge, but at that second, my heart lurched and the next thing I knew, my sword was in my right hand with the jambiya in my left!'

'Then what stopped your sword hand, father?' asked Baji, thrilling to the story though he could probably recite it in his sleep.

'They were a sight! Dark as the night with flowing mustaches covering most of their faces. Rough woolen headgear and the armless woolen vest their tribe wears, cinched in at the waist. Tightly wrapped knee length dhotars and the traditional thick silver band around their left ankle. Each held a battle axe at the ready position! And they quickly stepped to either side of me so that I would have to fight on two opposite fronts on that hemmed-in path.'

'Do you know where the word *Ramoshi* comes from?'

'Yes, father. It is derived from *Rama* and *vansh* which literally means they are descendants of Lord Rama'

'Good!' smiled Kanhoji.

'Learning is as important if not more than weapons-training. I'm glad to see your tutor's fees are being put to good use,' and Kanhoji resumed the tale after this slight detour.

'I was debating whether to attack the right-hand man and push beyond him into the forest to gain a temporary respite, when suddenly the man lowered his axe, and transferring it to his left hand, bowed respectfully. He saluted me with the usual *muzra*, raising and lowering his right hand, palm up, from the ground to his temple thrice. After a pause, the man on the left did the same.'

'The *Raje* awaits you at the temple,' was all he said.

'Thankfully, I had been recognized. I sheathed my weapons and continued along the path. I looked to neither left nor right, but I could feel an itch starting in the small of my back, half expecting a spear or axe blade.'

'Presently the path opened out to a small clearing at the center of which was a small stone temple. From the stone *nandi* or bullock, which was Shiva's ride, set right at the top of the three worn stone steps, I guessed this temple was dedicated to the Great Destroyer.'

'The entire edifice was constructed in the black basalt of our region, and the classical simplicity of the structure took my breath away. The top of the simple structure was surmounted by a stone dome, ending in a *kalash*. I automatically touched the cold stone of the *nandi* with my right hand and brought the fingers up to touch the center of my chest, paying obeisance to Shiva's ride, companion and first line of defense and entered the sanctorum.'

'*Om namah Shivaya!* I pay obeisance to you Lord Shiva,' came unbidden to the man's lips.

'What did you see next, father?' from a rapt Baji.

'The room was around twenty feet by twenty feet and lit with torch *mashaals*, made of dried brush soaked with oil and tied to wooden stakes inserted into brackets on the walls.'

'The soft yellow flickering light illuminated a strange set of fellows! There was Tanaji Malusare! Bhimaji Wagh! Hiroji Farzand! Partially hidden by a pillar I spotted Suryaji and several other warriors. There was Raghunath Ballal Korde, who stood out because of his slightly more refined manner.' 'All in all, the gathering was strange because there was no method to tribe or social hierarchy. It was a wide spectrum of our society as far as I could see.'

'You should know by now how I choose the men I hire,' and Baji nodded

'I grade them by weapons skill, horsemanship, and whether they will abide by my iron discipline. The men tend to fall into a few familiar patterns, but this was a motley crew!'

'Korde nodded to me and indicated with a sweep of the hand that I should approach the group. I acknowledged him with a quick gesture and moved forward. Only then did I see Shivaji, at whose invitation I was here. He had knelt in front of the shrine of the mother-goddess, Bhavani, set into an alcove in the wall, directly in front of the *Shivalinga*. The column of smooth black stone was positioned right in the center of the room, underneath the domed ceiling. The stone moat around the tower was dry, as no offerings to the deity had yet been made.'

'*Jagdamb, jagdamb,*' came from Shivaji's lips as he touched his forehead to the cool stone of the alcove. Having recited the *stotra*, he straightened and only then turned to look at me.'

'Tell me, what was your first impression of Shivaji *raje?*' pleaded Baji. However many time this tale was recited, it still made the hair stand on the nape of Kanhoji's neck and it had a similar electrifying effect on the son.

'You have to remember I had known him since he was a boy. I had seen him grow from a mischievous child to a responsible, moral and caring man. His father, Shahaji had entrusted part of his rearing to me, but this was a side of him I had never seen. He could have lived a life of luxury. His father's *jagir* grossed him over 2 million *hons* per year. Had he wished, he could have spent his entire life eating, drinking and womanizing, sending his *shiledars* to fight for whichever Sultan paid the highest.'

'Instead, he had embarked on a dangerous, and potentially fatal journey. He had taken the fort of Torna from Mohammed Adil Shah without virtually a fight and was slowly but surely expanding his hold on the countryside. Veteran soldiers who should know better were charmed by the lad's guts.'

Kanhoji paused as a memory from almost ten years ago came to him.

'Remember these Sultans merely tolerate us. If any of us looks to become too powerful, they act swiftly to cut the person down to size.'

Baji looked a question and Kanhoji replied, 'When the great Vijaynagar empire was destroyed, it threw confusion into their vassal states, like Madurai, Thanjavur and Srirangapattan. It was Shahaji who proved a unifying force and covert support to these states, else the Sultans would have picked them off one by one. Mohammed Adil Shah never forgot how Shahaji thwarted his plans despite being nominally his vassal.'

'The Bijapur Sultanate had decided to teach this Bhosle family a lesson once and for all. Mohammed Adil Shah used the excuse of Shivaji's rebellion to do three things at once. He dispatched Farhad Khan with five thousand cavalry against Sambhaji, Shahaji's elder son. He also sent Fateh Khan with ten thousand cavalry against Shivaji, and at the same time tricked Shahaji and had him imprisoned.'

'Shivaji was only eighteen when this existential threat to his immediate family and kingdom was thrust at him. Bigger, more experienced warriors would have crumbled, but not this boy,' said Kanhoji in wonderment.

'He realized that his fledgling army of about fifteen hundred or so was no match for Fateh's force. Also, he could not allow the enemy into the kingdom. The usual trend of loot, rape and pillage would ensue and the people's faith that this kingdom would protect them was still too fragile.'

'Fateh Khan had meanwhile. already taken Supe and Shirwal, as well as the tiny fort of Subhanmangal.'

'Shivaji decided to take advantage of the Sultanate's unchallenged record of victory and prod the beast into making a tactical error. First, he chose the fort of Purandar, which really lay outside of his kingdom, to act as the theater of war. Somehow, he touched the dormant pride of the old fort commander and wonder of wonders, the man threw open the doors of the fort to Shivaji!' chortled Kanhoji.

'Shivaji knew he could never withstand a prolonged siege of Purandar either, so the only way was to get Fateh Khan to attack the fort with all his strength.'

'In an act of supreme personal bravery, he led a commando raid with two hundred cavalry at the dead of night on Fateh Khan's encampment himself!' and Kanhoji's spine tingled with the calculated bravado of the gambit.

In the next instant his face suffused with pride at another memory. 'And you proved that the Jedhe blood ran through your veins during the same battle!'

'The two hundred cavalries cut through the outer periphery and made straight for Fateh Khan's tent at the center of the encampment. The plan was to do as much destruction as possible and retreat to Purandar with the enemy in pursuit.'

'But things never go exactly as planned, do they?' remarked Kanhoji rhetorically.

The men, mad with blood lust and thirsting for revenge, plunged on and broke formation. It was in one such individual knot of skirmish that the Marathi colors fell to the slowly awakening defense. The cavalryman carrying the colors was run through and the flag fell into the enemy's hands. Immediately a chorus of '*Allahu Akbar!*' rose at this unexpected development. The awakening troops saw hope, and the outcome hung in a delicate balance.

It was at that point that a young Baji Jedhe, barely sixteen years of age, sensing the precarity of the situation mounted a sole attack on the knot of enemy cavalry that had taken control of the flag. His attack was swift and deadly in its ferocity and single-mindedness. He charged the enemy cavalry with a sword in either hand, controlling his horse with the reins held between his teeth.

He made straight for the saffron swallow-tailed *zaripatka* banner, slicing through the knot of riders guarding the man who had just started to celebrate the capture. Baji's mountain pony shouldered the larger Arabian horse the man was on, throwing him off balance. In a delicate choreography, Baji dropped the sword in his left hand, sliced off the enemy trooper's right hand at the shoulder with the sword in his right, and caught the falling flag in his left as it dropped across his own horse's neck. He kicked his heels in and turned his scrappy pony around charging back through the opening he'd created a few minutes ago while the enemy scrambled to cut him off. The wheel of fortune had made two round trips in less than a few minutes.

The Marathi force wheeled away with only ten fallen and made for fort Purandar at a gallop. Meanwhile, Fateh Khan incensed at this insult to the Sultanate, rallied his troops and set out in hot pursuit.

The small Marathi band entered the fort and the gates were slammed shut. They didn't have to wait long.

About an hour later the entire Sultanate force arrived baying for blood. Cries of '*Allahu Akbar!*' rent the air as the entire mass stormed the fort. Discipline was forgotten. All the attackers wanted was to put the impudent Marathi force to the sword. Strangely, Purandar was silent. Only the usual number of sentries could be seen atop the bastions. Emboldened by the lack of response, the Sultanate force swarmed up with renewed vigor.

And suddenly there was one plaintive wail of the *tutaari* war horn. The sound is a staccato high-pitched keening wail that ignites fire in the Marathi mind like nothing else. Immediately the *naubat* war drums crashed and it seemed like the forces of hell were let loose on the Bijapur force.

Arrows, some muskets, boiling oil, but above all a hailstorm of deadly stones enveloped the attackers. The Marathi force were all farmers and most could hit a bird on the wing with their deadly *gophan* slingshot when it came time to guard crops heavy with millet and amaranth. For them, it was child's play to pick out a human head at that distance.

Shivaji let the slaughter continue for a full thirty minutes till he sensed that Fateh Khan realizing his mistake was calling for a withdrawal to reset the battle.

At that point, the gates of the fort were opened and he unleashed his cavalry on the battered foe. The veteran Baji Pasalkar, almost sixty years of age, Kanhoji Jedhe's father-in-law, headed the merciless charge that erupted from the fort. The onslaught was so ferocious and determined that the Sultanate line completely broke. The Marathi force rode down the panicked men slicing, smashing till the rout was complete.

Fateh Khan who had been observing from the rear, sensing the battle was lost, turned tail, and ran with his personal guard following him.

This was the first victory that a self-proclaimed Hindu kingdom had seen in Hindustan over the Sultans since the collapse of the great Vijayanagar empire, almost a hundred years earlier.

Shivajiraje had himself honored the fifteen-year-old Baji with a gold bracelet and the title of '*Sarjerao*' or lion along with several others who had distinguished themselves in the battle.

Kanhoji resumed his story as a painful memory creased his face. 'Your grandfather, the crusty Baji Pasalkar, for whom you're named, died with his sword in his hand at that skirmish.' Both men said a silent prayer, that the great man's soul, find *moksha* or release from the endless cycle of birth and rebirth.

'It was only a matter of time before *Badi begum*, wife of Mohammed Adil Shah, took serious note and ordered an even larger force to crush the *kafir* uprising.'

'But back to that fateful meeting.

My first impression of him, was of intelligence. There was a twinkle in his eye as he greeted me in typical fashion, by embracing me thrice, with his own head once to the left, then to the right, and back to the left of mine.'

'The second impression, was one of physical vitality. His complexion is fairer than average, perhaps because his mother, Jijau saheb is extremely fair. I casually clasped his arms when we embraced, and I touched hard muscle there as well. He is of average height, and I topped him by a few inches. He wears unusual headgear, a conical silken *jiretop*, adorned with a simple string of pearls, but other than that, no foppish ornamentation. He effects a clipped beard, I suspect to lend a certain gravitas, at his tender age.'

'How old was *Raje* at the time?' again from Baji.

'I will stop my story if you keep disturbing my train of thought!' chastened Kanhoji in mock anger, once again ruffling his hair.

'The third thing that struck me was, that he held every man present there, in the palm of his hand. When he embraced me, every sword in the room was loosened in its scabbard in case I had treachery in my heart. This was not simple obedience, this was devotion in the eyes of everyone from the youngest Ramoshi stripling, with barely the beginnings of a mustache, to the venerable Korde himself!'

'Kanhoji, you honor us all with your presence, said Shivaji, with a slight bow of his head.'

'This is a gathering of the damned, Kanhoji!' he said with more than a touch of irony.

'Every man here, has vowed to fight, for a Hindu homeland or die trying! The Gods themselves demand this homeland!'

'Our temples lie desecrated; our lives and property are forfeit to these Sultans. Our very religion and existence lie at their mercy while we fight among ourselves for scraps off their table!! What use is this life if not to right this wrong? Will you join me, us, in this fight Kanhoji? We cannot do it alone. His eyes glowed like embers in that dim torchlight and he seemed to grow in aura right before my eyes. I am not a credulous fool, you know that. In that instant, I felt as though all my life had been leading up to that moment…'

'The *Raje's* voice had increased in volume and intensity, and his eyes flamed with emotion. A murmur passed through the gathering and these warriors stood a little straighter and gnarled hands dropped unaware to the hilts of their swords.'

'He had me then, son. It had been more than three hundred years since the majestic kingdom of the Yadavs had fallen and had been stripped piecemeal of all its wealth and glory. It was documented that it took three months to carry the loot away from Devgiri by elephant and bullock.

The old king, cowardly to the end, had even given the crown princess, Jeshtapalli, lovingly called Jethai by the people, to the Afghan invader in an ill-advised effort of pacification.'

At the recounting of this distant shame, Kanhoji's anger flared bright in his eyes and he had to take a moment to get his speech under control.

'The son, Shankardev had fallen valiantly in battle trying to take back the kingdom his father had lost. By then though, Alauddin Khilji had called for troops from the north and built up a large army at Devgiri.

The son-in-law Harpaldev had risen up in revolt as well, but it was his misfortune to be taken prisoner. Khilji had had him skinned alive with heated pincers like an overripe tomato and the blood red mass suspended from the ramparts of our own Devgiri fort, for carrion birds to peck out his pleading eyes, while he screamed in pain and terror.

The populace watched in abject terror as the cries died away and the body was finally dropped for stray dogs to feed on, denying him even a simple cremation. '

Kanhoji shuddered with loathing and disgust. 'I have killed scores of men in my time, but never understood this butchery. What is it about the people of this religion that pushes them to this level of depravity?' he asked rhetorically.

'Here was a young man, who had made it his life's mission, to fight back against centuries of Islamic oppression. What use is this life boy, if not to serve God and to preserve dignity and religion?'

'I made up my mind right then! I saluted him with the *muzra*, and the gathering roared in approval!'

'He embraced me again, and then turned to the priest who sidled up to him. The priest looked threadbare, and as old as the temple itself' and Kanhoji smiled at the old memory.

'It is time for the *abhishek* offering, lord. Will you do the honors? lisped the old priest in a thin, quavering voice,' offering up a small pot of milk for the ceremony.

'Of course, said the *Raje*, but this will be a special *abhishek*. With that he moved to the center of the room and the Shivalinga.'

'*Jagadamb, jagadamb,*' came unbidden to his lips as he invoked the family patron goddess, before a silent '*Om namah shivay…*' to the Shivalinga in the temple.'

'With an ease and economy of motion, he slipped the dagger from his waistband, and sliced open his left palm! His eyes closed as he recited the *shiv strotra* incantation under his breath. We all stood transfixed as the lips of the wound peeled open and the first ruby drops came forth, quickly running down his palm to drip onto the Shivalinga, in an *abhishek* of his own blood!'

'For once, the priest was shocked out of his usual chatter. What a sight that was! The *Raje* stood like a proud statue, with the blood from his palm, dripping onto the black basalt of the Shivalinga and pooling with the dried milk from earlier offerings, before flowing out through the stone channel at the base of the structure.'

'The moment was electric. No one quite knew what to do. Tanhaji roused himself first, like a huge shaggy bear. His thick handlebar mustaches quivered with emotion, and with his own '*Om namay shivay!*' he slashed his palm adding to the offering. Soon each warrior there was adding his own lifeblood to the stream.'

'I am not ashamed to say, my son, that tears rolled down my cheeks as I gave over myself to the cause that day.'

'It was at that moment that our Swarajya, or Hindu independent homeland was born and I was privileged to have been there at that moment!'

Chapter 3

Village Pali

'Just as a person sheds worn garments,

Does a soul shed the earthly body.

Water cannot wet, wind cannot dry,

Fire cannot burn, arrow cannot pierce,

Was never born, and therefore, can never die,

The soul ever is and returns to the godhead…'

The funeral rites from the timeless *Bhagvad Gita,* the song of God, washed over, offering scant comfort. The old Brahmin administered the final rites for Savitri and Vitha in a frenzy of haste. Ramaji and his son had spent the evening gathering wood for the pyres, which now blazed, aided by the clarified butter added to the dry kindling. Hiroji twinged at the memory of the pride the women had harbored at the quality of *ghee* butter they routinely made from the milk produced by their single cow. The village people had wisely stayed away, knowing that retribution was sure to come, and the priest had been induced, only when Ramaji threatened to cut off his ear, threat of excommunication notwithstanding, if he did not administer the final rites.

Presently, the fires burned down. Hiroji sent a silent prayer to Vishnu, the Preserver, that their souls be granted *moksha* and be released from the endless cycle of death and rebirth. The priest departed, having received his *dakshina,* gratuity in the form of the single *hon* coin that Ramaji had paid for his services.

Finally, the enormity of what had happened sunk in. The four soldiers would be missed and the *jagirdar,* whose contingent these Janjira *siddis* had accompanied would doubtless send out a patrol to check on their whereabouts. Either fear, gold or both would finally point the finger and then they would be hunted down like the periodic culling of the jackals. The only difference was that their deaths would not come quick...

Pali fell under the control of the Adil Shahi Sultanate of Bijapur. It was rumored that Mohammed Adil Shah was ill and increasingly, decisions were being made by his first wife, the Badi Sahiba. Taking control of the instability, Fath Khan had probably asked his men to align with a local lieutenant and their party had stumbled across the simple hut.

Savitri's dying remark irked like a *babli* thorn. The entire region south of the river Tapi and north of the river Koyna, had known no other reality than rule by the Sultans for generations. The ancient *Yadav* kingdom of Devgiri, which had always been a bulwark against invasions from the Muslim north, had finally fallen to Alauddin Khilji over 300 years ago. Corrupt officials had substituted stocks of grain for salt and the fort had been unable to withstand the siege. The fort had capitulated and what followed was three centuries of utter darkness. Since then, the land, grain, livestock, wealth and women had been at the mercy of one Sultan or another and the men had been reduced to selling their fighting abilities to the highest bidder, often against their own. It was rumored that the slave markets of Arabia as well as Kabul and Kandahar were awash with men, women and children from Hindustan, to the extent that prices had crashed.

The last Hindu kingdom that lay to the south, the mighty Vijayanagar empire had been decimated a hundred years ago, when the Sultans finally put aside their bickering and came together in the name of Islam to defeat the only Hindu kingdom in their way. When the geriatric king Alia Rama Raya of the Vijayanagar Empire had surrendered, the Nizam Shah, who had 'observed' the battle from the rear had stepped up and decapitated the old man. He had gifted the head to Adil Shah, who had had the skull artfully cored of brain, blood, flesh and tissue by a colony of ants, and then installed it in Bijapur so that the sewage from the city flowed out of the open mouth.

How could then he, Hiroji, a simple farmer-soldier staunch this tide?

The men made their way to their hut and meager belongings, knowing they had probably only a few days to leave the village. The little plot was tilled for the *patil* so there was nothing to lose. In a last farewell, Hiroji hugged Sarja and stroked his neck, sobbing uncontrollably while the old bull regarded him gravely with his large, liquid, heavily eye-lashed eyes. Sarja and he had practically grown up together since the day Ramaji had bought the skinny little calf home.

Ramaji gifted both him and the cow to a distant relative in the village along with their goat and few chickens. There was never any money and the single *hon* they possessed had paid for the funeral rites for the women. The only possessions of value were the weapons, which they packed carefully.

Ramaji had purchased his sword from a master armorer and sword maker from the detritus of the shattered Vijayanagar empire in exchange for a season's share of millet. It was a beautiful weapon. There was no ornamentation other than some words in their strange tongue inscribed on the blade. The pommel, tang and hilt were simply worked and complemented the three-foot double-sided blade. It was Hiroji's job to keep both sides razor sharp; with any lapse quickly earning a cuff on the ear.

In addition, each had a spear and wooden shields, banded across with strips of iron. The family treasure though was the *danpatta*, belonging to an ancestor, which had been presented to him for bravery by Malik Amber himself.

The weapon was lovingly cared for. The grip was inside an iron gauntlet that encased the hand and extended to the elbow. The arm was inserted into the iron shell, past a floating cross-piece which pressed against the inside forearm, to grip an iron bar, attached transversely lower down in the gauntlet. Attached to the metal gauntlet was thirty-eight inches of springy steel blade. The overall effect was to create an extension of the arm encased and protected in a steel sheath from elbow to fist ending in a double-sided razor-sharp blade.

The *danpatta* was the Marathi calling card, and the reason why the Sultans were willing to pay a premium for their services. Hiroji had made a name for himself when at the age of fourteen, he had held a pass for a critical hour against Turkish regulars sent by the Mughals against the Sultanate of Bijapur. At that time, he had been hired by the *Deshmukh* from the Hirdas Maaval, Krishnaji Bandal, who maintained five thousand cavalries for the Adil Shah. Hiroji, was young, foolish, and reckless, and armed with two *danpattas* he had stopped repeated assaults in that tight bottleneck allowing the rest of his colleagues to slip away before he too melted away into the surrounding forest. The repeated clockwise and counter-clockwise *pavitre* or plays traced within a grid of six by ten feet, had presented the enemy with a wall of razor-sharp steel against which their repeated assaults broke down.

Where could the men go? They had no fixed employer in the constantly shifting sands of the politics of the region. When the harvesting was done, the men of the region sold their sword arms to whoever paid most and left home to fight other men's wars till the planting season arrived again. The cycle repeated endlessly as it had for generations.

The only alternative was to seek employment with Shivaji *raje*. The entire region had heard the name of Kanhoji Jedhe, a prominent *deshmukh* chieftain from the twelve Maaval cantons. He nominally maintained a force of three thousand cavalry for the Bijapur Sultan, but who it was rumored had recently decided to throw in his lot with Shivaji, and who would welcome two more men into the fold.

'The Siddi will send men east expecting us to travel hard for the mountain passes to reach the Pune jagir' remarked Ramaji slowly mixing lime and the rough tobacco in his left palm with the stubby thumb of his right hand.

'The party will soon learn what happened and press east trying to catch us before we reach the badlands.'

The Sahyadri mountain range ran north to south, about fifteen miles, to the east of their village. The range was thickly forested and riven by numerous gorges and valleys and whole armies could lose themselves in that dense, thickly forested region.

'Why don't we travel west towards the sea, and the Siddi himself?' Hiroji remarked. 'Nobody will expect that, and we'll try to get a fisherman to take us down the coast to Rajapur or Dabhol.'

Ramaji chuckled, before carefully inserting the plug of tobacco into the side of his jaw, 'So, you did get some of your mother's smarts then.'

The women had prepared a heap of millet flatbread *bhakhris*. Hiroji loved the purple millet flour, especially when his mother served the piping hot flatbread straight from the griddle, over which she ladled a dollop of freshly churned butter. His eyes watered, thinking of the many times he had driven her to mock frustration, especially when returning from the wrestling *akhaada* pit, she'd complain he was eating the household out of home and hearth…

Ramaji took down the bundle from an alcove in the mud wall set high enough to keep the food safe from vermin, while at the same time keeping it cool, and distributed two each.

The men were seated cross legged on the simple but clean, floor that the women smoothed over with cow dung daily and let dry to maintain a smooth, cool surface. Hiroji took a white onion from the braid hung from the rafters and putting it on his brass plate, crushed it with one blow of the heel of his hand. Giving half to his father, the men helped themselves to a few green chilies and salt to eat the bhakri with.

Presently the simple repast was done, and they drank from the well and packed to leave. Each man carried a small bundle with millet flour, salt, dried red chilies and a few utensils. To that, they'd added the almonds and raisins, taken from the men they'd slain. Muslim soldiers were always better provisioned and their saddlebags were the first to be picked over after a raid.

Their shields were strapped to their backs with the leather thongs that normally went over the left forearm, and the spears and swords were carefully wrapped in an old sari. The nine yards of material completely encased the weapons and made sure there was no sound of metal on metal when the bundle was hefted onto Hiroji's head. He increased the heft by adding a sizable number of dried branches and twigs and tied the bundle carefully with twine. Finally, the men donned loose tunics over their dhotars to hide the shields and smeared their foreheads with horizontal stripes of ash taken from the hearth. To add to the disguise, Ramaji took a pair of *chiplya*, or castanets, while Hiroji took the *zhanz* or small brass cymbals with which to keep the beat while singing the Lord's praises.

To any casual observer, the men now looked like two *warkaris*, or seasonal pilgrims on a holy journey, relying on the charity of strangers to feed them as they went their way. Since they planned to travel westward, anyone questioning them would be told they were making an annual pilgrimage to Mumbadevi, the patron saint of the coastal *koli*, or fisherman community.

***

The men had set out once the village had bedded down after dark and made good progress west. Four hours of steady travel had seen the moon cross the sky and the false dawn tinge the east. Hiroji balanced the bundle of weapons on his head, with an ease born of practice, carrying loads of firewood from the forest, and Ramaji set off with a ground-eating trot. The men could lope for hours at this rate, eating up the ground while still prepared to burst into action at any threat. Nature had adjusted the physiology of the men of the Sahyadris, such that their heart rate was lower than the inhabitants of the plains, allowing them to scale these peaks with an ease that was the envy of others. The plan was to reach the small fishing village of Revdanda, where they figured they could pay a fisherman, to ferry them down the coast.

The men rested after four hours of the steady trot for a drink of water at the village well of a nondescript group of thatched dwellings.

Presently, the false dawn broke and the small huts along the way began to come alive, with roosters self-importantly announcing the start of a new day. The sun came up behind the mountains, and the first rays burned the cold off their backs. Ramaji stopped and Hiroji dropped the bundle to the ground in relief.

Both faced the rising sun and cupping their hands, joined them in prayer and turned to look at the ascendant newborn orange disc.

'O creator of all things,

Who, though Brahman, manifests to us as the sun

Allow me to meditate on your infinite brilliance

To further myself on my journey to enlightenment...'

The ancient Gayatri prayer calmed as always. Each soul had come from Brahman and to Brahman would return in the fullness of time. But on this earthly plane, Hiroji still had one important mission. He had to avenge Savitri.

The family had not always been poor. One ancestor had fought alongside the last Yadav king at the great battle of Devgiri in 1297. The entire continent, south of the Narmada, had been plunged into misery when that great Hindu kingdom fell, to the Afghan invader, Alauddin Khilji.

For three hundred and fifty years, the five Sultanates that came after had raped, pillaged and stolen the wealth of the people. Thousands of temples were destroyed or converted into mosques. Libraries were burned. People were forcibly converted to Islam at the whim of petty functionaries. If they resisted, they were butchered to set an example to others. Just recently, the Mohammed Adil Shah, on the occasion of his birthday, had ten thousand Hindus forcibly converted to Islam.

These were stories that were whispered when people gathered in the recesses of their homes, or in temples. In this feral climate, even a modicum of protest invited an inevitable and cruel death. Every boy was told the story of the king's son-in-law, Harpal Dev.

The manner of Harpal Dev's death was to show the population, 'Here, this is what we can do to your prince, imagine what we could do to you…'

Khilji had decreed that any Muslim could order any Hindu to open his mouth to be used as a spittoon. To protest was to face instant execution.

The people had fought and fought again. Entire clans had been decimated. The weak had converted to Islam. The strong had chosen either resistance or death. Generations had gone by and it was only the innate understanding of scriptures, that the body was but a temporary abode for the soul, that kept the people going.

Khilji's chronicler had noted three peculiarities of the people east of the Sindhu River. They were truthful to a fault. They were unafraid of death. And they were proud of the wisdom of their civilization, to the point that it bordered on arrogance.

Ramaji's ancestors had moved into the recesses of the Sahyadris, away from the hustle and bustle of the plains to eke out a simple and solitary existence, venturing out only on mercenary duties to augment the meager crops the poor soil provided. It was as though even God had turned his back on the populace. The poor soil and meager rainfall would not support wheat or rice, so people got by in small, tucked away mountain plots growing the hardy jowar, bajri or rajgira.

The great philosopher-saint Ramdas anguished,

'The Sultans have destroyed all that was ever good,

The populace has neither shelter, succor nor food,

Tell me, Lord Rama, where do we go?

But in the very next breath, his martial spirit emerged in his writing

Struggle, struggle to the very end,

Sway, evade, strike and never bend,

God to you will the strength lend,

As you light the fire of rebellion…

Savitri's last words had tormented Hiroji every single moment since that fateful day. Was it even possible to rid the land of the Sultans? To even think that was madness! The Nizam Shahi, Barid Shahi, Qutb Shahi and Adil Shahi, could between them field a combined army of over three hundred thousand men, with cannon, modern matchlock muskets, mobile camel guns, war elephants, cavalry, and all the material necessary to sustain a campaign of several years.

His thoughts were interrupted rudely by the sudden clatter of hooves, and a low warning whistle from Ramaji. A party of ten horsemen had been lying in wait in a little copse of trees beyond the road and they swung smartly to block the way when they saw the travelers approach.

Seeing *warkaris*, the leader visibly relaxed. He was a huge man, dark as coal, and sat on a superb gelding that clearly showed Arab bloodlines. He carried the sickle sword of the Abyssinian Muslims strapped to a broad leather belt at his waist. He was dressed in baggy pantaloons and a loose cotton shift. Resting his left hand on the hilt at his waist, he leaned from the saddle, and directed a stream of brown tobacco juice at a spot a foot away from Ramaji's legs. The drops spattered Ramaji's calves, but he gave no visible reaction and continued to click the *chiplya* while soundlessly moving his lips as though in a private trance.

'*Ram, ram*, son! Where are you from and which illustrious lineage do you belong to?' asked Ramaji in a calm greeting.

The warrior did not reply, looking first at one, then the other, noting the sinewy builds and dust-caked legs. The cogs in his mind were moving, but half his party were Hindu soldiers, as could be seen from their dress and the vermillion *tila* mark on their foreheads, and he did not want to risk upsetting them by wrongly torturing these mendicant-holy men.

'I am Karim, son-in-law of the Siddi,' emanated from somewhere deep within his chest.

'Where are you headed, old man?'

'We are making a pilgrimage to Mumbadevi, lord,' replied Ramaji quietly.

At the mention of the goddess, the Siddi once again spat in the dirt, before hooking his finger into the angle of his jaw and expelling the spent wad of tobacco. Busying himself with preparing the next batch, he asked,

'Did your paths cross with two men, roughly of your two ages making haste for the mountains? Think before replying old man, or I will cut off your penis and feed it to the jackals tonight.' The last few words were slurred on account of the huge plug of tobacco the man inserted by the side of his gum.

'No sir and I would never dream of lying to an important man such as yourself,' murmured Ramaji, with downcast eyes, a near perfect picture of complete humility.

The rest of the bunch had lost interest by then and several horses had dropped their heads to crop the grass by the side of the path.

'Get going, before I change my mind, and hang you for a bit of excitement,' said Karim digging his heels in to get his horse going back in the direction of the trees.

The men wasted no more time, grinning like simple fools and hurrying through the narrow gap the horsemen had created. Just as they were through, Karim shouted,

'Baji' get your lazy *kafir* ass over to those two and check their belongings before letting them through..' to a soldier in his group.

Baji hastened to comply. He dismounted in one fluid motion and walked his horse over. The men saw a lean, tough boy, with a mustache barely flowering on his upper lip. The vermillion stood proud on his forehead over clear brown eyes, strong with intelligence. He wore a simple tunic of rough cotton, cinched at the waist, with leggings of the same material tucked neatly around his calves. A sword was tucked at his left hip, and his feet were shod in thick leather *chadhav*.

As he came up to Hiroji first, his look was quizzical, as though he could not understand why a young man had chosen the ascetic path. Hiroji had lain down the bundle, and slowly but surreptitiously was rotating his neck and shoulders to limber up. If it came to a fight. The position was near hopeless, as all the weapons were in the bundle. Nevertheless, it was better to die fighting than the alternative.

He motioned for Hiroji to stand aside and started patting down the side of his rough tunic to check for weapons. Ramaji had angled away to one side, seemingly disinterested in the whole situation. Both knew he could explode into action at any second, and lend direction to the fight, as had been established in countless other situations. Ramaji considered all possible approaches and quickly decided the best way would be to hold onto the spears and back away from the path to try and find broken ground. The spears were their only hope of keeping the horsemen at a distance unless one of the riders had a bow, in which case they were lost. Ramaji appeared to stand idle, but he'd already transferred his weight to his right leg waiting for Hiroji to initiate so he could push off his right leg and reach his son's side in a quick lunge and grab a spear.

Baji's fingertips patted down the shoulders and his eyes widened slightly as he felt the bulging deltoids, and then widened ever more when he touched the edge of the shield strapped to the back.

Hiroji was a second away from effecting a palm strike to the man's throat when Baji's fingers moved away without reaction. He was turned away from the rest of his group so only the two men saw the minutest shake of his head. He schooled his expression and continued patting Hiroji down after which he made a cursory inspection of the bundle before turning to Ramaji. A knowing look passed between Ramaji and his son. Time stood still, as both men waited to react depending on which direction her fickle mind took.

'Just dirt-poor farmers on their pilgrimage, sir,' retorted Baji leading his horse back to the group.

Karim waved the men away, instantly losing interest and turned his attention back to the direction in which the track wended.

It took an iron will to move away at a sedate pace. Hiroji's shoulder blades twitched, feeling the eyes of the men, fully expecting a spear to find the small of his back at any instant.

'I know... He suspected we were the men they're after, and yet he let us go,' in a whisper, when the men had turned the corner.

'Did you know him? Or his family?'

Ramaji shook his head, and resumed his trot, taking his time before replying 'It's not as though we've taken it lying down for the last three hundred years. There have been countless uprisings, but they share one thing. They all failed. Hope is a dangerous thing. And Shivaji is giving hope to the people. We are beginning to dream.'

In his mind's eye, Hiroji pictured a guttering flame, struggling to survive, in the midst of mighty crosscurrents of air.

The sun had climbed to its zenith, and the heat came off the surroundings in a white glare. As the men neared the coast, the land became greener. The surrounding fields had been furrowed to plant rice once the rains started. Every living thing conserved energy in this heat though, and all was still. Life in this coastal strip depended on the monsoon clouds that once a year came in off the sea and battered themselves into oblivion against the crags of the Sahyadris, unloading their beneficence to the area below, so that rice, barley, millet could grow.

The men passed a small village – barely ten huts. Nobody was around, the men probably out with the cattle to find grazing, the women probably in the cool of the huts. The age-old tradition of the land had been to welcome any and all travelers with a drink of the left-over water from cooking rice, collected from every home. The liquid was sometimes but not always sweetened with palm jaggery. The starch provided an instant boost to weary travelers. The welcome was in the spirit of *'atithi devo bhava'* equating a guest tantamount to God. Alas, those days were gone.

Women dared not come out in the open because of the fear of the marauding Muslims. It was rumored that in the north of this ancient land, the Hindus had switched the timing of marriage ceremonies to the dead of night. The Muslim nobles had discovered a new pastime. Where better to find an abundance of Hindu women including the bride in one place than a wedding.

The tiny village ended at the communal well. The men dropped down in the shade of the red *chira* stone of the breastworks. The water smelled of moss and a deeply unpalatable fishy odor. The rains would freshen the land and fill these wells with sweet water, but that was still a month away. After slaking their thirst, the men found a large mango tree, and finished the last of their *bhakris*.

The men knew they'd need to travel during the night, so they rested under that magnificent mango, the shade underneath which was almost black in comparison to the white heat of the afternoon.

One man kept watch while the other slept, and presently they set out again when the sun had started its slow descent towards the far horizon. They knew the coast was at hand when the heat was tempered by the cool winds off the western *Sindhu sagar* sea. The air was spiced with the tang of salt and drying fish, and their pace quickened in anticipation of the first glimpse of the sparkling expanse.

The road bent left to head south, in the direction of the Portuguese settlements around Mumbadevi, but the men chose a simple cattle trail that veered off in the direction of the small fishing village of Shirgaon. The surface gave way to drifts of sand and the smell of drying fish became stronger. The path turned, upon itself in a gradual descent to the shore and as the path rounded a big basalt boulder, the gigantic, jaw-dropping, majestic expanse of the sun-dappled blue of the ocean extending to the far horizon came into view.

On the other side of that body of water lay *Aravasthan* or 'Land of the horses', once a thriving Hindu kingdom, peopled by the *Smritic* tribes. *Smriti*, means interpretation or commentary on the ancient Vedic texts. Those people, lying on one extremity of the Hindu cultural expanse, had probably evolved their own variant or *smriti*, of the mother religion thousands of years ago. Hiroji yearned to travel and see those lands.

'Good God!' exploded Ramaji, and Hiroji's contemplation of the red orb of the sun, sinking into the sea, was rudely interrupted. He looked in the direction in which Ramaji pointed.

To the north and almost lost against the brown background of the meandering coast but turning into a natural cove fed by a largish creek was an Arab dhow. It was only because the men were at an elevation had they seen it. The people of Shirgaon were probably blissfully unaware of its presence. A thought flashed through Ramaji's mind; careless of the village to not post a lookout on the plateau above the beach, especially when the monsoon was only a month away. Once the rains hit, the seas would become deadly and all seafaring would stop for a couple of months.

It could only mean one thing – Arab slave traders! They were laying off the coast, waiting to strike after nightfall.

The men gave up all attempts at safety and raced down the simple track to the village. The sight of two *warkaris* running towards the village caused not a little alarm. A young man saw the pair and raced to intercept them after yelling out an alarm. He was disoriented at the sight of the two mendicants rushing down but he had still unsheathed the short, heavy, wickedly-curved *para* at his waist.

The men slid down the incline and tumbled to a running stop and Ramaji raised both palms outwards in a gesture of peace. 'Arab slavers!!!' he panted.

'Gather your women folk immediately! A raid is coming!!' he gasped out between breaths.

By now, a small group had raced to the aid of the first man, similarly armed. Surprisingly, there were women among this group too. As sinewy and lean as the men, they too carried the large *koyta* blades, that normally gutted fish, but which could as easily take off a human head, or slice open a stomach. The way they wore their saris was different as well. The fabric was very tightly wrapped allowing extreme agility of movement, whether for work or battle. These women would not be going down without a fight any time soon!

The villagers were mostly *kolis* and *bhandaris*, making their living from the sea. The men were all uniformly burnt black by the sun. Each man wore only a *langot* or codpiece, with a short wooden holster at the waist to hook the hilt of the para. Their upper bodies were massively muscled, no doubt from the effort of rowing their seagoing canoes and each right hand held a para blade.

Both men had by now been forced to their knees by the crowd and Ramaji squeezed out between labored breaths, 'I am Ramaji, and this is my son, Hiroji. We are fleeing after our home was destroyed… We mean you no offense. We just wanted to warn you that we saw an Arab trader anchored off your coast…'

A short, bull of a man shouldered to the front. From the way the other made way, the men sensed he was of importance.

'I am Shankar, the patil of this village'. He stood only a few inches over five feet, but his short bowlegs supported a barrel chest and huge shoulders and arms. Part of his ear was missing, no doubt from some ancient sword strike, and there was a deep scar running from navel to the edge of his ribcage. His chest and skull were covered in tight peppercorn curls, running to white. He was the only person of the group who had still not unsheathed his weapon.

'How big was the boat, was it a gharib? How far away is he docked?' he asked after coolly assessing the two men.

'It was single masted, so I would say they have not more than ten men on their raiding party,' gasped Hiroji.

Shirgaon was a tiny affair, with about twenty huts clustered around a natural small cove. About fifteen *machwe* fishing boats were pulled up above the high water mark and were festooned with rope nets. To one side, there were simple wooden frames built of driftwood on which were hung fish set to dry; *bombil, bangdaa,* and salted shrimp laid out on coir mats on the ground to dry.

'Gather your belongings and take the women to the hill,' shouted Shankar and the men dissolved in a flurry of activity.

'Baba – I am tired of running from these people. Why don't we make a stand? There are ten of us. Let us show them that Shirgaon is not to be trifled with..'. These words were uttered by a mere boy. He was not yet fourteen and a mustache was just starting to appear on his upper lip.

'You are a young fool, Ram!' chided Shankar, but not without a hint of pride.

'He is my grandson, my girl's boy. Both his parents were lost to the raiders a few years ago. He burns for vengeance with the anger of the young'.

'Ram, say we prevent this attempt, what then? They'll just come back with more people.'

'Ram has a point,' said Hiroji, despite a sharp look from Ramaji.

'If they find the village empty, they will burn your huts and trash the small fields to the side that I see are heavy with millet and vegetable.' Hiroji was already untying the bundle of sticks and laying out their weapons.

The villagers looked on with ever-increasing surprise as the two 'ascetics' hastily strapped on their swords, and hefted their spears, finally looking like the farmer-soldiers they were.

'I head a platoon of ten men with the rank of *havaldar* when the harvesting is done and it is time to fight,' said Ramaji, by way of explanation. Upon this revelation the mood of the crowd changed.

'Will you fight alongside us?' asked Ram with hope visible in his eyes.

Ramaji spat on the ground before answering, 'It appears we must pay for the foolishness of our young ones. My son spoke in haste, but his word is binding on me. Will you do as I say? Only on that condition will I put my son's life and mine in danger.'

'Also, by some miracle if we do succeed in thwarting the raid, will you help us find passage down the coast in one of your crafts?'

'Done,' said Shankar. 'You have a *koli's* word.'

The women and children hurriedly gathered their meager belongings and set out in a convoy, up the path to the plateau, that the two travelers had recently descended. They would bisect the path at the top and continue into the foothills of the Sahyadri mountains, in the maze of broken rock, trees and shrubs, which would swallow them whole.

That left ten males in the village, ranging in age from twelve to sixty. Of these, only Shankar and two other men had actual battle experience, albeit as foot soldiers. The group hunkered down in a circle in the center of the village while Ramaji laid out his plan.

'The raiding party will split into three. They will station two men on the boat, one man to hold the horses at the rear, while the main force circles the village.'

'The raiding party will ride down the coast to about half a *kos* away, leave the horses and approach in a wide ring on foot from the landward side of the village. That way they will ensure all the escape routes out of the village are blocked.'

'Bhimaji, I want you to set out immediately and travel landwards to the boat,' said Ramaji addressing a fifty-something grizzled man.

'Wait till the raiding party departs and are out of earshot. Then take out the men on the boat. When, and only when, you hear the fight break out at the village, set the boat on fire, and make your way back. That way, even if we perish in the fight, there will be no way for the party to transport anyone back to sea.'

'*Ho ji!*' affirmed Bhimaji, one of the men with prior experience. He set out in a long loping trot to find the boat and was lost in the foliage and fading light in about twenty paces.

'Ram, I want you to take a vantage point in the small copse of trees that abut the main road that lies above the path to the village. Once you see the main force leave their horses, you need to circle around and kill the man holding the horses. Remember this is not a fair *dharmayuddha* fight. These people do not abide by our ancient code, or any code for that matter, because they consider all non-believers as sub-human species anyway. There is no need to challenge anyone to a fair fight. Approach from behind and use your para to strike at the neck or slip between the ribs into the heart.

Once you've done that, send us a signal. What bird songs do you know, son?'

'I'll imitate the *hola* warble; these motherfuckers won't know that the hola never warbles at night,' suggested Ram with evident pleasure in his quick thinking. Ramaji nodded appreciation.

'Only when you hear the fight start in the village will you then take all the horses to where the women are hidden or return to the village depending on what happens. Do you understand?'

Ram visibly swelled up with pride on the unique honor done him. The old hands, of course, realized that Ramaji had purposely given him the easiest job of all, to shield him from the main brunt of the fighting.

After Bhimaji and Ram left, there remained eight fighting men. By now the light had faded. A huge fire was lit in the middle of the village *chowk* clearing.

The group ate a hurried dinner of rice and dried fish curry which was the staple food of these villagers. The final touches to the plan were decided over the susurration of blades systematically being ground over whetstones by each man in the group.

Ramaji's sword drew admiring glances from Shankar. The blade was indigenous *wootz* steel, and the weapon had been crafted by Arunachalam, the famous swordsmith from the once majestic city of Hampi. As Ramaji drew the whetstone across the blade, the firelight threw into sharp relief the alternating wavy patterns of blue and black, that rippled across the blade like spilt ink.

As the full moon slowly rose, each man chose a hiding spot in a rough semicircle drawn around the village, about ten steps into the dense vegetation that began after the cleared area where the village ended. The plan was to allow the enemy to filter through their net and into the village before beginning the attack. Each choose a thicket, or low tree to hide in awaiting the signal to attack. It was decided that Ramaji would herald the start with a war cry and only then were the men to fall upon their picked-out targets. The men settled down to wait, the experienced ones with the stoic patience of infantry anywhere, careful not to look at the fire to keep their night-vision intact.

Hiroji chose a thicket of *kewda* bushes after carefully checking that nothing slithered underfoot. The kewda served a dual purpose. Both the thorns as well as the belief that cobras preferred to nest at its base, would deter any approach towards the hiding place.

This fight was going to be at close quarters. Hiroji laid his sword across his lap and settled down to wait. For some people, patience was difficult, but he had a hunter's skill. He had learned to lay for hours, in wait for prey, barely moving a muscle or even an audible breath. Eventually the forest closed around him again and assimilated this foreigner into its presence. His breathing slowed, till he was conscious of each metronomic individual heartbeat as he dropped into the inert, waiting state. The small night songs started up again and the village looked the picture of peace and quiet, with the small fire in the central clearing, slowly subsiding into red, glowing coals.

Chapter 4

Shirgaon beach

Bhimaji threw a coir net over his shoulders and set out briskly along the beach. The sea was to his left and the surf broke in a white foamy line that was barely visible in the gloom. The sound of the waves and the salty air did not bring him the usual pleasure today.

He heard horses, but they were inland. No doubt he was being watched, but to all intents he looked like a fisherman making his way home. These jackals preyed on the defenseless, using treachery and deceit to first eliminate any opposition.

The moon rose, and Bhimaji turned inland, as though to head for some predestined village. He could feel unseen eyes on him but knew that they would lose interest as soon as they thought he was moving inland and away.

Once he reached the shrub line, he carefully laid the coir net at the base of a *suru* tree to lighten his load. The net would be retrieved later, but now he had to move fast and rely on his *para* blade, tucked into the waistband of his loincloth. He climbed steadily inward in a huge semicircle, paralleling the coast. The shore lay serene in front of him, but he could not spot any craft, large or small, anchored in the shallows. A small creek washed into the sea a little further on.

Bhimaji intercepted the creek after about fifteen minutes of steady climbing. At this point he had two options. One was to ford the creek and continue, or the second, to swim down the creek. Though it was possible the raiders had dragged the boat inshore and hidden it, that would make a quick getaway that much harder, so Bhimaji chose the latter option.

Kolis going about their chores do not normally carry swords, so all Bhimaji carried in the way of weaponry was his *para*, which was ten inches of a heavy broad blade, with the business end curving sharply inwards. The grip was fashioned out of the rough wood of the coconut tree. Normally, the curved tip is used to break a coconut's thick outer husk while a flick of the wrist can peel the rough outer layers as one would of a banana. Today the humble *para* would have to do more bloody work.

The water was warm, and Bhimaji waded in till it closed over his head. The creek was about thirty feet broad with lush vegetation sloping down to the water's edge. There was a good current, and Bhimaji used the push of the water to float down the channel with only his head tilted back above the water, careful to make no noise. The smell of decaying vegetation from either bank washed over him

The night was peaceful, and the chittering of birds indicated his presence had not been discovered by the creatures of the forest. Bhimaji used the natural buoyancy of the mixed salt and sweet water to float downstream on his back with his body at a forty-five-degree angle under the surface. The creek twisted and turned and presently, Bhimaji could make out a sandbank starting to appear on his left. From memory, he knew this was the place where during low tide, fish were caught in small pools, and the children of the village had easy pickings of the *jitade*, and other small, trapped fish. He slowed his pace in the water and hugged the left bank, sniffing the air like a hunting dog.

He smelled them before he saw them. The smell of dried fish, and shit wafted momentarily, and was gone again, but as he crept along the bank, the stern of a thirty-footer came into view. The square mast had been rolled down but she was pointed downstream so she could get going to the sea in a hurry. With infinite slowness, Bhimaji drifted closer. Presently he could hear snatches of conversation as the wind tossed the words his way. One man was on the boat and the other was on the shore, perhaps to help the raiding party load their human cargo and cast lines.

While Bhimaji pondered how to take one man without alerting the other, fate worked a hand. The fight at the village started up, and faint cries and the harder clash of blades drifted over. Bhimaji sensed rather than saw the men freeze. Both turned their attention landwards which was instinctive but futile since the creek bank was completely overgrown with bushes and visibility was barely twenty feet inward. The man on the boat was obviously no fighter, and just the distant sounds loosened his bowels, so with a shout to his companion, he pulled up his dirty robe, and moved to the side of the boat. The boats had no privy, of course, and the usual manner of doing one's business was to hang your haunches over the side, holding onto a knotted rope affixed for that express purpose. Because of this arrangement, the sides of these boats were often marked with lines of dried human excrement. The man chose the mid-channel side of the boat, and Bhimaji quickly approached the empty stern. Grasping the raised edge, he drew himself on deck slowly from the water like an apparition of the sea. The faint sounds of water dripping from him were masked by the soft grunts from the man hanging from the side ten feet to his right. Bhimaji drew his *para and* crabbed along the side of the boat till he could see the knuckles of one hand holding onto the side of the deck.

With one smooth motion, Bhimaji cocked his arm and rose above the deck. There was barely enough time to register the youth of the man squatting over the side with his robe gathered around his armpits, who stared at him goggle-eyed in shock and fear. Bhimaji in one smooth motion chopped his blade down from above, taking off the man's chin and demolishing his windpipe before lodging in his neck. As he wrenched the blade out, the body tumbled into the water with the eyes still looking shocked back at him.

Hearing the splash, the man on the bank turned, thinking his partner had slipped and fallen but his retort froze on his lips at the sight of this dark, near-naked man, who had apparently appeared out of nowhere. He drew his sword and rushed to board the deck of the boat.

In that split second, Bhimaji paused. In a fair fight, there was no way a *para* could match the reach of a sword, and the outcome would be predictable. He feinted and instead chopped the line mooring the boat, and the boat shuddered as the current bit into it. The Arab realizing Bhimaji's ploy made a concerted effort to board but Bhimaji parried the strokes, containing the man to the riverbank for the few heart beats it took for the boat to edge into the stream. Finally, realizing the impossibility of reaching the boat, the Arab could do no more than spit curses at Bhimaji and watch the boat center in the creek and glide safely downstream.

Bhimaji found his hands were shaking. It had been decades since he had last fought, and to calm himself more than anything else, he set about unfurling the simple sail in preparation for turning along the coast to the village at the point the creek emptied into the sea. As the rush of adrenaline faded, he realized his mouth was dry, and he sank to the rough deck to keep from stumbling.

'Goddess *Ekvire*, who holds the world in her palm, help my brothers repel these attackers, and I will sacrifice a cockerel at your feet,' came the unbidden prayer from dry lips, as he cleared the breakwater, and turned the small craft along the coast.

***

A *prahar* passed and the moon blazed down from above. It was very close to midnight. The fire in the village *chowk* clearing had banked and the village dogs lazed around the fire. Hiroji's wandering thoughts were suddenly interrupted by the soft warbling of a *hola*, repeated once again.

He moved his cramped legs slowly, and individually tensed each thigh and calf to prepare them for instant action. Stripped down to his *dhotar* he was almost invisible in the gloom of the thicket. With senses now on full alert, he waited for what was to come. The blood seemed to thicken, and each heartbeat felt as though the heart was working to push suddenly thick blood out to the extremities. His temples cramped with fear and anticipation.

And just then, the unthinkable happened.

There was a slight pressure on his instep and looking down, saw to his horror a cobra begin to glide across his foot. In the daylight, the creature would have been magnificent, with an underbelly of creamy yellow and a brilliant pattern on top. He continued his journey, taking the foot to be a tree root. Just as Hiroji was ready to release a breath again, the creature stopped, and the man realized the serpent's sensors had picked up an alien vibration. It was probably the tread of multiple feet approaching the position.

Just as the dogs lolling about the fire picked up their heads, three men glided silently past the hiding place, one from the left and two from the right. All three halted at the perimeter of the forest looking into the village *chowk*, no doubt waiting for the rest of their party to get into position.

Hiroji categorized them swiftly. The first man to the left was an Arab. He was of medium height but looked lean and tough. He was dressed in a stained and filthy robe. He held a long, curved *shamsher* in his right hand.

The two men to the right were *habshis*, Abyssinian natives. Even in the moonlight Hiroji could see each was over six feet tall. The nearest one was younger, and his upper body was shockingly packed with muscle. His black skin glowed nearly blue in the moonlight and glistened slightly with oil. He was close enough to see the muscles of his forearm stand out in ridges as he gripped a broad cleaver-like sword in his right fist. The man to his right was taller and older, with a leaner build. Hiroji rightly guessed he would be the most formidable fighter of the three and the one that'd need to be taken care of first.

The snake had tensed, no doubt picking up the tension that flickered in the air. The lessons of a street fight had been drummed into Hiroji in a dozen different campaigns. The key was always to hit first with overwhelming force. This moment was electric. Life and death in their purest forms hung in the balance and the situation begged for release.

Hiroji breathed out slowly through an open mouth and inched his left hand to where a glance out of the corner of his eye told him the snake's head was. A cobra's vision is poor; the serpent tastes the vibrations in the air with its tongue, reading movement at levels far below human understanding.

He quickly grabbed the head of the serpent at the jaw hinge with the thumb and index finger of the left hand and stepped on his tail with his right foot. The reptile's entire body exploded in a surge of muscle but expecting that, Hiroji quickly grabbed the tail between the middle and ring fingers of his right hand. He straightened up, effectively holding five feet of very angry cobra in his hands.

The men in front were completely unaware of what had happened behind them. Now timing was everything. The other members of the raiding party would already be in position awaiting their own prearranged call, which could come at any second. Panting slowly with anticipation, Hiroji raised both hands, cocked them overhead, and bunched his muscles. With an explosive grunt, he threw the snake overhead and onto the Arab who stood looking away ten paces to his left.

The other members of the village force were each at least thirty paces on either side and he could count on no help to eliminate the three raiders before him.

The snake landed on the man's shoulders with a soft thump, and in a movement reflexive to the species, immediately wrapped a fold around his neck. The man's cry of horror was cut short as the snake sank its fangs into the side of his head.

Both men to the right turned in amazement hearing the grunt to the horrific sight of a cobra draped down the front of their comrade who had dropped his sword and was clutching his neck. Before they could react however, there was a flurry of cries of '*Har har Mahadev!!*' from somewhere along the perimeter!

The attacker's surprise was almost comical when they realized things were not going according to plan.

Both men instinctively tore their gazes away from their comrade and looked to the center of the village for the source of the noise. Hiroji used the cover to slide out from ambush and in four long strides was upon them from behind.

He chose the neck of his first adversary. The neck is a relatively fragile column of muscle, gristle, and bone. His last lunge was timed perfectly with the backhanded first draw cut which went across his body and neatly severed the head of the younger man where the neck emerged from his thick shoulders. The head cartwheeled in midair, and the eyes widened in shock and surprise even as his brain died. Hiroji was already turning with the power of the blow and setting up to take on the last man.

The older man had superb reflexes. Somehow, he sensed the movement at his side and knew instinctively this was an ambush. Instead of turning to face the threat, he threw himself violently to his right.

Mid-flight, Hiroji changed the angle of the underhanded reverse strike to counter the man's move. Instead of cutting across the man's front, the blade crunched cleanly through his left shin before plunging into the soft sand of the undergrowth.

Almost comically, the first *habshi's* body had dropped to its knees as though in prayer. The neck spouted geysers of blood with each beat of the still beating heart, turning a five-foot radius of sand black with the rich blood.

Hirohi stood panting with battle lust and the exertion and stress of the last five seconds. The *habshi* was destroyed but he slithered back on the ruin of one leg and raised his sword: his left foot lay cleanly severed by his side. Blood pumped out of the stump with each beat of his heart. The sand near his calf was quickly turning black with pooled blood.

Hiroji looked back to the Arab to check his blind quarter but saw that he was keening slowly to himself and out of the fight. The cobra was nowhere to be seen.

Torn between going to the aid of the villagers or finishing off the injured man on the ground he quickly decided on the latter; one less raider to threaten the shores. The man's teeth were gritted in pain, but his eyes were malevolent with hatred. He was right-handed, and he used his left hand to support himself while he tracked his opponent's approach with the cleaver held aloft in his right hand.

Hiroji feinted to his left and the man quickly used his right heel to swing his body to face that direction. When the feint was done and Hiroji shifted to the other direction, he knew the man's stump was useless and he had only his left hand to try and swing his body around. While he tried to keep his eyes on the changed direction, as well as move his cleaver to counter the threat, his arm was bent nearly backwards and Hiroji quickly cut down on the length of the upper arm that was exposed. The sword sheared through bone and the man's cleaver dropped to the sand. With arterial blood flowing from two horrific wounds, the man would be dead within a few minutes.

Hiroji spun on his heel and raced to the center of the village.

Two *kolis* lay sprawled near the fire. One had been nearly disemboweled with a sword stroke while the other had half his neck severed. Shankar was fighting two Arabs with an ancient wooden shield held in his left fist and a *talwar* in his right. His bare chest gleamed with sweat and his loincloth was discolored by rivulets of sweat and blood running down his body. He fought well, moving rapidly using the fire pit to keep both assailants from flanking him, but he was tiring.

Three other skirmishes were taking place as Hiroji raced to Shankar's aid.

'Har har Mahadev!' The centuries old battle cry of the land mixed with the *'Deen deen'* of the attackers. This was a ballet that had come into being since the seventh century. Barbarians spreading outward from Arabia had brought death, destruction and forced conversion to every single place they visited. And each place of conversion became its own epicenter of further death and destruction.

'*Har har Mahadev!*' growled unbidden out of Hiroji's chest with no conscious thought and one of the attackers turned to face him.

'*Yella, come*' he grinned, panting shallowly showing black rotted teeth. He had on a stained robe, that had once been white, but while his appearance showed disrepair, the *shamsher* he held in his left hand gleamed dull blue in the firelight with ribboned blood.

He mistook youth for inexperience, and that was his undoing. Hiroji let his blade drop to below the horizontal to feign uncertainty, and the Arab went for the big kill. His sword swept in an overhead blow that had it landed, would've cleaved from shoulder to navel. Instead, Hiroji sidestepped to the left and brought up his sword outside of the blow and flicked it away to the right, using the man's momentum to retrace the tip of his blade against the man's face.

Hirijo saw with satisfaction the tip of his sword, slice open the man's left eye, and continue down till the hilt slammed against his jaw breaking it with his own forward momentum. The injury while not fatal, was extremely painful and the man dropped his sword and tried to hold his face in place with a keening cry.

In the countless hours of weapons practice, Ramaji had continually drilled in his students, he always said the common mistake was to go for the kill blow. It was much easier, to effect a lesser blow to an extremity, say an ankle, a finger, or face. That distracted an opponent, causing enough injury and pain to then allow you to deliver the kill blow at leisure.

Hiroji turned away to find the second attacker renew his assault on Shankar. Two hurried steps and Hiroji swept his blade horizontally across the man's back, rupturing both kidneys and the man dropped his sword with a scream, everything else instantly forgotten

Barely five minutes had passed since the fight began, but as Hiroji turned to look for the next threat, all was empty. It was the strange silence that comes after intense action.

Presently Ramaji walked in along with two other *kolis*. All were breathing heavily but were apparently unhurt. Seeing the Arab with half a face keening to himself one of the *kolis* swept his *para* down at the juncture of the man's neck and the keening stopped as he toppled over.

The ambush had worked flawlessly. All twelve men from the raiding party had been taken by surprise and killed. Only one group of two had managed to pass through the net and engage Shankar, and these were the two Hiroji had killed.

Chapter 5

Janjira fort

The party set off when it was still dark and only a pale lightening of the sky could be seen on the eastern horizon. The breeze was beneficial, and the dhow made good progress down the coast. Bhimaji and Ram, the grandson of the village chief, had volunteered to drop the men, down the coast, beyond the active control of the Siddi. The *deshmukhs* or chieftains in the area always had an eye out for good sword arms to fuel the constant fighting between the Sultanates. The men figured that'd be the entry to Shivajiraje's kingdom.

Hiroji had never traveled in a boat but took to it immediately. The day opened with magical suddenness and the scenery was magnificent. Palm-fringed shores cut by narrow creeks with the Sahyadri mountains in the backdrop lay to the left, and the azure seas to the right with soft, perfumed winds blowing off the waves.

Only the vast unbroken *Sindhu sagar* sea separated Hindustan from one set of enemies, the Arabs and Abyssinians who came looking for rape and plunder. This they did, of course, with the zeal of religious sanction. The dhow kept to coastal waters where the swells were enormous. The boat alternately pitched and plunged in four-foot troughs as the breeze freshened. The sun beat down out of a blue, cloudless sky and when Hiroji stuck his tongue out, he could taste the salt on the breeze.

The only boats seen were small canoes paddled by fisherman well within the shallows, with the men casting their lead-weighted circular nets. They froze when the dhow appeared, testifying to the malice that the Arab slavers employed in casual fashion in these waters. The relief was palpable when they realized the dhow was not out to plunder. At least not today.

In a couple of hours, Bhimaji called out an alarm, and the reason was clear. The craft was approaching the bay near Murud, the den of the *Siddi* ruler. Ramaji and Hiroji both went into the simple cabin, so as to present the picture of an Arab boat piloted by the serfs, with the owner staying in the shade of his quarters. Presently the coast turned in, and the massive fort of Janjira hove into view.

The fort was situated on a huge island just outside the mouth of a large bay. The island looked to be at least a few miles around, and the walls of the fort had been built right on the rocks rising out of the sea, so that the entire fort looked like it had been planted right in the middle of the surging surf.

The fort was stupendous. From the west, at least eight bastions were visible at any point. Cannon could be seen through the ports guarding all approaches to the bay as well as the shipping lanes themselves. The walls of the fort rose sheer out of the crashing surf. Black granite blocks well cut and fitted to form an impregnable barrier rose to a minimum height of thirty feet. While the main gate faced the strait separating the fort from the shore, there was a small postern gate facing the sea, and small craft could be seen making their way to and from the small gate. All in all, it was an awe-inspiring and fearsome sight. Spear-carrying helmeted *Siddis* could be seen stationed on each bastion. Very soon the men's small craft was sighted and an intricate system of hand signals could be seen conveying a message inward to the offices on the fort.

The original wooden fort on the site of which this behemoth stood, had been built by a local *koli* fisherman chieftain, Ram Patil. He and his descendants had used that base to repel attacks from marauding Arab and Abyssinian pirates, out for slaves and loot for hundreds of years.

One stormy night, an Abyssinian merchant had sought shelter from the storm, and it had been granted in the leeward side of the island. As a supposed mark of gratitude, the merchant had broken out casks of the moonshine he had on board. As the kolis knew that no ship was going to be abroad in the face of that storm, the guard detail had gotten well and truly drunk. At the lowest ebb of the night, the 'merchant' had thrown open the hold of his ship, and the Siddi pirates who had hidden there rushed the guards. Most of the kolis were senseless with drink anyway and were dispatched immediately. A few, who were sober raised the cry and rushed to the defense. The current Patil was roused by the commotion and dressed only in a loincloth, without armor or helmet, rushed to the fore with shield and sword and tried to rally the defense. What kolis remained fought bravely, but their stand was pitiful against the concentrated attack of the *Siddis*. To stop his men being slaughtered to a man, the Patil surrendered to the Siddi captain.

The *Siddis* gave the kolis a choice; convert to Islam or be put to the sword immediately. To their credit, not one of the kolis was amenable to the former choice. All the koli men were summarily beheaded. All the women were raped and imprisoned to be shipped with the children to the slave markets of Arabia.

The Hindu flag came down off the fort to be replaced by the green ensign of Islam. Several attempts to take back the fort were made, but they all ended in failure. Over the next couple of decades, the *Siddis* allied with their co-religionist the Nizam who financed the building of the stone fort on the site of the old wooden fort. Since then, the *Siddis* had played their cards carefully, siding either with the Nizam, or the Mughals, depending on which side looked to be winning at that current time. The ace they held was the means to control all shipping from the Mughal port of Surat, to the Portuguese-held port of Goa.

As the craft neared to within fifty feet of the postern gate, the chop increased till the bow rose and fell five feet, and Bhimaji had his hands full keeping the boat on course to pass the seaward side of the fort. A few minutes later, a swift *machwa* or canoe steered by four muscled *habshi* oarsmen peeled off from the gaggle of boats concentrated by the side of the fort and fast approached this new craft. There was probably a narrow gate used for the express purpose of letting out these small fast boats, without having to open one of the main doors of the postern gate. A white robed official balanced in the bow and called up a hand for the craft to stop. The skill of the sailors was incredible. They brought the canoe alongside and kept pace with the larger boat at a distance of not more than ten feet.

Bhimaji had already taken down the sail, and now held up a parchment to the official for inspection. This was the official permit issued by the Portuguese allowing fishermen to ply these waters. It was an official-looking leather cartouche, emblazoned with the seal of the Portuguese viceroy, and outsize in nature for the very purpose that it could be seen at a distance. In these waters, all crafts had to have either a Bijapuri, or Portuguese cartouche to ply their trade, or risk instant confiscation of the craft and all its goods.

In this travesty, the natives of the land required permits issued by foreign invaders to travel in their own land. The Portuguese had come in the fifteenth century and finding the Hindu kingdoms engaged in internecine warfare had established themselves along the coast. To their surprise not a single Hindu king had moved against them

The Portuguese had destroyed and looted over three thousand temples in the island of *Sahasashti* or sixty-six villages in the province of Goa itself. These temples had been lovingly built by the Kadamba kings over thousands of years and operated as stores of capital, in addition to the obvious religious function. The loot was enormous. However, the Portuguese did not stop there. Their leader was a monster called Xavier who was a priest belonging to the Jesuit denomination. He led the looting and destruction of hundreds of Hindu temples in that region. It was unfathomable to even the simplest Hindu soul how a so-called man of religion could visit these barbarities on the holy places of another religion. Did their long-suffering pale God whose images adorned their churches teach them this? Did he ask his followers to visit the same agony on others that he was going through?

Xavier quickly realized that forcible conversion did not stop the newly converted from reverting to the ancient Sanatani Hindu faith. The central tenet taught in this ancient land from birth was, 'there was one central truth, but various avenues to approach it'. The apparent polytheism was wrapped around a central monism. People saw no problem with adding Jesus to their existing panoply of gods. This, however was not acceptable because the Christianity inducted by Xavier required a fanatical cleaving to monotheism; one god and one god only. The converts had to forsake everything that came before, including language, music, dress, and even cuisine.

To address that Christianity did not easily 'stick', he ushered in the Inquisition, which was meant to convince people to remain in the new religion. Examples were important to persuade non-conformers. One common tactic was to organize public gatherings where defaulters were fried alive in giant vats of boiling oil. Another was to douse the clothes of a family patriarch who refused to relent in oil and set him on fire in full view of his family. It was recorded that Xavier danced with joy when young children, newly-converted to Christianity were forced to tread on the smashed idols of their previous faith.

The people of Hindustan wondered, 'were all foreigners barbarians?'

'Where is the owner?' asked the official stroking his beard with his right hand while keeping balance holding on to the shoulder of an oarsman with his left.

'Haji Usman is asleep, lord,' replied Bhimaji meekly. 'Too much palm toddy last night…' While the *machwa* was approaching, Hiroji had pulled both spears out of the bundle and had stacked them against the side of the cabin wall.

'We'll take out two oarsmen with the spears and then cut across the bay and beach the boat and try to escape ashore,' whispered Ramaji. 'Better that than be sold like cattle…'

They both knew escape was virtually impossible. The *Siddis* controlled not only the fort but also the coastal area for at least ten miles north and south and a few miles deep.

The official pondered over the fact that the owner was a 'Haji' in that he had made the pilgrimage to Mecca at least once. Disturbing such a man was probably not wise, despite his un-Islamic consumption of alcohol, so he waved magnanimously and instructed the *machwa* to be turned around. The men fell to with a will. These were Siddi soldier sailors, stripped to the waist, and their shoulders bulged with strain as they fought the outgoing current to steer the shallow craft back towards the narrow gate.

The waters swirled, gurgled and thrashed to cream all along the walls of the fort indicating currents, eddies and hidden reefs. No wonder all seaborne attacks to storm the fort had failed even before men could deploy scaling ladders onto the walls of the fort.

There was a collective sigh of relief as the men watched the back of the official and Bhimaji raised the square sail again.

The rest of the voyage was uneventful. They saw several boats flying the Siddi's colors, but the fact that this boat had come from the direction of the fort implied that it had the necessary permission, so no one accosted it again.

Bhimaji had brought along a simple meal of smoked fish, bhakri and raw onion, and around noon, with the sea like green glass all around, the four men sat in the shade of the cabin and divided up the meal.

As the sun began its eventual descent into the sea, Bhimaji started looking for a place to come ashore. To come into a port would be too dangerous, as all of them were controlled by the Bijapur Sultanate. Better to beach and abandon the dhow as far away from the site of its capture as possible. The two fishermen would then make their way back up the coast by sea or land and rejoin the village.

In the gathering gloom, the lights of a settlement far ahead on a promontory came into view.

'Dabhol,' muttered Bhimaji, while continuing to scan the shore. In a minute or so, he turned the boat in. He had seen a small creek emptying out into the sea. The dying wind was used to tack the craft closer inland. Ramaji stood at the stern with a spear to ensure that the group would not walk into a welcoming committee. The boat kissed a sandy spar and the men quickly jumped into the knee-deep lukewarm water. Bhimaji quickly hacked a small opening in the bottom of the craft with an axe and turned the sail, allowing the outgoing current and a gentle breeze to take the craft back into the sea, where it would slowly fill with water and sink beyond the surf line. Satisfied with his handiwork, he waited till the craft was well away from the shore before jumping into the sea and swimming to shore with quick, strong strokes.

Chapter 6

Rajgad fort

The sweat and blood, mixed and ran down his chest in rivulets, staining the waist of the dhotar he had hurriedly changed into after a wrestling practice into a delicate shade of pink. Today had been particularly brutal. Shivaji stood with his hand on the stone wall to the right of and high above the Konkan door of the Rajgad fort, watching a pair of eagles ride the thermals. The birds used the updraft to stay stock still in the air, with only the tips of their wings feathering for control while their hard, yellow eyes scanned the forest far, far below for prey. The breeze coming off from the west cooled his skin, while he fought to get his breath back to normal.

'Jagdamb, jagdamb…' that Sambhaji Kavji was a beast!

As usual, Shivaji had reached the *aakhada* gymnasium, located in the common area of the fort, at the crack of dawn. Here there was no king or commoner. All came to be tested in the rich red soil of the wrestling ring.

The large stone slabs that ringed the pit were pleasingly cool to the touch. A lamp lay lit in front of the idol of Hanuman, the god of strength, and Shivaji paid his obeisance and quickly moved to change into the orange langot, or codpiece that all wrestlers wore. Several men were already limbering up, some starting with the *jor*, or push up that started and ended with a full body stretch, while others started on the *baithaka*, or squats. His presence caused an immediate stir, with several men stopping their routines and saluting him with the *muzra*, bending at the waist, while bringing the upturned palm and tips of their fingers to their forehead thrice in the usual mark of respect paid to their king.

"At ease, brothers' smiled Shivaji as he took off his simple cotton vest and dhotar before tightening the thin cotton straps of the codpiece around his waist. Next, he took up the slack in the panel of cloth in the front, pressing all the important parts firmly against his body, and doubling the cloth panel back down and between his legs, tucking in into the back of the codpiece. It was as streamlined a garment as possible that protected modesty but allowed total freedom of movement.

With a force of over five thousand men on the fort, it was inevitable that there was always someone new at the aakhaada. There were two on this fort and he chose where to go each day at random. The men self-consciously resumed their routines, but Shivaji could feel their eyes on him.

What they saw was a man of about thirty, of medium height, and fair of complexion. What set him apart though was his gaze. It was at once piercing, insightful and still gently watchful. They saw the broad shoulders and the depth of chest, attesting to a youth spent in heavy training on the *kripan* sword and *danpatta*. The several pale colored worms of scars across his forearms, and one particularly vicious one on his left triceps spoke of his battle experience.

Shivaji ignored their gaze and strode to the place on the floor that had been obligingly made for him. Jiva, his bodyguard, and virtual shadow took position with his back to the nearest wall, his gaze sweeping back and forth over the men in the gymnasium for possible trouble. He was armed as usual with the curved kripan, worn in a scabbard at his waist.

Shivaji began with a set of a hundred *jor*, or full-motion pushups, followed by a set of two hundred squats. He came up easily out of the last squat and welcomed the burn in his thighs with pleasure.

The old *vastad*, or head of this gymnasium, had per custom emptied a full clay pot of buttermilk into the rich red earth of the wrestling pit. There was a rack of shovels to one side, and several men had already started turning the earth over, making sure the buttermilk was completely mixed in; this too was a part of limbering up.

The earth was special as well. This earth was the lifeblood of the Konkan region, rich in ferric iron, and therefore a dull red in color. The pit was twenty feet by twenty feet and sunk about five feet below the stone floor of the gymnasium. The rich red soil was two feet deep so, the feet sank comfortably in, adding a level of difficulty to the grips and throws.

Shivaji vaulted lightly into the pit, and scooped up the earth, rubbing it onto his chest, shoulders and arms. Not only did the fat from the daily portion of buttermilk act as an emollient for the skin, but it also made getting a grip on an opponent that much more difficult. The earth felt deliciously cool against his body.

There were already two pairs engaged in two corners of the pit, and Shivajji looked expectantly up into the general area to look for a sparring partner. Most of the men refused to meet his gaze, but one cocky youth met his gaze and grinned, and on Shivaji's signal jumped down into the pit.

He looked to be about the same age. The shoulders were heavy with muscle, and the ears already clubbed with scar tissue, attesting to years of practice. 'Chandji, *raje…*' said the youth after a quick *muzra* to Shivaji.

'Ah, so you are Kanhoji's then?' said a surprised Shivaji. 'He's never presented you to me before. Though I know your eldest brother well!'

'My lord, father sent me with a hundred men to end the bandit raids that were plaguing the area around Jani temb. We killed half of them and got the remainder to join our army,' said Baji with an infectious grin.

'So that was you then. I did read about those raids from the report from Kanhoji. Well, don't assume you get any special treatment today,' grinned Shivaji as he bent and took a handful of earth and threw it across Baji's shoulder as a mark of respect, and to signal the start of the bout. Baji did the same to Shivaji. The anointing of dirt across the opponent's shoulders, arms and thighs not only served as a form of mutual respect, but also to help grip a sweat slicked body part. A wrestling bout had no prescribed time limit and went on till one wrestler forced the other in touching both the upper and lower corners of his back to the ground.

Baji did the same, and immediately the two came face to face in the traditional *salaami* or greeting, with both palms clasped with the opponents, fingers intertwined, wrists rigid, in a preliminary test of strength.

The ancient form of *malla-yuddha* or *mushti-yuddha* practiced by the Hindus for over five thousand years had undergone changes with the advent of Muslim rule. Lord Krishna had been a master *mushti-yodha* warrior. That form of physical warfare was based on blows and kicks. However, Persian, Turki, Uzbek, Georgian and Mongol influences had all crept in to make *kusti,* which itself was a derivative of a Persian word, more based on grapples, pins, locks and throws than strikes and kicks.

Shivaji was at the peak of his physical prowess. However, he quickly realized that a protracted bout with the much younger Chandji would be an error. Chandji clearly had an edge over him in stamina and would wait to tire him out.

After the initial clasp, the wrestlers separated and circled each other warily. All the other action in the aakhaada had stopped with all eyes on this bout. Shivaji sensed that Chandji was enjoying the attention and would try for a sensational play very soon. The men came together again, each man trying for a grip to the upper arm, or neck, to go through into a lock and the other as easily shrugging off the attempt.

After a few minutes of this, both men were blowing with the concentrated bursts of strength. Chests and bellies were pumping for air. Shivaji let his left leg drift forward a fraction more than was necessary, telegraphing an attempt to center his mass on his right, Immediately Chandji fell for the hook and slapped Shivaji's left ankle with his right in preparation for a *pat khech* move.

This was exactly what Shivaji wanted. He let his left leg slip out but immediately dropped to his right knee in front of his opponent. With his left hand he gripped Chanji's right wrist and passed his right hand between his legs. Before Chandji could correct his balance Shivaji, in an explosive burst of effort pulled the man's left wrist down, and throwing his bicep between Baji's legs, powered upwards, using his opponent's tilt to completely cartwheel him over his back and flat onto the ground in a *kalajung.*

One second, Chandji was thinking through the next move on his *pat khech,* and the next found himself on his back, with Shivaji having turned his own body was now on top pinning him firmly to the mud of the ring

'Well done, *raje!*' cried the vastad, as Shivaji stood up, still blowing hard and offered a hand to Chandji to get him off the ground.

The young man looked crestfallen, but he drew himself up and bowed again in the *muzra* to his king.

'Better luck next time, Chandji!' said Shivaji, more to assuage the young man's pride. The bout had lasted all of two minutes.

Before Shivaji could lever himself out of the aakhaada, a baritone asked, 'If I may, my lord?'

Shivaji turned to see who had spoken. What he saw set his mouth in a grim line. The speaker bowed and snapped off a *muzra* with just the wrong amount of casualness, designed to irritate but not insult.

Shivaji heard the sharp intake of breath from Jiva, and saw his hand move to the hilt of his sword. A barely perceptible signal passed from Shivaji and Jiva relaxed momentarily but took two steps to the very edge of the pit so that he was only a corner away from the newcomer.

Sambhaji Kavji Kondhalkar was a brute of a man. He hailed from the fertile plains of Kolhapur, which was beyond the Sahyadri mountain range and outside of the hardscrabble Maaval region. Generations of plenty showed in his build. He stood at 6'2" with huge shoulders and a chest crisscrossed with old scars. He had a belly to match, and thighs like small trees. Shivaji had heard about this warrior.

He had fought for sardars aligned both with the Adilshahi, and Nizamshahi Sultans, frequently changing sides for whoever paid highest.

Some vestigial part of his brain that allied to Hindu pride had brought him to this fledgling Hindu nation, to add his strength to this fight for independence.

There was a story making the rounds about this man. Apparently when he first arrived at Rajgad, a *shiledar* had laid a bet with Sambaji that he would never be able to control the former's sturdy mountain pony, let alone try to ride the beast. Sambhaji had walked up to the animal, which rolled its eyes and pawed the ground, alert for any movement. Rather than try to get into the saddle, Sambhaji had quickly ducked under the belly of the beast, and with an explosive grunt, lifted the surprised pony across his shoulders, holding a front and rear leg each in his meaty hands. The prize had been a mountain goat that the *shiledar* had been fattening up for an upcoming feast. The story also went that later than evening, Sambhaji had had the goat roasted and eaten half of it in one sitting

Something fundamental shifted inside the primordial part of Shivaji's brain. The urge was atavistic. He realized he *had* to best this man to win his respect and send a message to others who were flocking to his banner. He needed the loyalty of fighters like these if he was ever to realize the dream of an independent Hindu nation. He wiped the sweat off his brow, streaking his forehead a rich reddish brown, and reached up a hand to help Sambhaji down into the pit.

'Come Sambhaji, I'm glad to finally meet you…' said Shivaji,

Sambhaji rolled, rather than stepped in and after another *muzra*, started limbering up. He ran a few circles inside the pit, alternately smacking his right palm into the crook of his folded left elbow, and the inner part of this right quadriceps as he leapt into the air and pranced around the pit. This was designed more for show to awe and cow down the opponent in a sort of psychological preliminary. Each smack of the palm reverberated like a musket shot in the gloom of the *aakhaada*.

Shivaji meanwhile rolled his wrists and shoulders, and stretched his legs, rotating his neck counterclockwise, in preparation for the combat to come. Alternating strategies went through his mind. His first thought was to tire the man and wait for the opportune moment, quickly rejected because the chance of injury was too great. Sambhaji could easily break his arm or crush an elbow before the *vastad* could intervene. A better strategy would be to let Sambhaji's confidence in his own strength work against him. Shivaji did a few squats to limber up his legs and gathered the rich red soil, slightly damp with buttermilk and old ghee, and rubbed it copiously into his biceps and inner elbow for a plan that was slowly formulating in his mind.

Presently, Sambhaji stopped his prancing and stood in front of Shivaji. After throwing the salutary dusting of earth across Sambhaji's shoulders, several other wrestlers in the ring took handfuls of earth and liberally rubbed down Sambhaji's arms and legs, at a quiet signal from Shivaji.

Both men clasped hands perfunctorily and the bout began. By now all eyes were on the pair. Nobody even had the pretense of doing anything else. Sambhaji easily had six inches in height and over fifty pounds on his shorter, slimmer opponent. Shivaji eschewed the usual preliminary palm clasp and both wrestlers came together in the center.

Sambhaji immediately went for the neck slap. This was strictly illegal in a bout, as the blow to the side of the neck could immobilize an opponent. Shivaji was alert to the move however and tucked his head into his shoulders, deflecting the slap with his left forearm taking the reduced blow on his shoulder. With his own right he tried for a quick elbow lock more to test his opponent's reflexes than anything else. Sambhaji shrugged off the attempt and danced back.

Both men came together again in the more formal neck clasp, with one palm behind the opponent's neck trying to pull him in as needed, and the other hand dancing and twisting with the opposing hand, each trying for an opening to go into a pin or hold. Both wrestlers leaned in, with their heads touching and feet splayed back, alert for any potential play. Sambhaji had seen how Shivaji had converted the earlier ankle slap and was not about to make that same mistake.

A minute passed, then two, then five. Both men were blowing now, their breaths steaming in the cold morning air, and the sprinkling of mud now turned into rivulets snaking down their backs, their loincloths stained with sweat and exertion. The only sound heard now was the panting of the two men, breathing through open mouths. as the fort slowly came to life. The air was perfumed with the musk smell of the exertion of two animals in the prime of health mixed with the tang of ghee and rich red earth. All eyes were riveted on the struggle going on in the pit below.

Slowly but surely Sambhaji's superior strength was beginning to tell. Sambhaji bore down inexorably, and Shivaji had to sway and turn to left and right to keep in the game. Several times, Shivaji had attempted leg traps, but the man's legs were rooted like trees into the ground, and any attempt to shift his balance came to naught.

Shivaji made his movements appear fractionally slower, overplaying his exhaustion and waning strength. He allowed his hand to slip off Sambhaji's shoulder a couple of times. Any time now, Shivaji knew the move would come to bring him down to the ground where Sambhaji could bring the full force of his strength to bear.

Shivaji allowed a halfhearted feint with his right leg, and quick as an adder, Sambhaji dipped his left shoulder in preparation to grabbing the ankle, which would allow him to proceed in any number of moves.

Barely had the thought registered before Shivaji disengaged his right hand from Sambhaji's left shoulder, which as now dropping in preparation to grab Shivaji's right ankle and brought the back of his hand smartly below Sambhaji's left elbow throwing up his left arm into the air with own right hand and ducking below Sambhaji's left armpit while pivoting on his left foot. He had kept his left elbow above Sambhaji's right as each gripped the other's upper arm. Shivaji used Sambhaji's own force to pivot his body counterclockwise, till he was now behind Sambhaji, with his left elbow now wrapped in around Sambhaji's neck in a textbook *lokaan.*

In the same fluid move, Shivaji brought up his right knee into the small of Sambhaji's back, driving him down to his knees and grasped his own right elbow with his left palm, bringing his right forearm across the back of Sambhaji's neck trapping his neck, in the dreaded lock called the *khappa*.

Sambhaji realizing the danger of the situation again surprised Shivaji. He threw himself back, knowing that if Shivaji's back touched the ground, the vastad would call it a win for him despite the lock. As both men flew backwards, Shivaji twisted in midair desperately keeping on to the hold and arching his back to stop the vastad from ending the bout.

Sambhaji brought up his hands to try and break the hold but Shivaji held on fast knowing this was his last chance to end this fight. Shivaji knew it would be only a minute before the flow of blood to the brain drained Sambhaji of strength.

Sambhaji thrashed like a tiger caught in a net, battering Shivaji into the earth time and again. The cord of Sambhaji's codpiece cut across Shivaji's abdomen, opening a shallow cut, as Sambhaji twisted and turned but Shivaji held fast, counting the seconds. Slowly Sambhaji's struggles began to ease, and his movements slowed. Fearing a trap, Shivaji did not let up the pressure looking at the vastad who had jumped into the ring. Shivaji's face was smeared with blood. Sometime during the struggle, Sambhaji's head had smashed into his, pulping his lip and the blood smeared across his cheeks and flowed into his beard. His teeth gleamed white in his face as his lips drew taut in a rictus of effort and determination as the muscles of his left forearm quivered like steel cables with the effort of holding down the much larger man.

Finally, the vastad judged he moment and called the bout over with Shivaji the victor. Shivaji rolled out from under the dead weight of Sambhaji and knelt in the earth by his side holding onto his sides and gulping in huge draughts of air.

'Why did you not end this sooner,' panted Shivaji to the *vastad* with more than a touch of anger in his voice. The Sultans were doing a fine job of killing his men without him having to help them in their noble effort.

'He'll come to shortly *raje,*' said the vastad with more conviction than belief.

***

Shaking off the morning memory, Shivaji's thoughts came back to the present as his gaze traveled over the carpet of lush green forest far below. The forest became even more dense as the direction of travel went west towards the coast, and his eye naturally moved to the next fort in the chain. Pratapgad lay roughly thirty miles as the crow flies to the south-south west, deep in the jungles of the Maaval.

'Yes! That is where I need to draw him!!!' burst from his lips, startling Moro Pingale his chief advisor, who was accompanying him on his rounds today.

'Lord, who do you mean?'

'Moropant, our newborn independence faces a ravenous python in the person of Afzal,' sighed Shivaji, adding the '*pant*' as a mark of his respect for the brave and wise Brahmin.

Chapter 7

Dabhol port

The immediate danger had passed. By traveling towards their enemy's stronghold, rather than away as expected, father and son had eluded capture and were in the vicinity of the only Hindu kingdom in that war-torn landscape.

Maloji Bhonsle had begun as a simple village headman. By dint of bravery and ambition, he had risen to prominence while in the employ of the Jadhav clan of Sindkhed fighting for the Sultanate of Ahmednagar. So prodigious was his war talent and personal bravery, that he had become a favorite of the great Abyssinian general Malik Amber who was the prime minister of the Sultanate. His sons Shahaji and Sharifji were fierce warriors as well. Shahaji had made a name for himself fighting for the Deccan Sultans and ending up with five thousand cavalry under his command. Shahaji had changed sides often increasing his personal wealth and importance with each move. However, it was his son, Shivaji who had done something completely extraordinary.

Rather than live the life of a pampered young lord, the young man had thrown himself into administering his father's jagir and learning the rules of good governance. At the same time, he had ridden up and down the valleys and crags of the Sahyadri mountains, till he knew every hidden mountain pass, sweet water spring, and valley in the region crisscrossed by the rivers Godavari, Krishna, Koyna and Varna. Shivaji had befriended the fiercely independent, hardy hill-dwelling Mavle men, as well as understood the potential of their small, hardy hill-ponies. These horses were indigenous to the region. No one could say for certain where their blood lines started, but when it came to mountainous terrain, their stamina, agility and speed could not be matched. The horses were mostly mouse-brown in color and short in stature. They needed no special feed and very often could graze off the land. The men who rode them were deceptively small-statured as well. Arable land was scarce and rainfall was unreliable. These Mavles had learned to do with less. They were fierce of spirit, god-fearing in the extreme, and quick to slight. Both enmities and friendships carried through generations, but once these tough, doughty fighters called you friend, they would not think twice of laying down their lives for you. These were the people who Shivaji had gathered around himself.

Shivaji had based himself at Pune, and after consecrating the old Ganesh temple he found there, he had slowly and unobtrusively begun expanding his realm over the surrounding territory. Shirwal, Saswad, Supe, came into the fold, as did several of the nearby hill forts. After three hundred years of the Muslim yoke, a Hindu champion had arisen and a new hope was in the air. Of course, along with the expansion came jealousy and the list of Hindu chieftains that opposed Shivaji was long as well.

Ramaji was aiming to meet Kanhoji Jedhe. Kanhoji's village was Kari, but he was the *deshmukh,* or overlord of fifty villages in Bhor district near the city of *Punyapattan,* which is nowadays called Pune. Kanhoji was nominally in the employ of the Bijapur Sultan but had openly sided with Shivaji. This old, seasoned warrior had been entrusted with Shivaji's care and upbringing by Shahaji raje himself when the old warrior had sent his wife and young son to Pune with a cabinet-in-waiting. Slowly and surely, good governance and Kanhoji's persuasion, had caused several other *deshmukhs* to align to the fledgling Hindu empire.

Shivaji never proclaimed the kingdom as birthright or took any personal gain. This Hindu kingdom was God's kingdom and every action and decision merely proved the point. All wealth flowed back into roads, culverts, fort upkeep and salaries for the slowly growing army. Shivaji had recognized the perils in the existing *jagir* fiefdom system of creating feudal lords, who wielded absolute power of life and death in their land holdings. They collected whatever taxes they felt like and provided a set amount to the Sultanate.

While slowly garnering the support of these lords, Shivaji had managed to raise an army of five thousand independents, called *shiledars*, who brought their own horses and weapons. This number was augmented with some *bargirdars* who were supplied horses and weapons by the state but were paid less as a result. Each *bargirdar* was supplied with one sword, one wooden shield and one spear in addition to a mountain pony. In addition, there was a monthly ration of jowar grain and lentils, so that each man was self-sufficient on the campaign. All vegetables, pulses, grain and other supplies were purchased at market prices. By Shivaji's personal edict, the act of stealing, or otherwise forcibly taking anything from the populace by force, was punishable by death.

After three hundred years, the land had begun to breathe a sigh of relief.

It was adjacent to this little kingdom that father and son had landed. Ram had begged and pleaded to come along, and after Shankar's consent, the two men had taken young Ram under their wing. They had scuttled the dhow near a small creek before the delta of the Vashisti river on which the port of Dabhol was situated. Bhimaji had set out on his return journey, and the two men had stripped off their pilgrim attire, and now looked like the mercenaries they were. Hiroji and Ramaji wore tunics cinched in the front with drawstrings, and tight dhotars with their feet shod in sturdy leather closed sandals. Each had tied a turban to provide some protection from the fierce sun. Each had a sword cinched to the waist, and a circular shield strapped to their back. Each carried a spear. Hiroji carried the *danpatta* in a special leather sheath that hung down his back. The *danpatta* was not a quick retrieval weapon.

Ram on the other hand wore the short armless vest and the woollen skullcap of his koli community and had the para sheathed at his waist. His feet were unshod.

Neither of the men had ever seen, a settlement of the size of Dabhol and they looked on in wonder at the size and splendor of the town.

Dabhol's heyday had been almost a hundred years earlier when it was the primary port on the west coast. It did a robust trade in horses coming in from Arabia and Khorasan and slaves sent in the other direction under the Deccan Bahmani Sultanate.

Khilji's rule had devolved into the the Bahmani Sultante. Gangras brahmin had been forcibly converted to Islam. When he had appealed to the clergy of the time to take him back, that orthodox body, had refused with extreme myopia, that the ancient Hindu religion was a one-way street. The embittered man had taken the zeal of the convert to a fine point in the reign that followed.

The Gangu Bahmani Sultanate had broken up into five separate Sultanates, each headed by a foreign mercenary from Azerbaijan, Georgia, Turkey and Khorasan. Other ports had started to be developed and Dabhol's importance had declined. The entire city was located on the north bank of the river Vashishti, named after the famous sage Vashishta from the time of the Mahabharat.

The men circled to the north of the town using a circuitous route and approached the outskirts with caution. A pleasant breeze was blowing off the sea, bringing with it the tang of salt and a slight edge of rotting fish.

Dabhol was controlled by the Bijapur Sultanate and there was a steady stream of people flowing in from the north of the town. The three men folded themselves in among a group of Maratha infantrymen trudging along on the dusty path.

Like infantrymen all over the world, the men marched stolidly on with a mute acceptance of their condition, and the 'Greetings brothers!' from Ramaji was answered with a desultory response.

'Where are you headed?' asked Ramaji, sidling next to a man who appeared to be the leader, digging out his tobacco pouch and offering a small mound of it on one calloused palm.

The man gratefully accepted a pinch and spitting out the spent wad in his cheek in a well-practiced stream of red saliva by the side of the road, inserted the new plug sighing with satisfaction.

'We're looking to catch a boat out of Dabhol to go further south. Maybe Rajapur or even Goa. We figured we'd earn some extra money before the next sowing.'

'Do you mind if we join you? We're looking for work as well,' said Ramaji falling into step beside him.

'Sure, why not. I'm Tukaram, and oh… can this stripling fight?' with a nod indicating Ram.

Ramaji snorted, 'Don't worry about him, the lad can handle himself!'

'All right then, its settled. But since we're the larger party, I'll take a third of all your wages,' inserted Tukaram, with a cunning look.

Ramaji pretended to give the comment deep thought. In truth, all he cared about was to get inside the town without the guards at the fast-approaching gate asking too many questions.

'Deal,' he grudgingly said, clasping Tukaram's shoulder. 'These are Hiroji and Ram, my companions.'

The path passed by several stately houses. The town had outgrown the old walled enclosure and rich merchants and their servants had established abodes spreading outwards from the north bank of the river. The houses though palatial had seen better times. Trade had slowly shifted away from Dabhol and fortunes had declined. Many of the houses were built of stone and were designed to impress. It was easy enough to guess who they belonged to; the ones with intricate Arabesque motifs and minarets were obviously owned by the rich Muslim traders, while those with lotus motifs and small private temples were obviously owned by their Hindu counterparts.

The sun was approaching its zenith and every living thing sought shade. Only a pair of stray dogs sat next to the path, panting in the heat, their scrawny rib cages heaving, while idly watching the men troop by.

'Stop!' challenged one of the guards at a gate next to an opening in the eight-foot-high stone wall that sat like a rough semicircle around the town reaching the water's edge on both sides.

'Who are you? What village do you come from?' asked one guard stepping out and blocking the group's path, while the other watched propped in the shade of the wall. Both men were native Muslims as could be seen from their dark complexions. Each sported a beard while the mustache was shaved off attesting to their religious fervor. Each man held an upright spear for support and had a *talwar* strapped to the waist.

'We are from village Nagothane sir, mostly the Jadhav family and some extended members,' replied Tukaram nervously, wiping away a bead of sweat that had suddenly appeared on his chin.

'We lost our plot of land in family quarrels, so, we picked up and left. We're hoping to work for passage on any boat leaving here for southern shores so that we may find work. Please sir, we haven't eaten for a few days now,' casting a hand back to indicate his travel-worn crew.

The first guard raised an eyebrow and looked over the sorry bunch; all stooped shoulders, and scrawny necks, and realized there was nothing he and his partner could loot from them.

'Move you donkeys; you're holding up more important folks..' and he spat in the dust in disgust moving on to the next pathetic bunch of travelers, who had halted a few feet away.

Tukaram and the rest of the group visibly cast off their doleful expressions once inside the walls of the town. Each had spirited away a rupee or two, sewn into the folds of their headcloths to enjoy the delights of the town. Here there were bars along the banks of the river, as well as brothels to cater to the sailors that came from foreign ports.

'Let's meet on the docks when the tide comes in. Till then me and my companions will find somewhere to slake our thirst,' said Ramaji with a knowing wink to Tukaram, before peeling off from the group.

The plan was never to go further south. The men's best bet was to break for Shivajiraje's kingdom, where they were guaranteed the most safety. The group struck for the center of town where they figured they'd gather the latest news before making their final plans.

The town was situated like a blister on the north back of the river where it poured into the sea. The river's edge was faced with a stone jetty to facilitate the docking of sea-faring ships and the area had many bars, and lodging houses. To the north was the castle, a solid stone structure surrounded with its own inner stone wall fortifications. There were rooms for the five hundred or so famed *kizalbaksh* Turkish soldiers who kept the peace and were the pride of Adil Shah. He had had them specially imported from what he considered his motherland, a country he had never seen but paid fervent allegiance to. In fact, the *qutba* or official prayer that was conducted in the mosques of all the Muslim kingdoms in Hindustan were in the name of the Caliph, ruling from Baghdad, who nominally headed the universal population of Islam, the *ummat*. In essence, these kingdoms were all foreign pockets in the soil of Hindustan. Generations of Muslim rulers had been born in the very land that they treated as alien, and the populations as sub-human and *vazibul katla* or deserving only of death.

The streets from the north gate where they had entered turned gradually commercial till they came to the center of town. What they saw there shocked them to their core.

The center of town was a huge stone paved central opening, or *chowk*. The area was reserved for a different type of market depending on the day of the week, and the Sultanate earned a steady stream of revenue from a share of the daily proceeds.

Today was a slave auction. A wooden platform had been erected at the center of the *chowk*, roughly ten feet by ten feet and about five feet high, with a set of rough wooden steps leading up to it. An Arab slaver stood on the platform looking out over the assembled crowd of about fifty or so men or varying ages and ethnicities.

The red *fez* headgear of the Turks could be seen on a few soldiers along with the loose overcoat and baggy pantaloons of a few Arab noblemen. Among the crowd too, were several Marathi merchants who were easily identified by the religious vermillion *tilak* mark on their foreheads. There was a palpable excitement in the air even before the proceedings began.

The slave master strode back and forth on the platform, self-importantly fanning, the expectation of the crowd.

'Fresh goods!! Tender meat my lords!!' he leered winking at the crowd.

In a few minutes, a procession of bullock carts trundled into the clearing and made their way up to the platform. Each held a gaggle of humans, dusty, bruised and beaten. There were men, women and quite a few children, too scared to even weep, looking on wild-eyed in terror.

The slave-traders knew how to play the crowd. They'd start with an attractive specimen first to get the buyer's juices flowing and then introduce the middling specimens, keeping the best for the last. The slave-trader signaled to his assistant, another Arab who walked to the second cart and seized a woman. She was a girl, really of eighteen, and pulling her off the cart dragged her by her arm to the steps. The girl, exhausted, and bruised, tried to resist while trying to gather the rags of her sari to cover her modesty. Seeing their mother hauled away, her two children who moments before, had been clinging to her in terror, jumped off the cart and clung to her legs, a boy of two and a girl of about four, their emaciated, snot-covered swollen faces distorted in terror.

All three were unceremoniously hauled to the platform, and the slave-trader, who towered over her held her up by her wrists stretched above her head for the crowd to admire her lissome form. The children clung to her legs in terror and broke into piteous wails.

'Bruised, but still serviceable' the slaver leered, thru fleshy lips. 'And with two kids that you get with her, you know she is never going to escape! What do you say fine gentlemen, shall we begin at five hundred rupees?' saying which the man peered into the crowd, trying to make eye contact with his two plants whose job it was to up the bidding by pretending to be buyers.

With his other hand, the Arab tore the threadbare cloth off the woman's front exposing her breasts, and even the guards posted at each corner of the *chowk*, perked in interest. The woman moaned in shame, twisting and turning in the man's iron hold.

Ramaji's face was set in planes of stone. Hiroji had never seen anything like this. He looked in increasing bewilderment, disgust, and anger at what was going on in front of him. Was this the depth to what civilization had fallen to in this land? The same earth that had felt the footsteps of Lord Ram on his way south, and in more recent times the sages Gaudpaad, Dnyaneshwar, Namdev, Gora kumbhar, the potter, Chokha mela, and Samarth Ramdas were now witness to… this???? and a low growl escaped his throat. The girl so reminded him of his Savitri… though they had not yet been blessed with children.

Ramaji saw the warning signs in his son, and put a restraining hand on Hiroji's forearm, but the limb had gone as rigid as a bar of steel. The killing rage was on Hiroji, and while the older man saw the signs, there was precious little he could do about it. There had been a few instances in the past when Hiroji had gotten into this state despite Ramaji's counsel that a warrior's job was best done with a cool head and ample preparation.

'*Har har Mahadev*!!!' rasped from somewhere deep inside Hiroji, and in one fluid motion he reached over his right shoulder and pulled the *danpatta* out of its leather sheath, taking a second to slip his right wrist and forearm into the metal gauntlet and grasp the padded grip inside. With his left hand, he jerked the hilt of his *kripan*, and the oiled steel slid smoothly out, the metal scabbard hitting the paving stone with a clang.

In two seconds, even before the crowd of buyers and onlookers could react, Hiroji charged the platform, sword in left hand and *patta* in right and in four long strides was at the front of the platform, the crowd parting in panic and confusion.

The *patta* moved in a circular blur and both the Arab slaver's legs were sliced neatly off below the knees. One minute he was sneering, and in the next instant, he had no feet to stand on. Two fountains of blood erupted from his legs as his heart went into overdrive and he fell back, screaming in pain and terror, washing the platform with his life blood. The girl, suddenly released, gathered her children to her and ran down the steps and towards the cart.

All was bedlam. The assistant was a brave man and in a second, he had his *talwar* out and was charging Hiroji. The Arab style of sword play was different from the Hindu styles, but Hiroji knew what to expect and deflected the blow with his sword, while his *patta* came down, almost lazily in a downward stroke and bit into the man's side, above his hip bone, carving through spleen and left side before going back to the ready position. The man looked down at his severed left side, his eyes widening in shock, before a gush of blood erupted from his mouth and he dropped to his knees, keening in pain.

Barely five seconds had passed but now the guards and some of the men among the crowd had taken stock of the situation, and had pulled swords, while the guards posted at the four corners ran to the platform leading with their spears.

Hiroji put his back against the platform and faced off the crowd. With the only stairs to the platform behind him, an attacker would have to scale five feet to get to his back from the far end of the platform, so for the moment his back was secure.

He took a visibly calming breath, and cursed, 'Come on you mother-fuckers, who wants to die today?' The *patta* in his right hand was held in a horizontal position with the right elbow pointing forward, able to strike at a distance anywhere to the front or right side within a range of five feet. The *kripan* sword in his left hand was held at the read, to block, cut or feint as needed.

His chest heaved with battle lust and the explosive action of the last few moments, but his thinking was not clear. There was no hope here. Because of his stupidity, he had written a death sentence for his father and Ram. There was no way three men could hold out for long, especially since they were in the middle of the town, with rings of the enemy surrounding them on all sides.

The fight paused in that delicate moment when the first explosive action has passed, and the actors are deciding the future course of action in the milliseconds that follow. Time slowed down, and each breath felt as thick as honey.

When Hiroji had rushed to the front, Ramaji and Ram had been forgotten and had been left behind in the group of non-combatants. The fighters in the group reinforced with the guards from the four corners moved five steps forward to accost Hiroji. They formed a wide semicircle keeping a respectful distance from the reach of the *patta*. Even the spearmen had seen what a *patta* could do. It would reduce the seasoned haft of the spear into kindling in the blink of an eye.

Ram had gone bug-eyed in fear and indecision. His hand dropped to the short wicket blade at his waist, but Ramaji stilled him by putting a restraining hand on his elbow. He wanted the situation to develop before his attack could come out of the blue and cause maximum damage.

He put his mouth to Ram's left ear and whispered. 'Run son. Live to fight another day!'

Ram just shook his head and drew in a steadying breath. '*Har har Mahadev!*' issued from his throat in a rasp and he balled his fists.

Ramaji looked into his eyes and nodded. 'Steady son; now we get to show our gods who we are as men. Drift to the right, to the back of the right segment and I will move to the left. Attack when I give the word…

Do you understand?' With that he projected calm and confidence and peered deep into Ram's jumpy eyes to calm his nerves.

Ram swallowed twice, his Adam's apple working noiselessly and nodded. Ramaji held on for a moment more to his elbow and then rakishly smiled, 'Meet you in the next life!' and took ten steps to his left, as though seeking to move away from the fight.

Hiroji faced the ring of men around him, who were now slowly gaining in confidence.

'You die today dog!' cursed one Turk smiling through his bushy mustache.

The blade of Hiroji's *patta* was ribboned with blood, and the tips of both weapons made little circles in the air, to keep them ready for action. He was poised for instant action, left leg slightly in front and at an angle with the knee slightly bent, and the right straight and holding his weight, and his gaze swept from left to right through reddened, slitted eyes. His world had coalesced into that ring of men who now clamored for his life.

Even while he was moving, Ramaji studied the ring of attackers from the back. Most of the merchants were all bluster, despite the weapons they carried. They were the most vocal in shouting abuses, but he knew they'd be the first to run. The guards were fairly well trained, but he knew they'd work together only up to a point. Any immediate threat to their lives and they'd break.

The Turkish *kizalbaksh* were another matter. They were probably *janissaries,* Christian boys abducted from the conquered territories of Eastern Europe after their parents had been slain, and forcibly converted to Islam. Following this they were trained in one art and one art only, that of warfare. These hardened men were then turned loose on the civilized world, to perpetuate the cycle of death, destruction and rape.

There were four Turks, calmly assessing the situation among the semicircle of attackers. They could be identified by their headgear and they had already spread themselves out so that they could attack from equidistant points along the semicircle facing the man at bay. They wore loose linen shirts and baggy trousers with the leather sandals unique to that tribe. Ramaji knew that before long, more would arrive and every second counted.

He knew he had to use surprise and an excess of violence to demoralize the enemy at the first go. Ramaji saw that Ram had drifted to the back of the right segment of the attackers, roughly mirroring his position. Ramaji peered intently at Ram, mentally willing him into steadiness and in the guise of wiping his forehead, used his left hand to touch his turban and nod at the Turk nearest him. Thankfully, Ram understood and nodded back.

Timing was everything. Just when Ramaji sensed the first wave of attack would break on Hiroji, he changed direction from what appeared to be moving away from the fight and swiveling on the ball of his right foot, drew his sword in one fluid motion. He had already picked out his targets and in the same motion, he took off the head of the first Turk cleanly. The sword hissed cleanly through and sliced through half the neck of the man to his right and suddenly the world turned red with twin sprays of arterial blood. The head tumbled end over end separating from the *fez* and had Ramaji had the time, he's have apologized to the eyes that looked at him almost accusingly.

The second Turk, more by instinct and experience, than by any warning had already begun to turn. But he was to the right of where the attack had struck, and being right-handed, had to turn more than ninety degrees to face the threat vector. In addition, the man to his left, one of the merchants had frozen with fear and was blocking his way. Even so, he made a heroic effort shouldering the merchant out of the way to bring his sword to bear.

One quick lunge to his right, and Ramaji bending low, reversed the swing of his sword and struck at the man's left knee where he had begun to pivot, destroying the joint. He had not been able to put his arm into the blow and the sword stuck in the bone, but the damage had been done. The Turk dropped his sword and grabbed his left knee with both hands, dropping onto his seat as his left leg gave out. Rather than moving to the next victim, Ramaji counterwheeled his sword again, and chopped off the man's left hand, midway between wrist and elbow.

Satisfied that the wounds were fatal, Ramaji stepped back, panting heavily to assess the situation.

Ram had struck the Turk on his side, in the back but his inexperience was his undoing. The wound was fatal, but the curved tip of the blade had stuck in the man's rib and rather that jerk the blade up, Ram kept trying to pull the blade out. As the blade would not budge, he was now in a state of pure terror. The second Turk had whirled, and without a moment to lose had swept his *talwar* left to right across Ram's front, opening him as cleanly as one would peel an orange.

The principal actors in this melee, were facing the tunnel vision peculiar to explosive and bloody combat, and they were unaware that the people in the square and in the houses surrounding the arena had by now set up a pandemonium alerting the group to the threat to their rear. The effect on the attackers was electric.

Realizing that danger existed to the rear without knowing the extent, most of the men had turned to flee and only eight or nine men, of whom four were guards remained.

In the split second that the attackers in front were distracted by the commotion at the back, Hiroji exploded into action. He took two lunging steps forward, again returning to his starting balanced position and his weapons descended from above in two outward directions. The *patta* bit through a guard's face horizontally, demolishing both eyes and the man's spear clattered to the ground as he dropped to his knees with a keening cry. The *kripan* in his left hand described its own arc to the left and hacked off a man's arm between the elbow and shoulder carving a deep gash across the ribs.

The effect on the rest was electric. One moment they were looking to crowd one man from three directions and in the next, five of their own were out of the fight, with two mewling piteously from their wounds.

The fight hung in the balance. Had Ramaji and Hiroji decided to run, the remainder would have gathered courage and chased, so the two men stood their stead, while the four or five left in the attacking group considered whether to fight or flee in that pregnant moment. Both men moved towards each other, and the attackers parted to let them through, till the men stood, back-to-back among the dead and dying with the paving stones slick with blood, and the keening of the dying lost in the general shouts and screams from the populace. Among the dead was poor Ram, his open eyes staring sightlessly at the bright blue sky, his mouth frozen in a rictus of pain as he had died.

The decision was made for them when in that very instant, a flying column of *kizalbaksh* erupted into the square from one of the alleys, and the equation changed again. With cries of '*Allahu Akbar!!*' the column dissolved in disciplined fashion into pairs of men, as they all converged on the solitary pair in the center of the chowk.

'I am sorry *Taat,*' whispered Hiroji, using the ancient Sanskrit word for father. I did not think. All your advice, over the years, to keep a cool head was lost when that pig touched the girl. What will I tell mother when my soul meets hers in the afterlife?' As the two men took up the fighting stance as before and watched warily as the Turks settled into position.

While several had spears, these were laid down when the earlier survivor relayed the events to the new arrivals in their strange tongue. The mood changed like quicksilver and father and son realized that they wanted to finish this with swords and daggers in a more intimate manner. So, this was to be the end.

Instinctively, the cry rumbled up from deep within the men's chests, '*Har har Mahadev!! Har har Mahadev!!*' to counterpoint the '*Allahu Akbar!*' of the Turks.

The Turks were very, very good. There was no frenzied rush at the pair. Swordplay was all about footwork. The Turks spread in a circle and approached methodically, and the pair constantly shifted the positions of their feet to counter and recounter. Ramaji had picked up a fallen blade, and now each man held a blade in either hand, twisting and turning with the tactics of the Turks.

In a well-rehearsed but unspoken signal, four Turks swept in from the four cardinal compass points, and both men parried in a frenzy as sparks rang from the blades. Both father and son knew that now it was only a matter of time. Hiroji blinked to stop the sweat from getting into his eyes, determined to not let his guard drop even for an instant.

The Turks closed again and Ramaji saw one man, who wore the sash of a captain grin, showing very white teeth under his handlebar mustache. They were now toying, drawing out the pleasure of tiring out the pair, knowing they had limitless time and resources to bring the fight to a close whenever they wanted.

'Father, shall we rush them?' hissed Hiroji

'Shush, my boy... watch their hands and their eyes as I've told you, let's take as many of them with us to the abode of *Yama,'* whispered Ramaji intent on watching his semicircle of attackers. He too grinned at the Turk soundlessly conveying, 'You can kill me, but not scare me...'

By now about fifty men were arrayed in a circle around the pair, with the new arrivals jeering, and catcalling to the pair

'Kaffir dogs, we will roast you tonight, and feed your intestines to our dogs!' yelled one.

'You're going to beg to die you scum before I'm done with you!' hissed another.

'Farewell, my boy. I could not ask Mahadev for a finer death than going down alongside you. Remember, die well. We are being watched by our ancestors at this time.' whispered Ramaji in anticipation of the final onslaught that would end it all.

And suddenly a miracle happened...

'Marathas! Marathas! They are coming! Run, run!!!' came cries from the periphery of the crowd and the Turks who had been single mindedly focused on the pair were momentarily distracted.

Hardly had the cry arose, than a thundering of hooves filled the square as horsemen poured in from the two farthest entrances! The atmosphere filled with cries of *'Har har Mahadev',* and the snorting and neighing of the charging horses, with sparks flying off the cobblestones as the riders bore in.

These were the legendary *Maavle* or the inhabitants of the twelve *Maaval* districts that extended from the crags of the Sahyadri mountain range down in the westward direction to the sea through thousands of miles of evergreen impenetrable forests.

Seeing a crowd at the center, a knot of horsemen charged the mass. Each man carried a cavalry spear, balanced either over the shoulder, or tucked in an armpit and as they charged, they skewered the standing men from a distance out of the reach of the swords and once the lance was in, they quickly dropped the weapon and unsheathed the long straight blades sheathed at their waists.

The attack threw the Turks into confusion as they tried to stem the assault. Within a few seconds, almost half had been run through by lances and the rest turned to their heels and fled, chased by the horsemen who delivered death from high above with swords and clubs.

Hiroji and Ramaji had moved back to the edge of the platform and watched in slack jawed amazement, at the efficiency and brutality with which these soldiers dispensed with the Turks. By now the square was littered with bodies. Men lay in every conceivable position, most impaled by lances but some with their skulls caved in, and their brains bulging out in pink-grey masses. In a remarkable display of choreography, the horsemen who came in the second wave stooped low and grasping the haft of the lance stuck in a body, rode on, allowing their momentum to tear the lance out of the body, with the fluted tip causing maximum damage on exit, several times bringing out entire strings of intestines.

Both men had lowered their weapons but not sheathed them, not entirely sure if the horsemen were going to turn on them next.

The initial knot of horsemen had exited the square and the clash of weapons interspersed with war cries could be heard on the breeze that wafted in. Yet another wave of horsemen rode in at a more sedate pace, leading strings of captured Arabian horses. They were led by a lean, sinewy man who looked slightly older than the others. He wore no obvious mark of rank, but the others deferred to him. He carried the strange, long sword in his right hand, holding the reins in his teeth. His tunic and dhotar were speckled with blood, as though he had just returned from reveling in the festival of *Holi!*

'And who the hell are you?' he hissed between clamped teeth as he halted his mountain pony with a backward jerk of his head. Five riders fanned out in a protective cordon behind him, seeing the *patta* in Hiroji's hand.

Ramaji bowed low, and in a few short sentences relayed all that had happened in the last few minutes.

'Do you want to do something good with that worthless life of yours? Or just piss it away like an idiot?' the man barked at Hiroji, while giving him a quick once over.

'Sir, take us with you. We'd be happy to serve in your band of bandits, and as you can see, we know a little bit about weapons,' cajoled Ramaji. These men would be gone as fast as they'd appeared and then there would be certain death for whoever remained.

'Bandits? Do you take us for thieves, you imbecile??' sputtered the man, rage and emotion suffusing his dark face to a purple, and making the veins stand out like ropes in his neck as he shouted,

'We are the army of Shivajiraje and we fight for independence!! Not for personal gain, you fool!!!' saying which he prepared to wheel his horse away.

With a desperate lunge, Ramaji lunged for the halter, and hung on, while the horse bucked in panic. Trying to avoid the front hooves, Ramaji panted, 'Lord, pardon this poor fool's mistake. You are the answer to our prayers! We were trying to get to Shivajiraje's dominions to offer our sword arms. Please sir, please, take us with you!!' and with that he hung on, despite the man delivering him a few blows with the flat of his blade.

Ramaji bore the blows in silence and seeing that neither Hiroji nor Ramaji offered any resistance, the man calmed.

'Can you ride?' at which Ramaji, still looking down at the ground, nodded his head in a mute negative.

'Where would people like us get access to a horse? We barely own the clothes we wear. The only thing we have of value are our weapons and our pride,' saying which he stepped back letting go of the halter, the anger and emotion plain in his lean, taut face.

'Dattaji, Kondaji,' and two of his riders straightened in their saddles.

'Choose two of the captured Arabians and take these two behind you. Your horses can follow along. You two, hold on to these men for your lives. If you fall off the saddle, we will not be turning back for you.'

With that he was gone, leaving the two riders who quickly dismounted and selected two of the captured horses for the men to ride.

'This must be your lucky day! That was Mankoji Dahatonde, the head of our cavalry himself. He must have seen something in you or your boy. Normally, we don't wait a second beyond our planned maneuver. We hit, plunder, kill as many of the swine as we can and we are gone before they even know we've arrived,' the man said by way of explanation.

Chapter 8

Vijaypura (the city of victory) – bastardized to 'Bijapur'

'Amina was always the plucky one' was the thought that came unbidden to Afzal's mind as he ran his thumb idly over the blade of his *katar*, or war dagger. It was a vicious weapon. Almost ten inches long, the grip was unusual in that two transversal metal slats formed part of the handle, such that when held, the *katar* pointed in the direction along the arm. The stabbing action was akin to throwing a punch. The thick pad of callous on the pad of his thumb was sliced neatly as he stopped just short of drawing blood. His aide Sayyad had done a good job honing the blade and Afzal grunted in satisfaction, tucking the *katar* back into his waistband.

Afzal was feeling good today. Sayyad had taken care of an important chore for him. All sixty-two of his wives had been disposed of. They had been invited to a special outing, and they had jumped at the chance to get out from behind the latticed screens of his harem. The party had proceeded to a tiny village on the outskirts of the capital Bijapur, in a procession of gaily decorated bullock-carts. The women were all in purdah of course, and protected by twenty of his personal guard, not that there was any fear of the Marathas this far south.

Sayyad told him the women had sung and clapped hands, and a big feast had been prepared for them underneath the shade of a giant peepal tree. Water had been drawn from an adjacent well and the ladies had freshened up while their maidservants had spread cotton dhurries on the ground, under the shade of the giant tree.

Hamida as usual had found something to complain about. The cotton strings tied by generations of Hindu women around the trunk of the peepal tree to wish long lives for their husbands offended her religious sensibilities. She proclaimed that she could not eat a morsel within sight of that offensive *kafir* symbol. The long-suffering Sayyad, had to depute one of the guards to slice away and burn all the offending cotton.

A small crowd of villagers had meanwhile gathered to watch the proceedings, hungrily gazing at the huge vats of steaming mutton curries and fragrant biryanis. Presently the ladies were served, followed by the soldiers, with the maids and cooks eating last. The sun had moved into the west by now and several of the ladies were sleeping off their meal. The villagers had disappeared once they realized they were not going to be getting anything. The soldiers had hobbled their horses in a single line and were standing guard at the cardinal points of the encampment.

Suddenly, there was a signal from Sayyad, and ten swords cleared their scabbards with a series of rasps. Half the soldiers suddenly turned inward and raised their weapons high. The other ten immediately fell upon ten of the women, who in this unusual turn of events, could only gasp in shock. The women were picked up, carried to the lip of the large well, called *Surungbavdi* by the locals, about ten paces away and unceremoniously thrown in. In the ten seconds it took for this to happen, whoever was awake began to shriek and suddenly all was bedlam. At the same time, the ring of ten soldiers tightened the circle, stopping anyone from leaving the camp. One by one, the soldiers returned and made seven trips in all, throwing all the Khan's women in the well. The air was rent with the hideous screams of the women in the water. They beseeched Allah for mercy, but there was none coming. Thankfully, some of the later entrants fell on the earlier ones, knocking them out and they slowly sank from view.

Afzal had been clear in his directions. None of the women were to be dishonored or suffer any physical injury. Their death was to be solely by drowning.

Afzal's thoughts were interrupted by a polite cough from Sayyad, who had narrated the successful conclusion of his mission, and was waiting further instructions.

'*Shabbash*! good job! now that I've cleared the deadwood, I can raid the Maratha's territory and capture other women to replace these; I was really tiring of them anyway.'

His leer in the lamplight made Sayyad almost feel that the women he'd killed were in a better place.

I hear the king exhorts the women in his land to exercise and train in the martial arts; breaking them should be entertaining!'

Saying that, Afzal flipped a gold *hon* in Sayyad's direction and waved him away

***

'Wise men put a question to Allah to mull,

Does a man exist who could best Afzal?

Click clack, click clack, the prayer beads speak,

The field is empty, there is only Afzal, Afzal!!

Afzal Khan was not his birthed name of course. He had been born Abdullah, of the congress between some unknown soldier and a maid in the employ of the Bijapur Sultanate. Abdullah had no memory of his father and his mother had never revealed the man's identity, if of course she knew it herself. To further his career and give himself airs, Afzal added 'Mohammedshahi' to his name, declaring that he was a bastard son of the Sultan Mohammed Adil Shah himself.

Be that as it may, what was evident was that his biological father must have been a giant. Abdullah had taken his build. He towered over six and a half feet with broad shoulders, forearms like hams and a barrel chest. He had very little hair on his body unlike the men of Hindustan.

He routinely preened in the nude in front of a mirror, especially when he had one or more of his numerous wives, concubines, or whores in his bed, which was almost every night. He effected the current religious fashion of shaving off his mustache and growing his beard, which tinged with grey now, reached almost to his chest.

Abdullah was very proud of his light complexion and green eyes, that set him apart from the dark complexioned *kafirs* of the Deccan. When he'd noticed his hairline starting to recede, he'd started shaving his head. His face with the high cheekbones and cruel gash of a mouth, routinely struck terror with the girls in the brothels of Bijapur. He worked out daily with the *danpatta*, which was the only grudging nod of respect he gave these Deccani *kafirs* for the weapon they had developed. At forty-six, he was still at the peak of his physical powers. He was a prodigious eater, polishing off a haunch of mutton in one meal. It was only now that his waist had started to thicken with the advent of a small paunch.

Though born dirt-poor, Abdullah had quickly realized he had a head for numbers and that was his route to growth. He had asked the *kazi* or instructor in his *madrassah* to go beyond the rote memorization of the Koran and teach him the *hisab-al-hind* or mathematics of the Hindus, as well as languages. He was conversant in Urdu, Pashto, Kannada and what he saw as the god-forsaken Marathi of the region. His pride though was in his use of Persian, the court language of all Sultanates, and in which he had composed his extremely self-serving seal.

He had started off as a lowly clerk, in the office of the extremely astute vizier of the Bijapur Sultanate, Ranadullah Khan, an Abyssinian *habshi,* who had risen in the ranks on the dint of merit. Ranadullah was almost universally respected by friend and foe alike and was a close friend of Shahaji Bhosle as well. Abdullah had risen along with Ranadullah and was a head clerk at the age of twenty with the authority to approve low level requests that did not merit Ranadullah's time.

It was around this time that Abdullah's path had first crossed that of Shahaji Bhosle. Shahaji was the scion of the Bhosle clan of Verul. His generalship, personal daring, and ambition were well-known. He had even had the gumption to prop up the Nizamshahi Sultanate by ruling with Murtuza, the year- old heir on his knee, till the combined forces of the Mughal and Bijapur had defeated the Nizamshahi forces and absorbed the Nizam's territory between themselves.

After the Nizamshahi defeat, not only had this *kafir's* head not been separated from his body, but Ranadullah, recognizing the potential of the man, had offered him a position in the Bijapur Sultanate as the head of ten thousand cavalry! Ten thousand cavalry no less!

One tiny victory that Abdullah had managed however was by the constant whispering in the *Badi begum's* ears which he'd accomplished by a circuitous connection made by one of his young wives.

'Keep the *kafir* away from the province of Maharashtra! Reward him if you must, but make sure his *jaagir* or baronetcy is far from this troublesome district near Pune. Strip him of his support base of doughty, hardy fighters; the clans of the various *deshmukhs* who hold sway in this craggy region'. He was therefore given a position far to the south, and Bengaluru was his capital, and he ruled there as a virtual king, with all the pomp and pageantry accruing to that position.

Shahaji was untouchable till Ranadullah Khan, who by then was a close friend of Shahaji was in power. Abdullah had struck immediately after the old vizier had passed away. Till then Abdullah was worldly enough to mask his seething jealousy with honeyed pleasantries.

On a campaign about five years ago after Ranadullah had passed, Abdullah, Shahaji and Baji Ghorpade, a distant cousin of Shahaji, but also someone who secretly hated Shahaji's guts and success were in the field on campaign and Abdullah had hosted a night of revelry. The wine flowed along with the entertainment provided by the dancing girls and it was very late till Shahaji, by then in his cups had gone to bed. Barely had the lights been doused and Shahaji's camp fallen silent than troops from Baji and Abdullah's contingents, lying silently in wait had launched a surprise attack on Shahaji's camp. The outer perimeter of guards had put up a fight but had been quickly cut down. Cries of '*Deen, deen*' and '*Har har Mahadev*' from both antagonist and protagonist camps had rent the air and Shahaji had suddenly come awake in a fog of confusion.

He always slept with his *patta* beside his bed and he stumbled out of his tent with *patta* and shield to find his horse tethered, but the groom lying in a pool of blood with two of Ghorpade's men finishing him off. With a shouted scream of '*Har har Mahadev!*' which came from an alcohol rasped throat, Shahaji sheared off the arm of the first man while simultaneously blocking the strike of the second man. The second man, seeing his companion staring stupidly at the stump of his hand which was spouting fountains of blood, panicked and fled. Shahaji quickly swung into the saddle and charged to the center of the camp where the fighting was the thickest, rallying his troops and showing them, he was still in the fight.

Shahaji was like a man possessed, enraged at this treachery, and used both his war horse and the *patta* to leave a trail of bodies in his wake. The horse was trained to not spook at noise, or men running at him, but to shoulder them aside so that the rider could finish off the off-kilter foe. Very few infantrymen knew how to take on a horse charging straight at them. Just when the tide was beginning to turn, tragedy struck, when a soldier plunged a spear in Shahaji's horse's abdomen and the beast shrieking in pain and terror went down, trapping Shahaji's left leg under his side. Before he had time to extricate himself from under, a sword strike sliced him in the bicep and the *patta* fell from nerveless fingers. Seeing Shahaji fall, victory turned to rout and the men laid down their arms.

Abdullah immediately had Shahaji clapped in iron shackles and taken in procession to Bijapur, with the latter, continuously protesting his innocence.

Just as Abdullah was ready to toast the end of Shahaji, his wily son Shivaji had produced an ace. He had written directly to the Mughal, Shah Jehan, offering him both his and his father's services with immediate intent. His note said that he saw only one problem. His father, who was hugely respected by the populace was currently imprisoned by the Bijapur Sultanate without any evidence of an actual crime.

Shah Jehan, who had been plotting the downfall of the Deccan Sultanates all his life, thrilled at the prospect of getting this father son duo to his side. He dashed off a stern letter to the Bijapur Sultanate, threatening dire action if his future subject were not freed instantly, since no crime had been established. Mohammed Adil Shah, knowing the far superior strength of the Mughal, did not want to give the latter any excuse to set out on a conquest of Bijapur and immediately set Shahaji free.

Abdullah had sulked for weeks, even killed a few *kafirs*, to extract his revenge on the community; his Persian titles of *buthshikan* and *kufrshikan* indeed called him the 'destroyer of deities, and the slayer of *kafirs*'. The irony was lost on him and others that '*buth*' derived from 'Buddha' and his ancestors had all been Hindu before converting to Buddhism. Thousands of years of civilization had been upturned by a few generations after converting to Islam.

Alas, though Shahaji escaped his fate, Abdullah was able to get his elder son Sambhaji, killed during the siege of Kanakgiri fort. Sometimes, Abdullah marveled at how credulous these Hindu fools were. As commander of the campaign, he'd sent a Marathi contingent under Sambhaji, to launch a commando raid on a convoy, coming to relieve the fort with the assurance that once they had engaged the enemy, he would follow with a larger force. He had of course done nothing of the sort and the entire raiding party had been cut down, right to the last cavalry rider.

With Ranadullah off the board, the Shah had turned his gaze on Abdullah, and rewarded his service by conferring on him the title, 'Afzal' or dear to Allah.

To his credit, Afzal was an excellent administrator in addition to being an extremely capable general, so the Shah had increased his prestige by ratifying his self-given honorific title *Mohammedshahi* 'or of the line of Mohammed Adil Shah,' adopting him in a fashion.

***

Afzal's thoughts turned to that fateful day in April of 1659. The heat was stifling, almost unbearable, and the earth yearned for the quench of the monsoon winds which were still three months away. As per court norms, Afzal had donned the long robe denoting him a high noble of the Bijapur court. He carried his favorite sword in his left hand. It was shorter than a *talwar* but extremely broad with an edge on either side. The style was called '*Jamdaad*' or the 'beard of Yama, the god of death'. The nobles all filed into the large audience chamber and stood on either side of the central passageway, in order of importance; the more important you were, the closer you stood to the Shah and the throne.

The large room was cooled by servants fanning air over rush curtains that had been soaked in a cooling and fragrant *khus* herb extract. After the white-hot heat of the outside, the room was cool and pleasant. It was no hardship to wait there for the official clerk to begin announcing the emergence of the Shah, which took more than ten minutes because of the long, and seemingly never-ending titles that he had bestowed upon himself.

Today was different though. Mohammed Adil Shah, the earlier ruler had died a few years ago, and his son Ali was a minor. Instead, the widow, *Badi begum,* Taaj Sultana, had decided to address the nobles, denoting the topic was urgent.

Only the highest level of nobles, numbering twenty-two in all had been invited, and Afzal nodded affably to Hussein, Ranadullah the junior, Ankush, and even to Sultanji Jagdale, the most prominent Hindu noble in this august gathering.

The women's section was in an area on the first floor in a balcony behind the throne shielded from public gaze by a loosely woven rush mat. Individual shapes and even some features could be seen without permitting a complete view of any woman.

All eyes turned to the balcony after the requisite announcements finished and a sole figure appeared behind the curtain

'Are there no men left in Bijapur????' suddenly shrieked the Begum and all activity stopped. People held their breath wondering what was going to come next.

'Are we left only with impotent *napunsaks*?? That scoundrel dog, Shivaji, does what he wants in the region around Pune, growing his power day by day and all the men I send to battle him come back with their tails between their legs??'

'I sent a letter to our servant Shahaji asking him to rein in his son, but the man had the temerity to reply that he has no control over a grown son and that we should proceed as we see fit..'

The assemblage could all feel her beady eyes on them, and they looked down and shuffled their feet. Life was good. The region was fertile and rich. The coffers were full and the biggest issue of the day on everyone's lips was the rising enmity between the Afghani Muslim faction and the local Muslims, whether born or forcibly converted. Who cared what that pest Shivaji did in his barren mountain region? For all they cared, he could take a few more forts if he wished. The entire annual revenue of his region did not equal even a day's earnings of the Sultanate.

Seeing the lack of response, the begum screamed again, with both hands raised in a prayer to Allah

'Save me from these worthless donkeys, Oh Allah! They do not realize that this spark needs to be extinguished before it can turn into a fire! For three hundred and fifty years, no Hindu in this region has dared to challenge the supremacy of the true believers. These fools do not realize that this dog's success could give hope to the Hindus and cause them to flock to his standard!'

With that, she made a theatrical gesture to an aide, and Afzal realized the entire performance, had been planned in advance. As if on cue, a servant entered the chamber from a side alcove bearing a large brass tray on which lay a collection of *beeda* or betel leaves wrapped around fragrant spices and coconut shavings. The lady was about to lay down a challenge!

Afzal's fists tightened in anticipation, and as expected, the lady in a more sedate tone said, 'if there is a real man among you, let him pick up a *beeda*. I want that rascal Shivaji dragged in chains in front of me, and if that is not possible, I want to see his head on a spear so that it can be paraded on the ramparts of Bijapur fort as a warning to any further foolishness from these Hindus.' She paused to take a few breaths. She was almost panting with excitement and emotion, 'Who will come forward? Who? who?'

And then Afzal took one step forward into the passageway and the air buzzed with an electric tension. He looked up to the balcony and somewhere from deep within him, came the low bass drawl,

'Do not fear *Badi begum*. I will lop off that cur's head and bring it to you' and saying that Afzal bent and picked up one *beeda* from the tray.

The room erupted in shouts of 'Well done! *Allahu Akbar!*' and other nobles moved to congratulate him and slap his back. When the commotion had died down, the Begum asked in a quieter tone, 'send me what you need Lord Afzal. Infantry, cavalry, cannon, elephants? The entire treasury of this Sultanate is at your disposal. I want Shivaji dead, his rebellion stamped out and his capital Pune destroyed just as we had done thirty years ago.'

And with that the lady left the balcony and the meeting dissolved.

Chapter 9

Bijapur

Muraqat-i-Abul Hasan

The emperor Aurangzeb learning from newsletters of the province of Orissa that at the village of Tilkuti in Medinipur (Midnapore) a temple has been built, has issued his august mandate for its destruction, and the destruction of all temples built anywhere in this province by the worthless infidels. Every idol-house built during the last 10 or 12 years, whether with brick or clay, should be demolished without delay. Also, do not allow the crushed Hindus and despicable infidels to repair their old temples.

Afzal read the transcript again with deep satisfaction. While Aurangzeb yearned to overthrow the Sultanates to the south and take over all of Hindustan, he was after all a true believer. The policy that his ancestor, the extremely cunning Akbar had devised to rein in the valiant Hindu Rajputs, was finally bearing fruit.

The Rajput clans were among the fiercest warriors known to the north of Hindustan. They were fearless in battle as had been seen during Rana Sangha's fight with the barbarian invader Babar. It was Babar who had established the Mughal line.

When faced with Babar's metallurgically superior cannon, the Rajput warriors had on a signal from their commander willingly plunged their heads into the bores of red-hot cannon to try to block and disable them. Unthinkable bravery!

Their downfall was their insistence to adhere to the age-old code of *dharma* or righteousness, even in battle. They overlooked that the enemy had no such restrictions. The Rajputs never backed down from a fight, even when faced with certain death. They glorified a warrior's death as seen by the ritual of *kesariya* where the tying of saffron headbands declared that the only path to the next incarnation led through glorious death in battle.

For a civilization as ancient as the *Sanatana* in Hindustan, war had existed for millennia. The Greeks had tried conquests many times before Alexander. They'd been roundly defeated again and again. To their credit though, they had assimilated the wisdom in this ancient land to the point that king Menander had taken the Hindu name Milind and even authored a treatise, the 'Milindapanna'. Alexander thought he had seen Hindustan when he faced a minor chieftain Puru in battle, but when his men saw the mighty Magadha empire to the east, they refused to fight and instead opted to return to their homeland.

The Shakas had come, followed by the Kushanas and even the Huns, each drawn by Hindustan's seemingly endless wealth. They came for material riches and stayed for riches of the mind. Each successive body of invaders marveled at the depth of science, philosophy, art and other wonders that were commonplace in Hindustan.

Islam was a different phenomenon. All these hordes wanted, was to kill, rape, and destroy. Nothing was sacred to these people. All manner of barbarity was allowable, nay, even prescribed by their Koran. They had no ethics, and *dharma* as a concept was completely alien to them. A central tenet in their teaching was *takiya*, which was the allowance to lie, cheat and do whatever was necessary to overcome the foe. In the face of this monstrously amoral and immoral onslaught, the Rajputs were left wanting. Hindustan had forgotten the sage lessons of warfare taught by Lord Krishna in the Gita.

In the years following the establishment of Islamic rule in Hindustan, the Rajputs had suffered a further horrifying ignominy. The barbarian hordes were known to practice necrophilia with the Rajput women who had chosen to take their own lives after their men went into *kesariya*. Out of that had evolved the practice of *Saka*. Rajput warriors on the night before a final battle, would feed their wives and children opium and when stupefied would feed them into a communal fire. In the morning, when the ashes had cooled, the men would meditate on the cold funeral pyres, coat their bodies with these ashes and sally out for a final battle with the Muslim invaders.

At the second sack of the great fort of Chittor in Mewad, the monster Akbar had slaughtered over forty thousand defenseless civilians after the fort had fallen and all the warriors had been killed. As a joke, he had then had the *janeyus* or the sacred thread worn by men taken off the corpses and weighed as a tribute to Islam. The weight had equaled seventy-two and a half *muns*.

Cunning to the core though, he had quickly realized that the inherently warlike Rajputs would never cease to resist. So, he had turned on a charming façade and invited matrimony with the biggest clans. Some had succumbed, giving their daughters to the invaders. The girls were uniformly converted to Islam first, since marriage with a non-believer was not valid. And the progeny, were all Muslim, of course. The code of honor among the Rajputs forbade the family to have any interaction with the girl once she had been converted. So, there was never any chance of a sobering or civilizing influence on the fruits of the marriage either.

Akbar's great-grandson Aurangzeb, in time-honored Islamic tradition, had dethroned and imprisoned his father and slaughtered his two older brothers Dara and Murad to seize the throne. Dara, the eldest, was a scholar of Sanskrit and in a sobering influence had even translated the Hindu texts into the Persian language in an effort at understanding and reconciliation. Alas he had fallen and the beast had ascended the throne.

Aurangzeb put on a huge show of piety, but for all that, the old lecher had hundreds of wives and concubines, imported for their beauty from the farthest corners of the world. Not satisfied with that, he also lusted after his brother's wives. What Afzal would have given for one unfettered night in Aurangya's harem!

Afzal touched the parchment bearing the news of more temples destroyed to his lips in a mark of respect and put it down on his desk.

There were more pressing matters now that he had picked up the gauntlet to eradicate Shivaji and his piddling Hindu rebellion.

His aide Sayyad moved aside the curtain to the office Afzal was seated in and politely asked permission to enter.

'Enter you dimwit, what is it?' barked Afzal.

'Lord, Naikjiraje Kharate has come to meet you per your invite. May I usher him in?'

'Yes, give me a minute, and then send him in,' said Afzal, taking a moment to don his turban and straighten the lapels of his robe.

The curtains parted, and Kharate entered. He was almost sixty years of age, but the years of ceaseless warfare had cured him into a strip of leather. He made a *kurnisaat* or bow in the Muslim tradition to Afzal and when indicated with a gesture, chose a small stool to park himself.

His hair and mustaches were almost white. He wore the tricorn *pagdi* or hat of the Marathas with a single strand of pearls at its tip as an adornment. His face was like old leather, completely devoid of any softening feature. His overcoat was simple, of white cotton, worn over a white dhotar with a crimson sash at the waist holding a dagger. On his feet, he wore chunky leather chadhav and in his gnarled left hand, he held a *talwar*.

He smoothed his mustaches with the back of his right hand and said, 'Lord, why did you remember me?'

Afzal took his time before answering. For this campaign, he had asked the court for ten thousand cavalries on Arab or Turkish horses and twelve thousand infantries. Of this twelve thousand, he had specifically asked for five thousand Pathans, with fifteen hundred of them being musketeers. In addition, he had requisitioned four hundred elephants, one thousand camel and four hundred and fifty medium bore cannon and mortars.

He doubted that upstart, Shivaji could field any more than eight thousand men and he had virtually no elephants or cannon. It was a little too much, but he wanted to swat this fly and be back in time for Ramzan in Bijapur, with a fresh complement of beauties.

'Raje, tell me, how would you proceed to defeat Shivaji, were you me?' asked Afzal, adding the 'Raje' as an embellishment to flatter the old warrior.

Kharate was surprised. It was not like Afzal to seek counsel. The man was mean, homicidal and opinionated, but brilliant, nevertheless.

'Lord, have you studied the battles of this Shivaji? He never stays long enough to wrap up any battle. He uses hit and run tactics, and constantly harasses larger forces. He knows he has neither the Arab horses with greater speed, or muskets, or cannon to sustain pitched battle. He uses the topography of the Sahyadri mountains to evade any attempt at pinning him down,' and the old man paused.

'Exactly my thought,' beamed Afzal. 'So now I need to pull him out of his mountain stronghold and onto the plains of the *Desh* where I can bring my cannon to bear on his ragtag army. And have you seen his *Maavle* so-called warriors?' he said with a sneer.

'They're more like monkeys. Small brown men. Any Pathan or *habshi* in my contingent could lay a dozen of them low and not break a sweat.'

'Lord, it would be an error to underestimate his men. They are wiry, determined fighters. And remember, Shivaji has adroitly thrown religion into the mix.'

'Bah! One battle with my Pathans and they'll be running back to their mother's wombs!' snorted Afzal derisively.

Afzal paused then while Kharate waited in silence patiently. Suddenly the Khan came to a decision.

'It's decided then. Let your men visit their families and be ready to mount up. We leave in one week.'

'Do we take the route north-west to fort Panhalgad then?' queried Kharate, rising out of his seat.

An evil smile crossed Afzal's face then, and despite himself, Kharate shuddered in involuntary fear and disgust. He knew from experience that whatever the Khan had planned was something he would rather not know of beforehand.

Chapter 10

24th May 1659 Rajgad fort

The simple audience chamber was lit by four-foot-tall brass *samaya* lanterns with cotton wicks held in open trays. The cotton wicks rested on ports around the circumference of round trays. Each tray had a depression, from center to periphery, that held the oil which the wicks took up. They cast a warm light over the people assembled in the room.

A wide settee was placed at the head of the room. Jijabairaje, Shivaji's mother, in a simple green sari sat at one end. The light played on her patrician features. She was a slim, fair skinned lady in her late fifties. Brown eyes blazing with intelligence and warmth coupled with a fine aristocratic nose and thinnish lips, spoke of a beauty in her past. A small crescent drawn in red vermillion adorned the center of her forehead attesting to her married status.

She was after all a princess of the great Jadhav family, descended in a direct line from the clan of Lord Krishna of the Mahabharata. The Yadav clan of Lord Krishna had become Jadhav in the Marathi language. Today though, her brow was furrowed in worry and her lips were set in a compressed line.

Next to her sat Shivaji. He was as fair as her and he wore a simple tunic and dhotar. His hair was loose and shimmered blue black as it tumbled to his shoulders. His mustaches were oiled to two points, as was his beard which was neatly trimmed and narrowed down to a dagger point. His forehead too was adorned with a crescent in vermillion. His earlobes had simple gold rings and he too looked worried.

Standing in a respectful group in front of the pair were Moro Pingale, Shyamraj Ranzhekar, Mankoji Dahatonde, Gopinath Bokil and Yesaji Kank.

Shivaji clapped his hands once, and an armed attendant materialized at the door and bowed low in a *muzra*.

'Send in our special guests,' ordered Shivaji and with that a motley group entered the room. All four newcomers bowed low in obeisance. The gathering looked askance at what appeared to be a Hindu holy man – a *sadhu*, a Muslim priest – a *maulvi*, a beggar and a prosperous trader dressed in an out- of- region fashion.

'What news Dighe?' Shivaji commanded and the sadhu shuffled forward. Vishwasrao Dighe was a middle-aged, completely nondescript looking individual of average height and build. He was balding and had a lazy eye, which gave his disguise a comic if not pathetic flair. While he belonged to the warrior kshatriya *Chandraseniya Kaayastha Prabhu* community, he was also fluent in Persian and routinely passed off as Hindu or Muslim. Rumor was, he had also gotten himself circumcised to pass muster if required.

'Sire, Afzal Khan left Bijapur yesterday with an enormous show of strength. My spies tell me he has over twenty thousand men in arms, along with scores of elephants, camels and cannon. What is funny though is that he did not take the road to fort Panhalgad, which would have put him in a direct line with us, but moved north instead to Solapur.'

Having delivered his report, the man stepped back.

Realizing the importance of intelligence, Shivaji had invested in a country-wide spy network for the last fifteen years, and the enormous expense had more than paid for itself over the years. Shivaji had personally honored Dighe with the title, '*Vishwasrao*', or one who could be relied on.

'Vallabhdas, Sunderji?' and with that, the merchant and the beggar, stepped forward and once again made the *muzra* to Shivaji.

'Aurangzeb is busy consolidating his power. He does not have time to look to the Deccan yet. As you know, the Rajputs were split down the middle supporting both Dara and him and now that he has seized the throne, he is setting about bringing the other faction into the fold. To mollify the Rajputs, Jats, Sikhs and other warrior Hindu clans, he has also slightly reduced his program of forced conversions and temple destruction.'

Vallabhdas and Sunderji were from the area of Gujarat, which lay to the north of Shivaji's territory and their area of operation extended all the way north, past Delhi and into the Punjab. Both were totally committed to the cause of independence. Their land had seen the most horrific tyranny from the invaders. Though Gujarat was the resting abode of Lord Krishna, the populace was peaceful and as a result had suffered horribly. Gujarat was also the westernmost part of Hindustan and therefore closest to Arabia across the *Sindhu sagar* sea. After the rise of the Mughals, trade had shifted from Dabhol to the port of Surat in Gujarat, and Surat was the point from which the faithful embarked on the voyage to Mecca for the annual *haj* festival as well. Surat was rich beyond imagination. It also housed the most prominent slave market in Hindustan.

The greatest number of women taken as slaves and sold into the markets of Arabia were from Gujarat. It was said that the women of Gujarat were more feisty than the men. The Muslims had therefore evolved the technique of sewing shut a particularly troublesome sex slave's lips, to be opened only to allow the poor creature to be fed; and resewn promptly thereafter.

Entire communities had been forcibly converted to Islam. Such was the case with the Khoja, a prosperous trading community settled along the coast.

Surprisingly, despite centuries of tyranny, there had not been a single uprising in that province.

Shivaji mulled this over, deep in thought and then finally nodded to the last man to come forward.

'*Muzra* raje' and with that, the *maulvi* was transformed into the *Ramoshi* he was. Bahirji Naik Jadhav was the kingdom's spymaster and controlled a huge network of spies all over Hindustan. When the old emperor Shah Jehan, Aurangzeb's father had fallen ill in the fort of Agra, Shivaji had learned of the development one day before Aurangzeb himself did. At that time, which was roughly four years ago, the prince Aurangzeb had been the Mughal viceroy in the Deccan with his headquarters at Burhanpur.

The day Shivaji heard the news, he sent off his lawyer, to a surprised Aurangzeb professing loyalty, asking for acceptance for the forts he had captured from the Bijapur Sultanate and asking for acceptance for any future transgressions. Since the territory captured by Shivaji was not his anyway, Aurangzeb had been delighted to provide his blessing, and had sent back a robe of honor before leaving post-haste for Delhi. It was during this journey back to Delhi that he'd thought through how to slaughter his brothers and seize the crown.

Shivaji, meanwhile, had immediately set out to plunder Junnar, an important Mughal trading center, knowing full well the Mughals were busy in other matters. The treasury at Junnar had yielded loot of around a hundred and fifty thousand rupees. Shivaji had again followed up the raid by writing a letter of apology to Aurangzeb for his transgression assuring him it would not happen again. The money was not given back and Aurangzeb could only fume impotently; but it was at this point that he realized this *kafir* was unlike the others.

'*Raje*, these men are right, we have only one opponent at the moment. Even the Portuguese and Siddi are relatively quiet right now,' he quietly remarked.

'Your order, to abduct five Jesuit priests from Sawantwadi and offer them the choice to either convert to Hinduism, or then lose their heads, worked perfectly!'

'This was exactly how the Portuguese devils have been forcibly converting our people to their strange faith. Obviously, the priests refused and obviously we hacked their heads off and sent them to Goa. I'm told the viceroy almost soiled his silk drawers when the heads were delivered to him,' chuckled Bahirji.

'Their destruction of temples has also halted after you made an example of the Saptakoteshwar temple in the village of Narwe that they had converted to a church. I passed on your orders, and we took great delight in burning all their stuff, including that funny wooden cross they seem to love and reconsecrated our deities in the shrine. I only suggest that we do that in earnest given the thousands of temples those ugly red-haired baboons have looted and converted to churches over the past few centuries.'

Saying that, the man saluted deeply again, bending at the waist, and stepped back to his original position in the group.

'Thank you, brothers,' said Shivaji holding his palms together in the traditional gesture of respect indicating their audience was coming to an end.

'Please hurry back to your positions and your teams. I need constant information on Afzal's movements. I need to know who his chieftains are, their strengths, weaknesses and any other information you find. Remember, no detail is too small, or too insignificant.'

The quartet left as quietly as they had appeared and Shivaji gestured to Yesaji to speak first.

'Yesaji, as commander of our infantry, how many men can we field?'

Yesaji fidgeted, and looking down at his hands replied, 'Sire, I could stretch to four thousand right now, but if you give me till after the planting is done, I can round up another thousand or so'

'Mankoji, our cavalry numbers?'

'Raje, we have nearly four thousand *Shiledars* and *Bargirdars* combined. If we enter the field against the Khan, we'll need Arabians though, and without control of any port, the overland route using smugglers is just too dangerous, not to mention expensive. It would be suicide to take to the plains with our hill ponies. They'll run their hearts out for us, but are no match for the Arabians for speed.'

'*Yasyashva, tasya rajya,*

Yasyashva, tasya swarajya' intoned Shivaji under his breath;

Where horses, there a state,

Where horses, there's independence.

With the entire coast controlled by foreign enemies, getting horses and weapons was a problem that Shivaji had to face each day.

'Moropant, what is your counsel?' Shivaji added the 'pant' for respect when addressing the old Brahmin warrior-administrator and Moro stood a little straighter at this request from his king. Moro was extremely fair, as fair as the English traders at Rajapur, those men with their ridiculous hats. Like almost everyone else, he fought when on campaign and was lean and fit. He wore the looser dhotar, robe and typical headgear of the Brahmin. His right ear was pierced in the upper region and held a gold ring from which dangled a pearl, another hallmark of the *Chitpavan* Brahmin community he hailed from. Hazel green eyes in a long, clean-shaven spare face exuded intelligence and power.

He pulled his *uparna* shawl a little tighter to give himself a little time to gather and frame his thoughts; it would not do to ramble in front of his king,

'Bijapur has already sent out threatening letters to all the *deshmukh* chieftains in our area. I wonder how many of them will still stay with us. Afzal will gather men and material as he rolls towards us, and I figure he will top out at around thirty thousand cavalry and infantry.

'Further, with our queen Sai in critical condition and Shamburaje just about two…' his voice trailed off.

Shivaji's mood deepened and he glanced at his mother, who had remained uncharacteristically silent during all the proceedings.

'Moropant, this kingdom exists to bring back God's rule to this tortured land. Our individual troubles are of no consequence. Please leave that out and give me your frank opinion,' Shivaji said with a wave of his hand and turned his piercing gaze back to the man.

'Lord, I recommend we sue for peace,' and with that there was a chorus of assent from the other men as well.

'Let us give back a few forts and live to fight another day,' said Moro in his quiet and chaste accent.

Shivaji looked around the room and saw his commanders nodding quietly at the sensible and sage advice. For once, the slight smile that always adorned his expression had deserted him and his eyes flashed dark and stormy.

Finally, he turned to his mother.

'*Shivba* (only she could use the affectionate term), have you forgotten the tales of Krishna and his slaying of the evil Kans that I told you as a child?

'This problem will not go away. How many more of your subjects will you see killed, raped and enslaved by these Islamic invaders? Sometimes it is better to go directly to the head of the snake and crush it with one blow,' she emphasized with a chopping motion of her hand.

The men had only known Jijabai's kindness; now they saw her anger flare briefly.

'Do you think these people know the meaning of *dharma?* Do you think a peace treaty is of any significance to them? If you do not stand up now, the tiny flicker of hope that the people in this tiny independent homeland feel after almost three hundred and fifty years of slavery will be dashed!!

'Do I need to remind you what happened to your grandfather and uncles?' And with that an old, oft-remembered pain flashed across the lady's face..

'I remember every word Mother, but maybe this group needs reminding,' retorted Shivaji while the men hung their heads, refusing to meet his eye.

'Listen up then,' the old woman commanded, and her eyes went focused on some distant point as she began narrating the tale.

Lakhuji Jadhavrao, Jijabai's father was a bulwark of the old Nizamshahi Sultanate almost twenty- five years ago. The Sultanate had its capital at the ancient fort of Devagiri which Khilji had renamed to Daulatabad meaning 'place of wealth' on account of the immense loot he had taken when it fell.

As a commander of ten thousand cavalry, Lakhuji had served the Turkish Nizam Sultan faithfully for over a decade. He was a fixture at the court and the Nizamshah looked to him for advice and counsel over and above the military capability he provided. This became even more prominent after the death of the great general, Malik Ambar, the Abyssinian who had humbled even the mighty Mughal empire.

The Muslim nobles at court looked at this rising star askance. How could this *kafir* enjoy the limelight and privileges in this most holy of empires. The inevitable whisper mongering began. This *kafir* was becoming too important, he'd need to be shown his place.

'One morning, my father Lakhuji arrived at court along with three of my brothers Achluji, Raghuji, and Yeshwant.

Achluji, was ever the prankster. He was the one who twisted 'his' ear during my marriage ceremony,' and the old woman flushed a shade of pink at the oblique reference to her husband Shahaji and the ancient custom. In that part of Hindustan, the bride's brother twisted the ear of the groom during the marriage ceremony to remind him to treat his sister well throughout her life.

'As was the court custom, all the Hindus had to surrender their swords before entering the audience chamber in the presence of the Nizamshah.

The courtiers all filed in, and Lakhuji observed nothing amiss. Several other nobles, both Hindu and Muslim asked after his health, and congratulated him on his recent military victories on behalf of the Shah. As was his position, he was in the front rank of the most powerful nobles to pay obeisance to the Sultan.'

Though every single man knew this history, all eyes were transfixed on the mother of the king as she narrated the tragic tale.

'After the usual fanfare and tedious minutes of self-given titles, the Burhan Nizam Shah III was ushered to his throne. My father thought he would be singled out for recognition given the lands and tributes that he had recently captured, and he straightened in anticipation of the announcement.

Instead, the Shah looked up at him, and suddenly getting up, disappeared into the interiors of the chamber via a hidden alcove.

This was the signal and suddenly, the Muslim nobles who not moments earlier had congratulated and backslapped the Jadhav clan in bonhomie, whipped out their swords and surrounded my family like a pack of wolves.

Can you imagine the confusion? The terror? What must my brothers have felt? The youngest was barely sixteen...' and with that her voice caught and she struggled visibly to regain her composure.

Shivaji put a hand on his mother's forearm and silenced her. Everyone knew how the tale ended.

The Jadhavs had seen the mood change and had whipped out the only weapons they bore, which were their *katars*. What use a dagger against swords though? The men had put up a fight but had been cut down mercilessly, right there in the audience chamber of the Shah. Not a single Hindu noble had come to their aid. What could they have done either, armed only with their own daggers?

Lady Jijabai composed herself with a visible effort and when her voice was under control, continued

'This Afzal not only humiliated your father, but also engineered the death of your brother Sambhaji, never forget that.'

'Recover Sambhaji's debt for me Shivba!!!!'rang out her voice. And Lady Jijabai quickly got up and exited the room using the private entrance lest her emotions betray her.

'*Jagdamb, jagdamb,*' came unbidden to Shivaji's lips invoking the mother goddess.

'We fight brothers! We stop this demon at all costs. I want all preparations to begin immediately. We do battle!'

Chapter 11

Dabhol port

The men exited Dabhol the same way as they'd entered, in a lightning exit cutting down anyone who stood in the way. The only difference was, the loot that they'd managed to capture, in the old port town which was tied to the backs of the Arabian horses they had managed to liberate.

The raid had been highly successful. They'd lost only two men and had killed almost fifty by most accounts. More important, they had gotten fifty-five Arabian horses, twenty muskets with ball and powder, and one month's payroll meant for the Turkish garrison, which was exactly as the spies had reported.

In the space of a mile from the gate of the town, the raiding party, numbering two hundred cavalry had reached the outer fringes of the forest and within another mile had completely disappeared. The pursuing Turkish *kizalbaksh* hussars on their faster Arabians had seen the Marathi band reach the forest and then... just disappear. To plunge into the forest after them would have been inviting certain death, and at a signal, the corps wheeled and after hurling abuses at their tormentors, cantered back to the town.

The Marathas slowed down once they entered the forest and the rearguard reported that the pursuit had stopped, even waiting a few moments longer to ensure this was not a feint from the Turks.

The road narrowed to a trail so that only single file travel was possible. Dattaji and his companion realizing that the father and son had really never sat in the saddle, had tied each man seated behind to his own self to keep them from falling off in the charge from the gates of the town to the forest boundary

'How the hell do you do this?' retorted Hiroji when the party stopped briefly to water the horses at a small stream, and he had been cut loose.

He had rope burns under his armpits, where the rope had ridden up and chafed him almost raw, and his seat felt like someone had whacked it repeatedly with a broad leather whip.

'Are you capable of fathering children even after days of this?' he retorted, at which general laughter broke out.

'So, you want to fight in Shivajiraje's army?' queried Kondaji with a broad grin on his handsome face.

'What happens when you fall off your horse? Who is going to come get you?'

'Why, isn't there any infantry? I'd rather not get back on that beast if it's all the same to you,' remarked Ramaji, more calmly.

'Suit yourself. We're making for Dholparya's mountain. The Raje built a fort on the mountaintop three years ago and named it 'Pratapgad' or fort of valor. You're lucky that we can only walk the horses in this terrain'

'If you can keep up and don't mind walking twenty hours straight, it's no skin off my nose,' saying which he hooked his index finger in his cheek, to dislodge the wad of spent tobacco, before inserting a fresh plug.

It was going to be a long day and night. As they proceeded into the depths of the forest, vision narrowed to a shaded green tunnel. The path rose and fell and doubled back on itself. All around were majestic trees that towered over them, trees of types they'd never seen before and in places the green ceiling closed over them and shut out the bright sunlight completely. It felt as though they were travelling underwater, or in some dark green grotto.

While there was no wind in this path deep inside the jungle, the men and horses were protected from the summer sun. The heat and humidity though, was another matter. Before long, tunics were soaked with sweat and the horses had worked up a fine lather. The little hill ponies gamely soldiered on, perhaps sensing that they were proceeding in the direction of home. The salt from his sweat made the rope burns under Hiroji's armpits sting even more.

The presence of so much activity had stilled the noises in the jungle, but the men could feel the eyes of small and large animals all around them. When the tree cover parted slightly, which was not often, Ramaji checked the position of the sun and deduced they were traveling steadily in a north-easterly direction

After six hours of steady march, through the by now almost impenetrable lattice of forest, the group came upon a meadow with a brook running through one corner. Before the clearing came into view, the horses smelled the water. Dattaji's pony's ears cocked forward and he knew they were halfway to Khed village, which was roughly equidistance from Dabhol and Pratapgad.

Mankoji gave the order to make camp for the night when there was still some light. All the scouts came in reporting no pursuit of any kind and their replacements went out on patrol.

Hiroji and Ramaji rested by the base of a large jackfruit tree. The spiny fruit grew abundant and Hiroji used his spear to cut off a large jackfruit ten feet up the tree trunk. The men fell to with a gusto on the fleshy pods after slicing through the thick spiny outer covering. They had not eaten for almost a day, and the sweet, succulent flesh that covered each seed felt ambrosial. As they spat out the large seeds, the horses waited expectantly, as the seeds were a delicacy for the hill ponies.

Discipline was strict and the men were ordered not to forage far. One youth climbed the jackfruit tree and it was liberated of all its ripe fruit. That bounty alone was enough to feed half the men. The staple rations of the Marathi army were handfuls of roasted horse-gram lentils followed by a gulp of water. It was the cheapest protein to be found in the war-ravaged land. The fruit were divided equally, and the men supplemented the jackfruit with handfuls of the salted roasted lentil. They drank freely from the clear mountain spring before laying down to rest for a few hours.

The light went as though on signal, but it was still quite warm. Since they were quite literally in the middle of nowhere, Mankoji had allowed fires to be lit. Sentries were posted out of the line of sight of the party. The horses had been hitched in lines and sentries posted. This was panther, leopard, and bear country. Hiroji couldn't remember the last time he'd been this full. There was a small breeze rustling the leaves of the forest. The earthy smell of the ponies hitched nearby coupled with the clean, resin smell of the branches crackling in the fire lulled him into comfort.

Suddenly there was a stir, and his eyes came awake, his right hand instinctively going to his *kripan* sword laid down by his side.

'Relax, son,' mumbled a figure dropping next to him in an easy squat.

Hiroji realized it was Mankoji Dahatonde himself.

The commander was dressed just like the rest of the men. Up close, Hiroji realized the man was easily past sixty years of age. His face was nut brown with lively black eyes, and his mustaches spread luxuriously and gray-black on his lean, weathered cheeks. The long vermilion religious *tila* mark on his forehead extended proudly from between heavy brows to his hairline. Gnarled wrists thick with corded veins held his sword across his lap

Mankoji just stared at Hiroji for a few seconds, and a wave of emotion swept across his face.

'I wanted to personally thank you, my boy. It was only later that I learned that my grandniece, my sister's granddaughter was going to be sold in auction today along with her children. Had it not been for you, she might have been bought and hidden away when our raid struck.

I couldn't have spared the time to look for her, as doing that would have meant my band would've been slaughtered by the garrison.

What you did was foolish, but very brave, and this old man thanks you for it!' saying which he clapped his hand on Hiroji's shoulder, and brusquely wiped the sudden, hot tears that had sprung from his eyes with the back of his hand.

Hiroji struggled to articulate a reply, embarrassed at the old man's emotion. 'Sir, how did you know of my deed?' He asked falteringly.

'Oh, our spies were already there for the past week. How do you think we knew of the garrison payroll coming in?' and the old man smiled, cracking the craggy face and showing very white teeth.

'They reported that your opening gambit and use of a blade in each hand was very impressive. Where did you learn to fight like that?' asked Mankoji curiously.

'From *taal*' replied Hiroji, jerking his thumb at Ramoji, who had been quietly listening to the entire conversation from where he had bedded down a few feet away.

Mankoji regarded the two men somberly for a few seconds more in silence, the dying firelight making shadows of his eyes and highlighting his sharp cheekbones.

'We need.. *Swarajya*, our fledgling independence, needs men like you. Rest now, tomorrow is going to be a long day. It is a hard climb to reach Pratapgad' he said straightening up and was gone as silently as he had come.

Chapter 12

Bijapur May 1659

The Khan left Bijapur with an impressive show of force. The mile-long cavalcade was preceded by *Fatehlashkar*, a bull elephant carrying the standard of the Adilshahi Sultanate. The beast was in the prime of his life and carried scars from numerous battles. His back was covered in a red velvet blanket worked with gold that came down on either side to his knees. The green crescent of Islam flew proudly beside the Adilshahi flag. He had a pair of magnificent tusks, almost a light orange with age and one of the tips was broken off in an earlier fight. He was trained to roll up his trunk and trumpet at periodic intervals or when the mahout seated on his neck, gently reminded him with his prod. The effect was at once terrifying and awe-inspiring as he swayed majestically past the gates of the city.

Following *Fatehlashkar* came Afzal himself seated in a gold plated, covered howdah on his own elephant. The howdah was equipped with racks of spears and baskets of arrows, with a stand for his bow and mace. In a showy display of his power, Afzal held a *danpatta* in each hand and the blades swayed rhythmically on either side of the elephant with its steady plod.

What followed were ranks upon ranks of elephants pulling cannons and mortars of all sizes and camels equipped with light guns.

Next came the cavalry regiments with each proudly flying their colors. Turks, Uzbeks, Pathans, *habshi* Abyssinians, Deccan Muslims and lastly the Hindu regiments were all easily distinguishable by dress, headgear, appearance and weaponry.

Last came the infantry. There were Pathans, Marathas, and *habshis*, among the assembled force, but the contingent that drew the loudest cheers was the thousand or so Pathan gunmen with the latest wheellock muskets. While the *toradar* or matchlock was still more prevalent in Hindustan, this new type of musket was a curiosity because it could fire during wet conditions. Everyone knew the fury of the monsoons was soon coming and this new-fangled weapon might just tip the balance.

In all, there were approximately ten thousand infantry and slightly more cavalry. This mini city was, of course, accompanied by an entire retinue of servants, merchants, dancing girls, pack animals and hangers-on that brought up a long, disorderly and multicolored tail.

The people of Bijapur stared in amazement at this gigantic procession as it made its way out of the city and made camp only about five miles away at the end of the first day.

***

Afzal was in a fine mood. The cooks had slaughtered a goat for his meal. He especially enjoyed the head, slow cooked in the fiery, but complex spices of the cooking of the Karnataka region around Bijapur. The *bedgi* variety of chili pepper was a huge favorite of his and the cooks knew to include the powdered spice in any meat prepared for him.

His chieftains had been summoned to his large tent, and presently the men began filing in.

Afzal sat on his camp chair leaning against a plush cushion, slowly masticating the post-prandial digestive mix of aniseed and spices rolled into a fragrant pan leaf *bida*. His son Fazal Khan stood to his right, as did Randulla Khan junior, or *Rustom-e-Zaman* as he was more popularly called.

The lamps cast a soft yellow light on the plush interior of the tent, all outfitted in silks and satins. Afzal had grown up hardscrabble but had vowed never to travel that path again. The men were already deciding how Shivaji's territory was to be carved up.

The attendant announced a new group and Ankush Khan and Musa Khan strode in together. Both were Pathans, and favorites of Afzal. While Fazal and Randulla had known nothing but luxury, the

128

newcomers looked like what they were; hardened warriors from the Hindukush, who had made their way to the Sultanate in search of fame and fortune.

Afzal expansively indicated the tray of *bida* in front of him, inviting the newcomers to partake, and both men gratefully accepted, tucking the fragrant bundles into their cheeks.

Just then, the curtain parted again, and Naikji Pandhare, and Naikji Kharate strode in. Both men were much older than the crew assembled there yet held themselves erect and in a soldierly manner. They bowed low in a *kurnisaat* of greeting to the Khan and took their place to one side, a little away from the others.

Afzal acted as if he hadn't noticed, but he was aware of the internal bickerings between the factions in his party. Hindustani Muslims versus those from outside, Maratha against Muslim, and Maratha against Maratha vied for prominence in the Adilshahi *durbar* and Afzal fostered that tension in order to keep everyone in their place, just so long as they feared him.

'Lord, my sword yearns to take *kafir* heads; when do we cross into enemy territory?' Musa set the ball rolling.

'Well said!' chorused Fazal and Ankush looking to the Khan for his reaction.

Afzal pretended to give the question some thought, but in truth, he had already decided upon a course of action.

'We go to Solapur first,' said Afzal evenly, looking around to see who was smart enough to guess the reason.

'But Solapur is north, while our destination is north-west. Why are we taking a roundabout route?' queried Fazal and the Khan turned to him in irritation. Had he been too soft? Or was the boy, just plain dumb? He knew he should never have married his mother, that chubby girl from Arcot. His sole interest at the time had been to forge an alliance with her father who held a small *jagir* in that rich province. How was this simpleton ever going to manage the large estates, that he, Afzal had managed to build after a lifetime of hard work and guile?

Only Kharate guessed the real reason and his brow wrinkled, but he did not speak.

'Let us have some sport lads! And while doing that, let's needle that rat Shiva. Maybe he'll emerge out of his hiding place sooner?' chuckled Afzal, directing an orange stream expertly into a spittoon held up by an ever-attendant Abdul.

Suddenly, there was a commotion outside the tent, and Afzal sharply remarked to Abdul, 'Go see what it is! Tell whoever is causing this noise that I'll reward him with fifty lashes if he's wasting my time,' and Abdul hurried out.

A moment later he came back in panic, and completely forgetting all etiquette, blurted out, 'Lord, lord, *Fatehlashkar* has died! What do we do now? It's an ill omen, our mission is cursed..' and so saying began wringing his hands in terror.

'What nonsense is this!' exploded Afzal, and swiftly picking up his sword, dashed out of the tent. To his surprise, he saw a collection of nobles and soldiers, both Hindu and Muslim, nervously entreating his guards for an audience.

Someone shouted, 'Lord, we must turn back and consult with the priests as to the auspicious time to depart. Please Lord! Please!' and a general hubbub followed.

'Silence!!' roared Afzal, and his deep growl carried over the entire crowd terrifying them into silence. His anger was a thing to behold. He held his arms wide, with his sword held by the scabbard in his left and hissed in what was now complete silence.

'Fools, all of you! We are sons of Allah! Have you been so corrupted by the ways of the *kafir* that you look at stars to tell you how to live your life? Shame on you!

'I, Afzal, am master of my own fate and I tell you that I will bring back Shiva's head on a spear to post outside the gates of Bijapur!

'Let me not hear any more of this nonsense!!' he thundered and issued a quick order to the guard.

'Ride back to Bijapur right now and get another elephant from the royal stable! I want to start at the crack of dawn tomorrow!'

Seeing this level of confidence in their leader, the men looked at each other and slowly but surely, the resistance broke down till they melted away into small groups back to their tents.

***

The day broke to a beautiful line of pink on the eastern horizon. Before even the first rooster had crowed, the assembly was treated to the spectacle of the Shah's personal elephant himself. A large bull in the prime of life proudly decked out with the royal livery bearing the official standard. As if on cue, the beast trumpeted when he saw Afzal step out of his tent.

A cheer started, and before long, it had become a torrent of sound, 'Praise be to Afzal, praise be to Afzal! *Allahu Akbar, Allahu Akbar*!!'from thousands of throats who had literally seen a man defy the gods on the strength of his own will and conviction.

They army reached Solapur on the fifth day and encamped outside the town. This was a major trading center in the kingdom of the Sultanate and prominent members of the town came to pay their respects to the Khan enquiring as to the reason for his visit.

'All will be revealed in due course,' smiled Afzal accepting their gifts and letting them know that he would grace their town the next morning.

***

The stone temple had stood for a thousand years.

The Rashtrakuta kings had ruled a thousand years before and they had left their legacy in the thousands of temples carved out of the hard basalt rock of the region.

Or who knew, perhaps it was even older, much older, from the time of the Satavahana kings. It was impossible to tell. After the thirteenth century, anything that the Islamic invaders could lay hands on, had been destroyed. Thousands of temples had been demolished and entire libraries had been burned by this or that Sultan. Millions of irreplaceable manuscripts had gone up in smoke.

What was undeniable was the beauty of the place, and the serenity on the face of the idol of Kalabhairav, the simultaneous destroyer and regenerator of the world.

The temple consisted of a shrine and a hall. The shrine was where the *Shivalinga* was placed in a sunken area with a channel to route the offerings of milk and *ghee* that were ritually offered by devotees. The idol of the *Kaalbhairav* was on a ledge on the back wall.

There was a raised stone lintel to enter the shrine. The hall had open bays with intricate stone latticework to let the breeze in. Carved stone pillars with lotus and mango leaf motifs supported the roof and the stone *kalash* shaped dome atop the temple.

The architectural ornamentation came from the recesses and projections in intricate patterns in the walls themselves, rather than carved figurines, or other embellishments. This was a hallmark of the temple architecture style of the region.

The stone idol of Bhairav, or Shiv, was four feet tall. A tall brass lamp with multiple wicks stood in front, casting shadows on the idol's face. A priest who looked older than the temple itself, sat silently reciting Sanskrit verses under his breath in front of the idol. A few devotees sat in the outer hall, hands folded, and eyes closed, tuning in to the peace and harmony of the place.

It was at this point that the party of Afzhal Khan rode into the temple courtyard. The meditative silence was shattered by the clatter of hooves as the men rode the horses up the stone steps past the outer gate and into the premises. The devotees looked shocked at this breach of tradition and as quickly their anger was stillborn upon seeing the heavily armed party. Afzal had been careful to bring only his co-religionists on this mission. Kharate, Pandhre, Mambaji Bhosle, Pilaji Bhosle, Shankraji Bhosle and the other Hindu chieftains had been kept in the dark.

Afzal swung off his horse, tossing the reins to a soldier and strode into the temple. The first thing he did was to kick the waist-high stone figurine of the kneeling *nandi* or bull at the entrance to show his utter contempt for these symbols of the *kafir* religion. The few people in the hall blanched to see him stride into the hall wearing his leather sandals, again an insult, but no one had the nerve to do or say anything. They cast their eyes down and moved to the corners of the hall, looking for the easiest way to escape.

The party of about twenty men trooped into the hall and looked curiously around. Most had never been inside a temple and the few that had, had been on a mission of destruction not prayer. Afzal crossed the lintel and entered the shrine.

The squeak of leather sandals broke the priest out of his meditative spell and he looked up in anger. Seeing the Khan and the rest of the men filing into the sanctum turned his bowels to water, and his protest when he saw one of the men park himself on the *Shivalinga* died on his lips.

Afzal savored the man's fear and desperation for a few seconds, and then barked, 'So this is your all-powerful god then?' with a sneer on his lips.

He extended a hand back without turning his head, looking intently into the serene sightless eyes of the idol, and a soldier smacked an iron hammer into his palm. The instrument was normally used to hammer tent stakes into the ground. Afzal pounded the head of the hammer lightly into his left palm to test the heft and stepped up to the idol.

Sensing his intent, the priest yelled, 'No, please no, Lord, I beg of you,' and broke into a piteous mewl, seeing which one of the men drew his dagger.

Afzal however, stopped him with a gesture, 'No, he needs to see this, and tell everyone what happened here… hold him.' And with that he swung the hammer back and brought it onto the face of the idol with all his considerable strength.

The hammer bounced off the granite and the nose cracked. The priest uttered a keening cry and tears rolled down the wizened cheeks as he averted his face in horror.

'Hold his head up and open his eyes! Cut off the eyelids, if need be, but he needs to see this' barked Afzal, swinging the hammer again.

Nothing could withstand those blows and bit by bit, the ancient idol cracked and finally the torso broke into a few large pieces.

'Gather the pieces of the head and take it with us. We'll make sure to bury those pieces under the steps of our Jama mosque in Bijapur so that the feet of the faithful trample these icons of the *kafirs* every single day,' he ordered between pants. Even his massive strength had been tested today.

Handing back the hammer to his man, he smiled at the priest, 'Tell that Shivaji who pretends to be the torch bearer of the Hindu religion that this is what happens when you cross the Sultanate. Tell him to come and face me and I will set him on the true path.'

With that he strode out of the temple and into the courtyard, where a knot of terrified villagers had gathered. They could not comprehend the hate that would want to visit this sort of wanton destruction. Several were openly weeping at the sight of the shattered remains of the idol glimpsed in the dim recesses of the inner sanctum. The old priest clung to the legs of the idol, sobbing uncontrollably, washing the feet with his tears at his inability to protect his god.

Chapter 13

Rajgad June 1659

'What news Bahirji?' asked Shivaji, accepting the man's *muzra* and indicating that he should speak freely.

Bahirji was in disguise that day as a *Vasudev*, a traveling minstrel who entertained poor villagers with tales from the great epics in exchange for whatever they could spare. Despite being dirt-poor themselves, people offered a handful of rice here, a few grains of lentils there. He wore the conical hat woven of grass adorned with blue-green peacock tail feathers that was the hallmark of that role. A simple, knee length cotton tunic, cinched in at the waist with a faded red sash on a tightly wrapped dhotar completed his dress. He held the single stringed drone musical instrument *ektari* in his right hand and *chiplya* or castanets in his left. A long, hefty cotton cross body sling held all his possessions and was also used to hold the offerings provided by his audience. His daily job was to go from village to village narrating the stories of the Ramayana and the Mahabharata in song and prose, educating children in the guise of entertainment, and connecting people to their roots.

The audience chamber was empty this early in the day save for the king. The room was situated in the fort's *ballekilla* or keep. This was the highest point of the fort to which the defenders would fall back in a last stand. The majestic sweep of the Maaval provinces cloaked in a sea of green could be glimpsed from the large windows. Outside the windows, a pair of kites were poised in mid-air, the tips of their wings making fractional adjustment to compensate for the shifting air currents while their sharp eyes scoured for prey far, far below.

'Sire, the Khan does not make for our territory! For some reason, he goes deeper into their own territory in a direction at right angles to Rajgad. It makes no sense whatsoever!' remarked a puzzled Bahirji.

'Stranger still, he just desecrated the *Kaalbhairav* temple at Solapur in full view of all the assembled populace. Why would he risk angering the Hindu chieftains in his own army on the eve of a battle?'

'Well, he does call himself a *buthshikan* and a *kufrshikan*,' remarked Shivaji drily.

'Still, this bears watching. Infiltrate his camp. I want daily reports on his movements. I want to know who his chieftains are, and which of our people are joining him,' saying which Shivaji dismissed his top spy. The man bowed low in salute again and departed.

***

The Bijapur army broke camp and in a decision that puzzled just about everybody, turned further away from Shivaji's territory, making its way northeast to the fort of Nardurg.

There, Afzal repeated his performance, this time smashing the main idol in the even more ancient temple of *Khandoba*, who was considered a reincarnation of Vishnu the Preserver. Again, this was done in full view of an audience, reinforcing that he could do whatever he wanted to the holy places of the Hindus with full impunity.

On the evening of that day, the Khan was in a joyous mood celebrating with drink and dance accompanied by his top chieftains. The biggest topic on his mind was which of the girls to order to his bed that night. He looked like a felled oak as he lay sprawled among the fine silk cushions and bolsters arrayed on thick woolen rugs in front of the dance area. Four musicians sat to one side providing the accompaniment to the troupe of dance girls. Ayesha, as lead dancer and owner of the troupe, was doing her best to be selected through veiled gestures and subtle hand movements. She was a little too old for this game thought Afzal; he preferred his meat tender.

Suddenly, the guard posted at the flaps to his tent entered bowing deeply and conveyed that Naikjiraje Pandhre wished an audience.

Afzal grimaced in disgust. Trust the old fool to destroy the mood of the evening. Ankush Khan and the others were already more than a little drunk, lying back on the bolsters around the dance floor.

However, he needed the Hindu nobles on his side to swat this Shivaji, so he raised a hand to stop the dance, and straightened up slightly to show at least a modicum of respect to the old warrior.

The flaps parted and Pandhre came in. He bowed in salute but did not accept the seat that Afzal indicated with an expansive gesture. The music stopped as the dancers retreated to a corner in confusion.

'Lord, why did you have to break the idol of *Khandoba?* Was the *Kaalbhairav* not enough? The men are restless,' spat out the old warrior, his silver whiskers quivering in rage and indignation.

'Shut up, old fool,' replied Ankush, clearly inebriated and forgetting all protocol. 'Do you think we care about the feelings of you filthy *kafirs?*? You are all *vazibul katla*, which in case you don't understand means deserving to be slaughtered.'

Pandhre froze, and his hand dropped to his sword. Afzal realizing the situation could get out of hand very fast, held up a hand and interjected, 'Forgive my brother, Naikjiraje,' adding the *raje* to fluff the old man up.

'He cannot handle his liquor and clearly speaks out of turn,' saying which he subjected Ankush to a withering glare.

'Do you not see this is the only way to draw Shivaji out of his burrow?

'Please think about this calmly and as a war strategy. Shivaji's fifteen or so hill forts are his hiding places. He descends on small raids and is gone before we can marshal our troops. I do not want to spend the next few months chasing him from one fort to another.

'He calls himself the champion of the Hindu religion, does he not? Well, what would a champion do when I openly defy his authority over his religion?' and Afzal halted, peering at Pandhre wondering if his comments had percolated.

Little by little, Pandhre relaxed and his hand fell away from his sword hilt. What the Khan said did make sense. His face, which had suffused with color, relaxed a little and he nodded in assent.

'Hmm… yes, we can bring our cannon to bear on the plains and blow his ragtag forces away without expending a single hussar or infantryman,' and he stroked his chin thoughtfully.

'My informants tell me that Shivaji is still holed up in Rajgad. I need to draw him out. If his people see him do nothing, he loses face, and he cannot afford that. This entire foolish movement of his is based on providing hope to the people and I plan to destroy that hope bit by bit,' and Afzal rested back after providing the winning argument.

Pandhre acknowledged the logic of the argument, also knowing that he really had no choice in the matter. 'So where next, Lord?' he asked.

'Patience, my friend' chuckled Afzal. 'This is a game of chess, and I plan to sweep the board! But all in due time,' said Afzal.

'Once I receive information that Shiva has descended to the plains and started gathering his army, I will plan the best place to meet his 'army,' Afzal said stroking his long beard.

'Meanwhile, letters have gone out to all the *deshmukh* chieftains of the Maaval provinces to immediately join our forces along with all their men. They cannot refuse, since doing so will invite certain death. Their possessions and their families will be forfeit to the Sultanate if they do not comply,' assured the Khan to Pandhre.

After Pandhre had left, Afzal turned his full fury on the sulking Ankush.

'You fool!! You can indulge your fantasies only when all of Hindustan is converted to Islam. Till then, learn to hold your tongue. We need Hindu swords for the moment, don't you realize?' said Afzal, his face mottled with rage.

Seeing Ankush penitent the Khan's rage cooled and he said more soberly, 'Your sentiments are correct, but they should be aired only in the exclusive company of the faithful, do you understand?'

And Ankush nodded meekly in reply.

***

And yet, there was nothing from Shivaji. No letter, no movement, nothing.

Afzal's spies reported that news of the temple's desecration had spread throughout Shivaji's kingdom. While the temples were within the Sultanate kingdom, people had nevertheless started asking questions.

Afzal chuckled at the predicament Shivaji must be facing. And decided to turn up the pressure.

The Adil Shahi army, was like a giant swarm of locusts, that devoured everything within five miles on either side as they passed through the countryside. The size of the force had by now increased to thirty thousand infantry and cavalry with the addition of all the *nayak* chieftains and Marathi *sardar* chieftains who had been pressed into service.

The *Badi begum* had opened the treasury to Afzal to put out this Hindu spark of rebellion mercilessly. The only way to keep a population twenty times their number under control was to wield terror so completely that no Hindu would dare of sedition.

The state was far worse in the plains of northern Hindustan. And had been steadily deteriorating for the last five hundred years. The province of Sindh had been completely overrun. Raja Dahir of Sindh had gone down fighting and his wives and daughters had become sex slaves to the invaders. The entire populace to a man, had been forcibly converted to Islam. The same was the case with the province of Kashmir with repeated waves of Hindus moving out, fleeing forced conversion. Kashmir was known as a seat of learning with the great

Sanskrit university of Sharda as well as the Martand sun temple figuring prominently as destinations for visiting students..

It was well known that Kashmiri women were prized for their beauty. The situation had become so desperate that fathers had taken to slicing off the noses of their daughters as they entered puberty in the hopes that the disfigurement might perhaps save them from Muslim eyes.

The Italian traveler, Nicolai Manucci, had recorded that in his travels from Pataliputra to Delhi, he had seen minarets made of Hindu heads every half mile. By his calculation, in that journey alone he had counted twenty thousand heads. Minor regional overlords like Abdullah Ferozshahi, had boasted to him, that his service to Islam had been to slaughter over two hundred thousand Hindus with an equal number sold into slavery. Going by the meticulously kept records of all the Muslim invaders in Hindustan over five hundred years, the total number of Hindus slaughtered exceeded forty million.

History weighed heavily on Afzal, and he too yearned to be counted among the front rank of the faithful in terms of the number of *kafirs* slaughtered.

Thirty miles in the same north easterly direction lay another ancient temple. The temple of Mankeshwar, had been built by the Yadav kings and was reputed to be among the most beautiful in the land. The Yadav dynasty had ruled for over a hundred years and had been patrons of art, sculpture, literature and music.

The army of the Bijapur Sultanate took three days to reach Mankeshwar. This time Afzal wanted to send an even stronger message.

The army of the faithful set about destroying the entire temple. Hammers and pickaxes were used by men in the hundreds to completely reduce the once magnificent structure to rubble.

And yet Shivaji did not react

Chapter 14

Pratapgad fort

Hiroji thought the forest would never end. This was the most god-forsaken territory he had ever traveled through. The tree canopy extended as far as the eye could see in every direction. Each path looked exactly like the next. Snakes and scorpions abounded and the mosquitoes that came out when the sun set were enough to drive a man mad.

Early that morning they had had to beat off a pair of leopards who'd come for the horses. One brave sentry, who'd raised the alarm and tried to beat back the pair, had been severely mauled. Already, his wounds were seeping pus and delirium, had set in.

The group was planning to reach Pratapgad fort on the evening of the second day. Shivajiraje had ordered his forces to conduct lightning raids, on the smaller Adhilshahi towns, to distract Afzal Khan and perhaps divide his forces to address these threats. Mankoji had led this raid on Dabhol, while other groups had raided Sangameshwar and Rajapur to the south.

Being the seasoned general he was, Afzal was not fooled. He had shrugged off these distractions. Shivaji had hoped to splinter the opposing forces, but that had not happened.

Dattaji had meanwhile, decided to use this opportunity, to teach Hiroji how to ride. The lessons also served the dual purpose of providing amusement to the rest of the men, watching Hiroji's determined but fruitless efforts to stay on, given the undulating terrain, and the hill pony's jaundiced attitude towards this useless human.

'How do you trust the guides to know how to get out of this jungle?' queried an incredulous Hiroji.

'Last night I stepped away from the campfire, for a little bit of privacy to do my business and chose the wrong path coming back. It was only by sheer luck that I found my way back, and that only because our column had several campfires going, and even then, I ended up almost half a mile from where I'd started,' remarked Hiroji idly scratching a mosquito bite on his arm.

'Lads, shall we tell him the story of Malik Uttujar?' threw Dattaji back over his shoulder, addressing the men immediately behind him.

'This happened more than two hundred years ago,' began Godaji enthusiastically. Godaji Jagtap was a quiet, taciturn man. He had a reputation as a swordsman but refused to provide any detail about his past life. He kept to himself, and Hiroji had seen some private tragedy in his eyes when he felt he wasn't being watched. The only time he came alive was when the talk turned to warfare.

'Alauddin Khilji, as you know was the first Muslim invader, to breach the south of Hindustan in the year 1296. After his death, power had devolved to the dynasty headed by the convert Gangras, who came to call himself Gangu Bahmani Shah.'

'The then ruler, was Alauddin Shah Bahmani, in the year 1453. This entire region of the twelve districts of the Maaval has always been an eyesore. The terrain is too difficult to govern and the people too proud and independent to fully bend to the Sultan's yoke.'

'Bahmani sent his vizier, Malik Uttujar, with a force of ten thousand hard men to subdue this region. Among them were three thousand hand-picked Arab warriors, noted for their skill, ferocity and Islamic zeal.'

'Uttujar decided to start with Shankarrai More who ruled Javli with his family seat at village Paar. When More got word of the army coming his way, he moved his men to the fort of Vishalgad which was a hundred miles south of here within deep forest. He could not have had more than five hundred men at arms under his command.'

'Uttujar laid siege to Vishalgad and after a month, More realized he could not hold out. He sued for terms, accepting the Shah as his master and agreeing to a yearly tribute. Uttujar however, had another demand. He insisted that More along with all his family and his clan convert to Islam.'

'After some thought, More agreed, but then suggested that their combined forces attack the Shirkes, whose family seat was at Sangameshwar, about fifty miles due north, but again deep in the forest. More suggested that why should the privilege of becoming a believer be his alone when the Shirkes too could be brought into the green fold of Islam.'

'Now everyone knew the ancestral rivalry between the More and Shirke clans,' chuckled Godaji. He was warming to the tale and all the men within hearing, though no doubt having heard this tale countless times before, hung onto his every word.

'Some hazy time in the past, some More had insulted some Shirke, or it may have been the other way around, but they'd been killing each other for generations. One wiped out the other's wedding party, and the other retaliated by slaughtering an entire family branch of the other, years after things had apparently cooled down. To these people, revenge is almost a religion,' said Godaji and one or two of the other nodded in assent.

'The combined army set out for Sangameshwar with More leading the way. For the first two days, the More scouts led them along well-defined paths. On the third day however, they took a turn into the depths of the forest and the men lost all sense of direction. The path twisted and turned and became narrower and more precarious. By the time the fourth day dawned, the men were completely lost and totally dependent on the scouts to lead them back.'

'After a long day of tramping through the forest, the men looked forward to setting up camp. A storm had been building up since afternoon and the evening saw the wind gusting in full force. Tree branches whipped in the wind and the ensuing racket and maelstrom of leaves and dust reduced visibility to only a few feet. There was also no clearing in sight. So, Uttujar gave the order for the men to eat dry rations as lighting a fire was impossible and bed down for the night.'

The men hearing this tale now all leaned forward eagerly, in anticipation for what was to come.

'At around midnight, when the men were sleeping, the sleep of utter exhaustion, a signal was conveyed, and Shirke's men, who had been shadowing the force the entire day behind thick cover emerged stealthily. The path was so narrow that there was not enough room to fully swing a sword. The More's men pulled out their *katars,* and with *jambiyas, bichwas* and an assortment of daggers, the combined forces of the More and Shirke clans set about slaughtering the sleeping enemy.'

'The work was done in utter silence with the racket of the wind providing cover for any groan and shriek that did manage to escape. The men were butchered like hogs,' reported Godaji gleefully.

'When daylight broke the next morning, only two men, though wounded, had somehow managed to survive, while the Mores and Shirkes had melted away. What those men saw was a massacre like none before. It is reported that jackals, hynenas, wolves, wild pigs and panthers feasted for a full month!'

'By the time those two made it back, they were half mad, with terror and thirst, and nobody at first believed their story. The fact of the matter remained however, that the forest had swallowed the entire Sultani force, including their vaunted commander Uttujar.'

'The Mores and Shirkes had temporarily declared a truce, only to destroy the common enemy!' hooted Godaji with laughter, slapping his thigh, and causing his pony to roll its eyes in astonishment.

'Say, I meant to ask you before,' said Ramaji when the laughter had died down

'All you men wear a sword of a type I've never seen before,' casting a look at the sword that Dattaji wore in a scabbard attached to a sash at his waist.

'Oh this? This is a *dhop*,' said Dattaji sliding the sword out of its scabbard and tossing it to Ramaji.

Ramaji caught it in mid-air and examined it with interest. Unlike the traditional curved *kripan* that Hiroji and he wore, this sword was straight, and much longer. The blade exceeded four feet, and the grip was padded with cloth to wick away sweat. The hilt ended in a metal disc from which protruded a dagger like short four-inch blade that he guessed could be used to stab an opponent who advanced from the rear. The sword was also much lighter than any existing model. His eyes looked a question at Dattaji.

'The Raje himself designed this!' said Dattaji proudly.

'To fight the taller Pathans and *habshi*s, we needed more reach, so he had the blade elongated. You'll see the blade is also much narrower and the resultant saving in weight means it is far less tiring to wield. Also, the extra reach helps during a cavalry charge. Raje has the steel imported and has set up special forges to turn out these blades,' saying which he returned the blade to its scabbard.

'This is now standard issue for all cavalry and for all infantry Havaldars,' he added.

'I don't have firsthand knowledge, but I was told, it is also being introduced into our fledgling navy, headed by Maynaak Bhatkar, who belongs to the Bhandari seafaring community that lives along our coast.'

As the sun crossed the mid-point in its fiery trail across the pale blue sky, Hiroji noticed an eagerness in the men and the reason was clear. Through gaps in the foliage glimpses of the Dholpara mountain crested with the fort of Pratapgad could be seen. Rest and food were now barely a few hours away!

'Halt!!!' the stentorian voice commanded and the line of troops, which had been making its way up the path to the first gate stopped. The gate was a sturdy wooden affair studded with brass nails, and almost fifteen feet high and ten feet wide. It was set within a stone tower that extended all the way from the hillside to the drop on the other side of the path. There was no way a force could bypass this gate.

The speaker was a huge man, black as basalt and thick with muscle. He was clad only in a tight dhotar with a *mundasa* cloth wrapped around his head to protect it from the sun. He stood like some sort of mythical creature on the rampart of the tower at the center of a line of bowmen who already had arrows nocked to their bowstrings alert for treachery.

He held an unusual weapon in his hands. It was a *pahaar,* a six-foot-long steel shaft, about two inches thick that ended in a chisel at its bottom. Its normal use was in earthworks, used along with pick and shovel to break rocks. He held it across his body as though it was weightless. Even from this distance, the men could see the pink scars of healed battle wounds on his massive arms and chest. They looked almost obscene on the otherwise unbroken black vista.

'*Naik,* it is I Mankoji, returning from the raid on Dabhol, and you my friend are a sight for sore eyes!!' called out the commander, cantering his horse to the front between the two forward scouts.

Naik was an honorific accorded to these tough men. Members of their tribe were normally called in when livestock died and their hereditary business was the production of leather. As a result, they were both avoided and feared. It was Shivajiraje's personal charisma as well as his actions in visiting their settlements and breaking bread with the community that had convinced them to join the forces for independence. A lot of them preferred to fight with an implement they were all too familiar with and they had devised their own fighting style when going up with a *pahaar* against spear, sword, axe or mace.

Vinayak, who had been referred to with the honorific, peered from deep set eyes under bushy black eyebrows and called out, 'I see you now Mankoji. How could I miss such an ugly face?' and before the soldiers at the gate could bristle at the insult, both men laughed heartily. They were old friends with the special bond forged in the heat of battle.

'One can never be too careful these days. Our king and kingdom are in danger, and I am afraid some of our compatriots might be thinking of changing sides.'

With that, he waved to the men below, and the massive gates groaned open, letting the convoy in.

Once past the gate, the crushed gravel path turned to stone steps and flagstones and turned sharply to the right, in an almost one-hundred-and-thirty-degree turn. This was designed so that if the gate was forced by the enemy, any charge would lose momentum in making such a drastic change in direction. The attacking forces would lose speed for a few seconds proving an ideal killing ground for the archers and musketeers posted on the next tower that adorned the main gate of the fort. The ascent was steep as well which would make it doubly hard for an attacking force to turn sharply and maintain speed at the same time.

The convoy entered the fort through the main gate and into the lower fort or *maachi*. The enclosure was in the shape of a rough rectangle about a thousand feet long and three hundred feet wide, surrounded by stone walls and bastions six feet thick.

The mountain ponies gamely took the ascent in their stride, sure footed as goats. Hiroji looked around him with interest. The men had told him the king's chief architect was one Hiroji Indulkar. Well, this man was a genius! He had used the natural ridge lines to further fortify the defenses. Perfectly fitted basalt blocks rode the ridges as they snaked their way to the top of the mountain. The heights of the walls ranged between thirty and fifty feet from the mountainside below which itself was so steep that neither man nor beast could ascend easily. The lower fort held stables, granaries, administrative buildings, barracks, and an open freshwater tank fed by a natural spring. There was also a small temple to the mother goddess *Tuljabhavani* the patron deity of the Bhosle clan. Shivaji had a temple built here, dedicated to her, as the original temple lay deep in Bijapur Sultanate territory.

The air was immediately cooler and sweeter at this altitude and the men gulped down deep draughts savoring the wind drying their sweat-soaked clothes.

From the lower fort, a narrow set of steps, easily defensible by two swordsmen, led steeply to the upper fort, or *balekilla* which housed the king's quarters, treasury and other sensitive buildings. The upper fort was a wonder of nature, a plateau completely flat measuring about five hundred feet by five hundred feet and about two hundred feet higher than the lower fort. It would be almost impossible to take by force against a few determined defenders. Next to the king's quarters was a small but beautifully appointed temple to *Kedareshwar*, an incarnation of Shiva, and the patron deity of the fort.

'All right men, listen up!' yelled Mankoji, getting the attention of the exhausted soldiers.

'Once you've handed all the horses to the grooms, grab something to eat from the kitchen and rest up.'

'I'll be going to the upper fort to report to the treasurer to submit the take from our raid,' and he signaled to his personal guard to accompany him.'

Every single man there knew the iron discipline that was enforced throughout the kingdom. Any and all material taken as spoils of war belonged exclusively to the state. Theft from the treasury, if proven, was punishable by beheading. The head was stuck on a spear and first taken to the man's family, after which it was rotated through the kingdom, to deter anyone with similar thoughts.

Every single man there knew that even the king himself was allocated a salary just as every other person in the kingdom. The contents of the treasury were used only for matters of state.

'We'll be given a couple of days to rest before we mount up and move out again; and oh, have that poor soul cremated first,' referring to the injured man who had succumbed to his wounds.

Chapter 15

Afzal Khan's camp – fifty miles east of Tuljapur

'What news of Shivaji's movements?' asked the Khan, eagerly of his informant Ali.

'Nothing, my lord,' replied the man fearfully. Giving bad news to Afzal Khan was dangerous but lying to him was fatal. He swallowed nervously, and looked down at his hands, which were twisting and turning the ends of the long scarf he wore around his neck.

'Nonsense! How can that be?' thundered Afzal flushing red. Ali saw that he was working himself up into a fine rage. This was the time of maximum danger. Afzal had such a high regard of his own intelligence and power, that he couldn't bear the thought, that his stratagem was not bearing fruit.

'Get out fool, before I gut you like the Shia pig you are,' spat Afzal dropping his head and glowering at him under an unbroken line of bushy brows and Ali almost tripped over his own feet in his haste to depart from the Khan's tent.

Ankush watched from one side, cleaning his nails with the tip of his dagger. Satisfied that he had gotten all the gunk out, he frowned at Afzal, and said, 'Lord, it appears we have to do something far more provocative to pull that rat out of his hole.'

'My counsel has always remained the same. We make for his territory and bring death and destruction, to every village we encounter. Emulate Timur my lord, and you will go down in history as the *gazi* to end all holy warriors. Especially, since you will repeat that feat in the land of these stubborn Marathi swine.'

'Hmm…' remarked Afzal, taking a sip from his goblet, and slowly his face cleared, and a smile began toying at the corners of his mouth, which soon turned into a chuckle, and then into a belly-shaking laugh.

'What?' asked Ankush, irritated at being left out of the private joke.

'What a fool I've been!' said Afzal, smacking his forehead in mock irritation.

'Does Shiva's family goddess not reside in Tuljapur? And that is only fifty miles due west of here, and on the way to his territory,' smirked the Khan willing Ankush to guess at his intent.

'Of course! Yes, oh yes, that is what he deserves. There is no way he will be able to ignore that!' and both men laughed in anticipated delight at the horror that was going to unfold.

***

The terrain through which the Khan's army traveled, while flat, was part of the enormous Deccan plateau, which lies at an average height of around two thousand feet above sea level. The plateau slopes down as it approaches the center of Hindustan. To the south it ascends to almost three thousand feet. The area is fed by mighty rivers which make most of the area arable supporting two crops a year.

This plateau is the breadbasket of the south of Hindustan and which filled the coffers of the four Sultanates there. To the west, the plateau abuts the Sahyadri mountain range, which is the rocky spine that runs along the western shore. West of this unbroken mountain chain, the land plunges precipitously down to the *Sindhu sagar* sea through thick, lush evergreen forests.

It was in the folds of the forbidding Sahyadri range, that Shivajiraje had built most of his forts and each had been carefully situated, to monitor critical passes or dominate valleys that scored the land.

The Bijapur army left Mankeshwar and reached Tuljapur, traversing fields heavy with millet, wheat and sugar cane that were in the process of being harvested. Just as deer sense when a tiger is not out for the kill, the villagers working the fields sensed a different purpose in the tramp of the army. Today at least, they were safe from random depredations.

News of the temple destruction had already reached Tuljapur and the priests were in a state of panic. Tuljapur, was one of the holiest shrines, in all of Hindustan. The idol of the warrior goddess Bhavani, who in mythology had slain the demon Mahishasur, was seated on a tiger and each of her ten arms held a different weapon. The idol was awe-inspiring. The lady was resplendent in her authority and majesty. Tuljapur was considered one of fifty-one *shakti peeth* or power centers that the mother goddess in all her various moods and forms had graced with her presence and was therefore a major center of pilgrimage for the Hindus of south Hindustan.

The morning prayers to the mother goddess were just about ending with hundreds of devotees singing the *aarti* hymns accompanied by cymbals and drums when Afzal strode through the gates of the main courtyard.

The courtyard was a largish space enclosed within an eight-foot-high stone wall. To the right and left, were small temples dedicated to other deities. There were buildings that housed the resident priests as well as a barn for the few cows that devout Hindus worshiped as part of their daily rituals. There were five mature mango trees within the courtyard with one right adjacent to the main Bhavani temple. Smoke from a *havan* ritual drifted up through the leaves of the tree. The smell of clarified butter used in the offering, the gentle lowing of the cows and the dying strains of the *aarti* created an atmosphere of civilized peace.

'Silence!!!' thundered Afzal upon entering the courtyard as his men fanned out behind him. The mood was suddenly shattered and the people who were in the hall of the main temple, looked askance at this new development. All movement and sound ceased.

Afzal advanced rapidly and in two quick strides bounded up the steps into the main hall tracking the dirt from the road with his leather shoes and made for the inner sanctum.

The devotees scattered as he arrowed through, elbowing those that were slow to move. Brass offering plates with pitchers of milk, *ghee*, coconuts, and flowers clattered to the floor. Behind him came a swarm of Pathans and others, with Naikji Pandhre and Naikji Kharate among them.

Afzal kicked over a brass *kalash* that a devotee had placed on the lintel to hand over to the priests in the sanctum and crossed over into the inner room.

There were three priests offering prayers to the goddess that day. One was young while other two were middle aged. The young one instinctively moved towards the idol in a futile effort to protect while the other two shrank to the sides, their hands folding in mute prayer to the Khan.

Afzal took a moment to savor the terror of the three men. There was nothing finer in life than enjoying the naked terror of a man or woman knowing he was the cause!

By now the sanctum had filled with his band, who all waited expectantly for what was to follow. Even Afzal had to admit to the skill of the sculptor who had created this exquisite statue. The lady was almost alive in her righteous rage, and from her seat on the tiger's back, she stepped on the headless carcass of the demon while several other demon heads lay scattered at her feet.

Afzal reached behind and a soldier handed a hammer into his open palm.

At that, the young priest uttered a keening cry and seizing a *trishul* or trident that was propped next to the idol charged at Afzal. Before he could cover the ten feet or so, an alert Pathan whipped out his sword and easily knocked aside the trident, but the young man cannoned into Afzal.

Afzal braced and absorbed the charge, holding the man helpless in a bear hug. The soldier meanwhile brought back his blade to plunge into the man's side, but Afzal shook his head.

'He needs to watch this first' and so saying he threw him to a group of soldiers, who quickly held him in a vise like grip.

The other two priests had meanwhile set up a wail, with tears and snot running down their faces as they entreated the Khan for mercy.

Afzal took his time walking to the front of the idol, and stood squarely in front of her, gazing into her sightless eyes. Behind him, most of his men, who had pulled out their swords after the priest's attack, had yet to return them to their scabbards. Even Kharate and Pandhre had their swords out and their gazes were locked onto the scene playing out in front in morbid fascination.

The Khan hefted the hammer in his right hand swinging it slightly back and forth to get the right balance.

'Where is your strength now!! Show me what miracles you are capable of now!!!' thundered Afzal addressing the mute statue.

And with that he swung the hammer up and behind his head in a massive buildup. His huge chest stretched threatening to tear his tunic, and his arms bulged as he brought down the hammer on the forehead of the idol.

The stone cracked and a sliver separated from the forehead. Afzal repeated the blow and the column of granite comprising the neck gave way and the head tumbled off the body.

The men were spellbound in the wanton brutality of the moment. Their lord had truly proven himself to be a destroyer of the *kafir* idols!

The priests were all crying inconsolably. This was the deity that they had given over their existence to and had spent their entire life lovingly worshiping.

A loud keening erupted from the few devotees who had mustered up the courage to gather at the doorway to the sanctum.

Afzal shook himself out of the religious trance he himself had fallen into. He was like a man possessed. His chest heaved with exertion and emotion and his face had gone red with the veins standing out like ropes in his thickly muscled neck. He turned on his heel and exited into the outer hall letting the hammer drop. His men parted respectfully and followed him out.

'What do we do with this Brahmin?' asked one of the soldiers holding the young priest.

'We need to show the townspeople what happens when someone tries to lay hands on a believer. Send out a party to drag any villagers you find to this courtyard. They have exactly fifteen minutes.'

The rest of his squad spread around the courtyard looking curiously at the strange temples, idols and offerings of these kaffirs, touching an image here or poking a statue there. The terrorized villages slowly started trickling into the courtyard prodded along by the spears of the Pathans.

'That's enough! This man needs to learn the consequences of assaulting a believer!' thundered Afzal standing at the top of the steps to the main hall, hands on his hips. He looked almost superhuman as he stood there, filling the doorway with his massive girth.

'Throw him over that stone bull there,' he indicated, and the young man was prostrated on his belly over the back of the huge stone *nandi* bull with four men holding him down, each to a limb.

Afzal looked around the courtyard. 'Bring one of those iron rods lying beside the barn,' he indicated to a pile of construction material piled in a heap there.

A soldier ran to obey and came back with an assortment of roughly five-foot iron rods, which would normally be used to reinforce a wall or roof. Afzal chose one that tapered to a rough point at one end.

He handed it to a Pathan. 'Yusuf, take the hammer and drive this through the *kafir*'.

The soldier looked confused for a moment till realization dawned and his face broke into a smile.

Taking the rod, he walked over to the young man, boy really, and gauging where his anus might be, twisted it in, tearing the man's simple dhotar. The youth's head jerked up in terror and pain, and a scream emerged from his throat as his face transformed into a rictus of pain.

The four soldiers holding each extremity held on tighter, and at least one of the men had the decency to look away, shamefaced at what was being done to this innocent boy. Blood erupted in a fountain, turning the side of the stone black and dripping onto the pavestones.

The soldier held the rod with his left hand, and swung the hammer with his right, driving the rod into the body, in a succession of blows. The cries of pain and terror reached a crescendo, as the poor man screamed, '*Aii*!! mother!!' in the universal call for succor. Several of the onlookers fainted while others broke into tears. A few old men stood taller though, and Afzal indicated them to his soldiers to watch for any resistance.

Presently, the cries decreased in volume and warbled off and the rod having destroyed everything in its path through the poor man's body emerged from the soft skin next to his neck. The youth had mercifully lost consciousness a while earlier.

Afzal looked around at the gathered villagers holding each person's eye till the other's gaze inevitably dropped.

But he was not done yet.

He jerked a thumb at the barn and ordered, 'Get the whitest cow you can find in that barn and bring her here. Take the rest back with us.'

A Pathan went to the barn and came out leading a pure white cow by her horn. The animal docilely followed him. Her liquid eyes placidly surveyed the knot of men she was being led to. She could not have had any inkling of what was to come.

At a signal from Afzal, another soldier walked up to her drawing the nine-inch *katar* tucked into his waistband. He gathered the folds of her neck in his left hand, and the animal turned her large brown eyes questioningly to him at this lack of etiquette. He inserted the point midway in the neck in one quick motion and sliced down with all his strength. There was a shocked gasp from the crowd as a fountain of blood erupted and the animal lowed in pain and terror. The man murmured the Muslim prayers as the animal's heart pumped out her lifeblood and she slowly cratered on her feet and finally folded and fell. The air resounded with her cries and several people clamped their palms over their ears and clamped their eyes shut, unable to bear it any longer.

The other men of Afzal's party immediately fell to, skinning and butchering the carcass.

By now, there was not one person among the villagers who was not openly crying, and several were beating their chests in futile torment.

But Afzal was not finished yet... 'Cut off a chunk of meat from the haunch,' he ordered, and one of the soldiers quickly hacked a piece and came to Khan; his sandals making bloody footprints all the way up the steps and into the hall.

Afzal took the raw piece of flesh and held it up for all to see.

'Bring me those other two priests,' he commanded, and the two poor creatures were dragged to him.

At an order from him, two soldiers forced open the mouths of the by now trembling and nearly delirious men with the flats of their daggers. Afzal walked up to them, and tearing the piece of flesh into two chunks, stuffed one each into their mouths, mashing the bloody fragments against their teeth while their limbs thrashed useless and eyes ogled with terror. Not even in ancestral history or genetic memory, had these Brahmins come even close to the taking of life. Why God? Why?? Their eyes seemed to beseech in mute terror.

He wiped off the congealing blood on the tunic of one of the priests and took one last look at his handiwork, satisfied with the way things had gone there, before signaling for the corps to depart.

Chapter 16

Rajgad fort May 1659

And yet Shivajiraje did nothing...

The atmosphere in the audience chamber was charged. Moropant Pingale, the crusty old Brahmin warrior paced, his hands gripping the ends of his *uparna* shawl tight. His face looked almost bloodless and his lips were compressed into a pale line.

Tanaji Malusare stood at attention, seemingly made of the same material as the stones used to build the fort. He was taller than the average *Maavla* man, pointing to ancestors who must have migrated from the fertile regions to the east. Though he stood stock still, at a parade rest, his eyes blazed with a quiet fury and his full mustaches quivered with emotion as though an internal tempest threatened to break out.

The old Brahmin Raghunathpant Hanmante was present as well. The king had given him an extremely important but unique task. He'd been asked to rid the Marathi language of the accursed Persian words that had crept in after three centuries of Islamic rule. He had already come up with over a thousand Sanskrit and Marathi words and was in the process of completely overhauling all the verbiage on court and administrative documents and official records.

He was a slim spare man, neat in appearance and was always studious and reserved in his responses. He sat quietly waiting for the proceedings to begin.

Yesaji, Suryaji, and the newly arrived Mankoji were among others, who stood quietly to attention, wondering what had transpired to create this buzz of anger.

There was a sudden rush as two attendants entered heralding the arrival of Shivajiraje.

All the men immediately stood and bowed in the tripe bow *muzra* to their king. Shivaji acknowledged their salutations with a gracious nod and took his seat. Only then did the rest take their seats. A half-smile tugged at his lips, and his wide-spaced eyes sparkled with intelligence above the aquiline nose.

'Bahirji, what news?' and a nameless servant posted at one of the columns of the chamber suddenly transformed in manner into the spy in front of their very eyes.

Bahirji bowed low thrice in salutation but could not meet his king's eye today.

'Sire, the news is bad' he whispered to a hall that had suddenly gone stock silent. Shivajiraje stayed silent letting the man frame his thoughts and articulate his words.

'Afzal crossed all boundaries of human decency yesterday sire,' he said looking up and meeting Shivaji's level gaze.

'He broke the Tulja bhavani into two and slaughtered a cow in the temple, lord,' and the man's voice broke off as he struggled to control his emotions.

The hall erupted into pandemonium, as those who had not heard of the event, lost all sense of court etiquette.

'Sire, just give the word,' the normally laconic Yesaji blurted. 'I will personally lead a *Sultandhawa* on that pig,' he said visibly trying to bring his surging emotions under control. Several of his lieutenants echoed him with cries of 'Yes, sire, yes, yes!!'

A *Sultandhawa* was the Marathi equivalent of the Rajput suicide charge. Knowing that the enemy was too strong and numerous and that death was almost certain, a concerted attack was made on the commander of the enemy himself, with the clear understanding that either he was killed, or no attacker returned alive.

The only emotion Shivaji displayed, was a slight whitening by the side of his lips as his eyes flashed fire. He held up his palm, and the clamor ended as quickly as it had begun.

'That is exactly what the Khan wants, don't you men see that?'

'Moropant, can you tell me,' the king turned to his advisor 'why has this sacred land of ours seen over five hundred years of this barbaric Islamic rule?'

Taken off guard at this singling out, and not having time to think, Moro stammered, 'Sire, these people have better cannon, better steel weapons…' but that sounded lame even to his ears.

'Wrong!! We have forgotten the lessons of our ancestors, whether it is Lord Parshuram or Lord Krishna,' and Shivajiraje looked around the room to make sure his words had carried,

'*Yo yathaa pravarte yasmin, tasmin tatha pravarte,*' he said quoting the ancient Sanskrit. This was the advice given by Lord Parshuram to Devavrata'.

Seeing the blank look on some of the men's faces, the king further explained, 'Devavrata later came to be known as Bhishma because of the monstrous vow he undertook for his father's happiness. Knowing that very few in the room understood Sanskrit he explained in Marathi, 'Treat your enemy exactly as he treats you'.

'Have you forgotten how Lord Krishna got the better of Karna? Or how he engineered the defeats and deaths of Shishupala, Dronacharya, and even Lord Bhishma himself?' and his voice cut through the room with volume and authority.

'Do you think the Pandavas would have won had they launched a *Sultandhawa* at the chariot of Duryodhana?' And looking around he saw the men suddenly beginning to rethink their reaction.

'But sire, we have the teachings of Lord Rama, to abide by, who was scrupulously fair even in battle' blurted one soul who looked down when the king's hawkish gaze fell upon him.

'There is a time for Rama, and there is a time for Krishna, and it all depends on what ideals your enemy follows,' replied the king to this direct question, and he saw several men nod in assent.

'So, tell me, Prime Minister, what is your counsel?' turning to Shyamrajpant Ranzhekar who had stayed silent while all this went on.

'Sire, he needs this fight more than us. He knows he could spend years in this terrain without seeing even one of our soldiers, let alone you. We will harry his troops at will and bog down his campaign.'

'If he wants to close, we need to choose the terrain to our advantage. We need to drag him into the forests of the Maaval, where his cannon and elephants will be useless and we can use the terrain to our advantage.'

'Exactly!!' responded Shivajiraje, pleased that at least someone was thinking straight.

'He wants to drag us onto flat open ground to bring his cannon and cavalry to bear, and brothers, we have to resist all his provocations, threats as well as temptations!'

'Speaking of which..' Ranzhekar quickly remarked and realizing he had cut off the king immediately bowed in a *muzra* saying 'begging your pardon my lord for my interruption.'

Shivajiraje laughed then, a pleasant laugh and waving a hand in his direction said, 'No man should ever apologize for speaking his mind here. Our independence and kingdom are pre-destined by *Shree* himself and we are all united in that quest.' At that remark, several men folded their hands in momentary prayer to the idol of Ganesh that fit into an alcove, lit with a five-wick brass lamp.

'Speak,' commanded Shivaji gently.

'Kanhoji Jedhe seeks an immediate audience sire. He has ridden hard from Kari just to meet with you Sire,' said Ranzhekar with worry written large all over his face.

Hearing the commotion, the king's mother Jijabai had entered the room, and immediately a flurry of muzre swept her way, and Shivaji bent down and touched her feet in respect and led her to a seat by his side.

'Kanhoji is here? It has been a while since I've had the pleasure of his audience. Do send him in!' she remarked, a smile lighting her patrician features.

Ranzhekar turned and made a sign to an attendant, and the entire assembly waited in anticipation.

Hardly had a few minutes passed than Kanhoji swept in like a force of nature. His five sons Baji, Chandji, Naikji, Shivji and Mataji followed half a step behind. They were all cut from the same cloth. Hard-bitten, tough, wiry sons of the soil comfortable with plough, sword or *patta*. They were uniformly clad in rough cotton tunics cinched at the waist and tightly wrapped dhotars with the traditional red Marathi tricorn *pagdi* on their heads. Each had a sword strapped to the waist as well as a dagger tucked into the sash and had circular shields strapped to their backs. It was evident they had ridden hard and had something urgent to say.

This raft of newcomers quickly bowed low and fired off a flurry of repeated *muzra* to the king and his mother, and acknowledging these, Jijabai exclaimed, 'Kanhoji, you have not changed a bit! And is that Baji I see there? He is a couple months older than my Shivba if I recall correctly!'

At that Baji flushed deep red, and Kanhoji just smiled, 'You are too kind mother.'

She called out to the guard, 'Has someone seen to these men? Have they been fed after their ride here?'

But Kanhoji urgently said, 'There will be time for all that mother. First I need to speak with Shivajiraje!'

When Shivaji indicated with a wave that he should speak, Kanjoji blurted out, 'Sire, I received an official letter from the Adilshahi Sultanate this morning, and immediately came here,' handing an official-looking document to Ranzhekar, who came forward to take the offered parchment.

While Ranzhekar scanned the document written in Persian, Kanhoji began,

'Sire, the letter begins by reminding me that I am a vassal of the Bijapur Sultanate. It goes on to inform me that their mightiest commander Afzal Khan has recently been dispatched with over twenty thousand troops to put down the rebellion of one Shivaji Bhosla and bring him back to Bijapur dead or alive' and Kanhoji gulped at vocalizing the impropriety.

'Do not worry Kanhoji, I am not offended. I know these are neither your words and nor do you agree with them,' said Shivaji gently urging him to continue.

'The letter orders me to report with all available men to join Afzal's army at the earliest. If I do not obey, the order says the Sultanate will confiscate my landholding. They will tear down our ancestral house. All the men will be slaughtered unless we agree to convert to Islam, and our women and children will be sold as slaves. The name 'Jedhe' will be forever be erased from the soil of Hindustan..'

And Kanhoji paused, his chest heaving, eyes reddened and narrowed into slits, hands shaking with fury. The sons looked confused and angry, perturbed at the emotion in their father's frame. All five looked expectantly at their king.

Ranzhekar coughed discreetly and pointed out, 'Sire, letters have gone to all the *deshmukh* chieftains in the hills with a similar message'

'How many have accepted?'

'Kedarji Khopde was always aligned with Bijapur, so he has stayed true to form. What is surprising is that his cousin Khandoji has switched sides and gone over to the Sultanate.' While saying this his gaze drifted to Kanhoji because everyone knew that Khandoji was a close friend and admirer of Kanhoji, and a frequent guest at his home.

Anger flared in the king's eyes at hearing of this betrayal, but then Shivaji's gaze moved over to Kanhoji and his face settled.

'We are doomed for destruction Kanhoji. Why do you want to follow down the same path? Go ahead! Align with the Khan. The Bijapur Sultanate will add more to your holdings and wealth,' remarked Shivaji quietly, with a sardonic twist to his mouth, to shocked silence from the entire gathering.

'What are you saying sire?? Take the path of treason?? Perfidy with this holy struggle?? You forget, this is Kanhoji Jedhe standing in front of you!!' exploded Kanhoji raising his voice a few decibels.

Pingle opened his mouth to remind Kanhoji of his place, but the king silenced him with a quick look.

Kanhoji turned to the low table that was placed in front of the royal pair. On the tray was placed a traditional brass pot filled with water for the king's use.

Kanhoji held the pot by its tapered neck in his left hand and held out his right palm upwards in front of the king. He directed a stream of water onto his open palm, letting the water fall to the floor

'Here!!! I wash away any attachment to my landholding!! I wash away any attachment to my hearth and home!! I wash away any attachment to family!!" he cried, spittle flying from his mouth in his anguish.

What followed was a moment pregnant with silence... till every throat in that room erupted spontaneously in '*Har har Mahadev*!! *Har har Mahadev*!!'

The king stood up quickly and his eyes moistened as he stepped up and embraced Kanhoji thrice in the traditional Marathi way, saying, 'Kanhoji, I was never in doubt!! I was merely checking your mind.'

Shilimkar spoke up next. 'Sire, my thousand sword arms are yours. We are ready to kill and if necessary, die for a Hindu homeland!! And I know I speak for my kinsman Bandal as well!!'

'The Shilimkars and Bandals are yours to the death!!' and the room erupted again in a flurry of bowed salutes as every warrior there, pledged respect and allegiance to the movement and to their king.

Chapter 17

Pratapgad – lower fort

Mankoji had ridden off with a small escort, to Rajgad fort the next morning, after the return from Dabhol, but he had left orders for the rest of the party to barrack in the fort pending further orders.

Hiroji had started the day with his usual thousand free squats followed by two thousand *surya namaskar* in four sets on the east bastion facing the rising sun. The sweat ran freely down his bare chest and arms and he cooled off with the wind coming off the ocean far to the west at his back.

Presently he descended the twenty of so stone steps from the bastion to the lower fort enclosure and picked up his *kripan* and shield. Of the various schools of swordplay prevalent in Hindustan, Ramaji's clan adhered to the Bhavani, or mother-goddess school. He initiated the several stylistic movements in an intricate choreography of cuts, parries, thrusts, and blocks simulating attack and defense from all the cardinal points. With each play, he increased speed till the sword became a blur and his feet danced over the flagstones, constantly adjusting his center of gravity, from foot to foot with the movement of the sword.

By now an interested crowd had gathered. After fifteen minutes of this, Hirjoji was blowing like a horse, and his *dhotar* was drenched with sweat.

He stopped, only to see that among the crowd was Godaji, the elite, feared swordsman laconically watching the display.

'Very nice,' he sarcastically murmured, 'but in a real fight you may need a sword in either hand. What will you do then?'

Hiroji realized this was a test of sorts. He had to earn the respect of these hard men

'Fair point,' he conceded, trying to speak while bringing his breathing under control.

'Sir, do you mind loaning me your *danpatta*?' he asked of Godaji, deferring to his age and status.

Godaji was taken aback momentarily. A *danpatta*? For this green boy? But he gamely gave over the *patta* he'd been carrying in his left hand, offering it hilt forward to Hiroji.

'Careful with that blade boy. I'll have your hide if you nick it on the stone'.

Hiroji, nodded in acceptance and laying the shield down, transferred the sword to his left hand and accepted the *patta* in his right, sliding his hand into the gauntlet. He moved ten paces away, because the flagstones where he'd been practicing were slick with sweat, and he needed a few moments to catch his breath.

He hefted the weapon to get a feel for the weight and flex of the blade as well as gauge the length. These weapons were made in bespoke manner to match the strength, reach and stamina of the warrior. The blade of Godaji's weapon had two tiny holes drilled where the blade met the tang. The holes had then been filled with gold. It looks like two drops of gold fallen on the blade. Each drop signified a hundred men killed in combat, and despite himself, Hiroji's gaze lifted quickly in shock and reverence to meet Godaji's level gaze.

Hiroji made a few sweeps with the blade and then respectfully turned back to Godaji, 'With your blessings, sir?' and Godaji inclined his head in assent.

What followed was an earthly rendition of what Mahadev's cosmic dance of destruction *tandav* must have been.

Hiroji was already limbered up, and he launched into the full flow of the *Bhavani vidya* or weapons science. The *patta* played the role of major strike weapon with the sword playing counterpoint in a blur of movement. The display of skill was both delicate in its artistry and brutal in its potential scope for destruction as Hiroji danced over a ten-foot killing ground. The blades whirled in a blur of movement as Hiroji turned clockwise and counterclockwise creating a tornado of razor-sharp steel. Men stepped back involuntarily though they were nowhere near the range of the weapons.

After only a few minutes of the amazing display, Godaji started clapping and exclaimed, 'Well done boy!! Mahadev himself has blessed you! You have a rare skill. From tomorrow you will be my right-hand man. I rest easy knowing there is someone like you to carry on our tradition!' and the rest of the men broke into whistles of appreciation and clapping at this rare praise from Godaji.

Humbled by the fulsome praise, Hiroji bent and touched Godaji's feet in respect, raising the same hand to his heart and lips and Godaji placing his right palm on his bent and damp head murmured '*Vijayi bhav*' rewarding him the age-old blessing for victory.

***

An hour later, bathed and having wolfed down the unleavened millet flatbread *bhakri* with a cup of milk served by the cooks, Hiroji made his way to the Bhavani temple in the lower courtyard to pay his obeisance and time permitting meditate in silence for a moment.

When he approached the outer courtyard, he saw Veero Ram, the *muzumdar* or archivist of records of the fort seated under the shade of the mango tree that stood in front of the simple temple. He was intent on perusing a book laid on the ground in front of him.

A slight breeze blew from the west ruffling Hiroji's hair and bringing some much-needed relief from the heat.

Hiroji folded his palms in greeting and the man responded in kind.

Seeing the strange script in the book, Hiroji enquired, 'Sir, what are you reading? And it appears you've already almost finished the book.'

Hearing that, the man smiled in a not unkindly way. He was middle aged and dressed in the traditional garb of the brahmin. Other than the single pearl in the earring that pierced the upper part of his ear, he wore no jewelry and affected nothing that broadcast his high office.

'This book is called the Koran, and it is the holy book of all Muslims in the world,' said the man patting the pages of the book.

'And this version is written in Farsi which is read from right to left, so in truth, I have just begin reading this book for the third time given my inadequacy with the language.'

'Why are you reading the enemy's book?' queried a puzzled Hiroji.

'Knowledge is knowledge son, whatever be its source. As Hindus we are constant seekers of truth, even if that means we must question our own scriptures. I'm hoping the contents of this book provide me an insight into the minds of the people of this religion.'

'Where are you from?' and when Hiroji mentioned Pali, Veero nodded and asked.

'Your village is fairly near the coast. Have you seen the Yehudis who are settled there? They have adopted our dress, customs and even our last names, but they do cleave to their religion and their language. Their religion is almost as old as ours. I met a Yehudi who was on his way to Rajgad to apply for trading rights and was lucky to spend several hours in discussion with him.'

'He mentioned that both the Islamic religion as well as that of the *firangis* arose from their religion,' saying which he saw Hiroji's interest quicken.

'They were hounded out from their own land by the followers of Islam and have found homes in many other welcoming lands, Hindustan being among the first to do so.'

'However, I trust only my own eyes and mind. So, unless I read the holy book of the Yehudis, I will reserve my opinion. And no, there is no translation of their book that I know of.'

Hiroji leaned down and looked closely at the unusual lettering that ran across the open pages,

'Surely their holy book chastises them for the sins these people do in Hindustan?' asked a curious Hiroji.

Veero looked up at Hiroji and said, 'You're giving me a crick in my neck. If you really want to know, sit here in front and listen to me,'

When Hiroji was seated in front, Veero took a moment to gather his thoughts and present in the most clear and concise matter possible. His eyes took on a faraway look.

'The more I read this book, the more I'm convinced, the followers of this religion are actually exhorted, by the writings in this book, to wreak inhuman torments on others,' said Veero to an incredulous Hiroji.

'And this book is considered holy and the word of God?' sputtered Hiroji in confusion.

Veero had marked several sections in the book with pieces of twine. He opened the book to the first section of twine and continued in his mild-mannered way.

'The main difference between our beliefs and those in this book is that we believe, every single thing that exists in this world--- human, animal, animate or inanimate --is a manifestation of divinity.'

'We are all free to give form to that divinity to enable us to grasp its essence. Hence, our profusion of gods and idols. Surely, you did not think we're stupid enough to worship pieces of stone, did you?' and Veero smiled at the range of emotions that crossed Hiroji's face.

'Divinity does not exist outside of us and that divinity does not prefer any one group over another.'

At this point Veero pointed at the book laid out in front of him for emphasis, 'This book divides all humankind into Muslims and others. And the God in this book sits in judgment outside of humanity.'

'Some of the verses trouble me. It says in chapter nine verse five, that the duty of every Muslim is to either convert people to Islam by whichever means possible, or then to kill them.'

'Killing innocents and taking their women and children, as slaves, is considered a 'spoil of war," he said disgustedly. Veero was known for his calm and collected manner, but Hiroji saw that the contents of this book had shaken him to the core.

'Chapter three, verse twenty-nine and one nineteen expressly forbids Muslims to take *kafirs* as friends or verse two hundred and twenty-two claims that even a Muslim slave is better than a *kafir*. And going against these principles risks excommunication. So, you will never be a whole person to any Muslim who obeys the instructions in this book.'

'So just because we do not convert to Islam, makes us criminals, in these people's eyes automatically?' asked Hiroji with increasing consternation.

'Surely, there is someone among them, who questions this on the grounds of basic humanity and decency?'

'That is the part I do not understand myself' confessed Veero with a shrug. 'That is why I've read this book multiple times, to try and understand, if there is some logic to this hidden somewhere.' And he left his sentence hanging in frustration.

'Both God and *Shaitan*, which this book defines as the Devil, I believe are creations of man. I wonder if the intent was to provide an outlet to man's most base instincts. What better way to do that, than to divide humanity, into two and sanctify all immoral acts as *kafir*-worthy? That way a person could act like a beast and feel in the right at the same time. Of course, a problem will arise when and if the entire world is converted to Islam. Who will they slake their thirst for rape, murder and loot on then?'

He closed the book and pinched the bridge of his nose in tiredness. 'It took thousands of years to bring about civilization as we know it.'

Have you heard of Panini?' and Hiroji shook his head in the negative.

'Panini was a native of the Swat valley, in Afghanistan and one of the greatest scholars, of the Sanskrit language. He lived more than a thousand years ago. He codified the rules of classical Sanskrit, to ease the way, through the dense thickets of *sandhi* grammar and syntax. The entire region was an engine of peace, prosperity and learning at the time,' and he paused,

'And now what does that valley produce?' he said rhetorically. No answer was necessary.

'I bet you didn't know that Lord Krishna travelled to Afghanistan to win the hand of the famously beautiful Lady Satyabhama!' he chortled seeing Hiroji's startled reaction. Seeing that the lad was more than just a knuckle-dragger, Veero persisted.

'Have you read the Upanishads?' he looked at Hiroji with a question in his kind, brown eyes.

'I have not sir' replied Hiroji ashamedly. 'I can read and write, but only just. Someday, when my fighting days are over, I hope to read the *Dnyaneshwari*' exclaimed Hiroji in longing.

'Understanding the *Dnyaneshwari* is a quest my son!!' replied Veero quickly. 'Saint Dnyaneshwar did us a favor by translating the teachings of Lord Krishna into our mother tongue. But don't wait till the end of your days. The advice in that book provides context to the world we see and gives us a framework to make right decisions at the right times.'

'But back to this book. Are non-Muslims not human? How can any system of civilized thought legitimize rape, pillage, slavery, loot and conquest by permitting these just as long as they are against the *kafirs*?' Veero could not keep the bitterness and sarcasm out of his tone.

'But my reading continues, son. There are several verses that talk of peace, kindness, and equity. However, to my mind, the humane verses cannot coexist with the hateful ones.

'*Only one set of mutually opposing principles can hold true.*'

The high priests of this religion need to decide what consistent message they want to provide to their followers,' saying which he closed the book and placed it in a satchel by his side.

Chapter 18

Afzal's camp twenty miles west of Tuljapur

'Has that rat, emerged from his hole?' queried a grinning Khan, of the envoy who had just entered his tent.

'Nothing Lord,' said the poor man, waiting for the eruption he knew was going to follow.

'Idiot!' yelled Afzal, throwing his goblet at the hapless man, spilling the contents of the sherbet onto his simple tunic, while the man dropped his gaze in terror. He knew his life hung by a thread.

'Are you sure the news of Tuljapur reached Rajgad?' hissed the Khan looking at the man through slit eyes. Today he had worn a simple white cotton tunic and leggings over his massive frame.

'Yes... yes... my Lord,' stammered the man. 'I myself traveled through the villages around Rajgad dressed as a *fakir*, and I saw that people are up in arms, and already enquiring, why their king does nothing. They ask of the *deshmukhs* as to what Swarajya is this, if they cannot even defend their temples.' The man's Adam's apple moved up and down as he swallowed spittle down a suddenly dry mouth, and a thread of sweat appeared on his hairline.

Afzal's look had become canny and his mouth twisted in the parody of a smile. 'This Shivaji is different. I thought I had given enough provocation, but it looks as though I need to do more.

'What lies to our west and is the holiest site to the majority of these Marathi *kafirs*' asked Afzal with an evil leer coming to his face, and the man in front shuddered.

'Pandharpur!!' cried Afzal in delight, answering his own question slapping his own thigh in delight. It sounded like a musket shot and the frame of the tent shook with the vibrations.

***

The news spread like wildfire in the camp, and for the first time the Hindu chieftains fidgeted in fear and resentment. The grand temple at Pandharpur was the abode of Lord Vithoba himself who was an incarnation of Lord Vishnu, the guiding energy that maintained the balance in the universe. Vishnu was part of the triumvirate that created, maintained and destroyed the universe instantly and constantly in a never-ending cosmic cycle.

Within the hour, Shivaji's spies in the camp had taken the news to Pandharpur and onwards to the king.

When Afzal arrived at the temple the next morning, he found the place deserted. No people, animals and no idols! All the idols, including the basalt statue of Lord Vithoba, had been spirited away by the head priest of the temple.

'Mother fucker!' retorted Afzal in disgust and anger finding his planned agenda thwarted by the quick-thinking man.

'Let's give these *kafirs* something to think about though' and the light in his eyes shifted as he quickly thought of a backup plan.

'Round up three cows and bring them here' he ordered a waiting Pathan.

'Slaughter them right here, in the temple, and tell our cooks to set up kitchen here for the day. I want beef to be prepared and served right here. One regiment will feast right in these premises tonight, and throw the head of the cow, guts, and the bones after you finish right here in all the inner shrines.'

'Now let me see what Shivaji makes of this' he said grimly.

***

and yet Shivaji did nothing…

Finally, the Khan played his last card. From Pandharpur, the army traveled the fifty miles or so to the trading center of Phaltan.

The town lay on the prime meridian, that traveled south through the major city of Ujjain, in the north of Hindustan. The ancient treatise on astronomy, the *Suryasiddhanta*, had already mapped the orbits of the major planets and calculated the distance to the sun and the moon thousands of years ago. The prime meridian had been set to run through that incredible center of learning, Ujjain.

Two of the major trading routes, bisected each other at Ujjain. One travelled north-south linking the great empires of the south with the erstwhile empire of the great king Lalitaditya of Kashmir, with his capital in the city of Srinagar (literally the city of Divinity) while the horizontal route connected the empires of Rome and China, both of which did a bustling trade with Hindustan.

Hindustani merchants sold steel, ships, cloth, pearls and spices to Rome and the same merchants brought back wine, and fair girls to entertain the men back home. It was claimed that the unequal trade with Hindustan had caused the Romans to bemoan the flight of their gold and silver and they had even started watering their silver currency of late. At any given point, at least six or seven Hindustani trading ships were berthed in the harbor outside Rome.

Phaltan had naturally benefited from the north-south trade and was a bustling city of merchants. Anything was available here, for a price.

One of the most prominent warrior chieftain families in Phaltan were the Nimbalkars. The men of that family had regularly lent their sword arms and cavalry to the Bijapur Sultanate for over a hundred years. What was even more important was that the chieftain, Nimbalkar's daughter, Saibai was married to Shivaji, and was the mother to the heir apparent Sambhaji.

The scion Bajaji, her brother was awaiting an audience with the Khan, following the arrival of his three thousand horses to augment the Khan's army.

'My lord,' said Bajaji respectfully bowing low in *kurnisaat* on entering the Khan's presence.

Afzal had decided on pomp and regalia that day and had worn a silk overshirt studded with pearls. His Persian-style turban was festooned with a triple strand of pearls and a single ruby the size of a small egg.

He was seated in his usual chair flanked on either side by his chieftains. He stroked his beard and regarded Bajaji through heavy-lidded eyes. The man was good looking, tall and broad and looked in excellent condition. He was dressed simply with no ornaments. He wore the tricorn headgear favored by the Marathas and had sweeping mustaches over clear brown eyes and a long, straight nose. Afzal saw that his sword and dagger were of excellent quality.

'I have brought three thousand of my best men, lord, as you ordered. We have set up camp next to Naikji Pandhare's men,' he said, indicating the chieftain who stood respectfully to one side.

Afzal continued to gaze at Bajaji till the latter started fidgeting, not knowing, what else he was supposed to say.

'Seize this man!!' suddenly roared Afzal, and the entire tent was thrown in confusion.

Ankush Khan, was the only person who had been given wind of this and he leaped to hold fast Bajaji's right forearm while the guard at the tent's door ran and grabbed Bajaji's left arm. Soon, the others had swarmed Bajaji and held him fast.

Not that Bajaji had any thought of resistance; in fact, his face had turned comical in disbelief and confusion as his hands were tied behind him.

'What is he guilty of?' queried a surprised Pandhre.

'Never mind that! Imprison him. Lock him in chains while I decide his punishment. But keep him away from the other prisoners,' ordered Afzal imperiously dismissing the others with a wave of his hand.

***

Barely had the news of the latest provocation at the holy temple of Pandharpur arrived at Rajgad than the news of Bajaji's arrest followed.

'He is your brother-in-law sire' nervously coughed Ranzhekar. The men were touring the battlements of the fort. The king made surprise inspections and woe betide anyone who did not follow the strict discipline laid down for every individual whether civil or military in the administration. This was one such and the king was inspecting whether the stockpile of arrows at this particular station was as per orders, and whether the gunpowder store had a sturdy lock.

'Yet he joins forces with the Khan and marches against me,' said the king coldly, giving the lock a solid shake, and looking to Ranzhekar for his response.

'Sire, these Sultans have ruled our land for over three hundred years. Almost twenty generations have seen nothing but the yoke of Islam. Servility and blind allegiance have been bred into most people by now,' he replied soberly keeping pace, with Shivaji's quick strides along the battlement.

'Mark my words, he will come around. And then there is Lady Sai to think of as well. I know her condition deteriorates day by day. I was told that she has been crying inconsolably for the last few hours, refusing to take her medicine.'

At this, Shivaji sighed and the rigid discipline he adhered to, slipped for a moment, allowing a glimpse of the husband, father and man shrouded inside, as his face twisted with a personal pain.

Ranzhekar looked away in embarrassment and the moment passed.

'Call Balaji Awji!' the king commanded as the two men swept through the doors of the audience chamber, with the guards firing off a flurry of the bent salutes as they passed.

Barely was the king seated that Balaji hurried in. It did not do to keep the king waiting. He was scrupulous about timeliness and work ethic and no detail was too small to not warrant his interest.

'Come Balaji,' smiled Shivaji indicating that the man should seat himself and take up pen and parchment.

'I want letters with my personal seal, sent to every Hindu chieftain in Afzal's army. Ask whether they can really trust a commander, who arbitrarily imprisons his own man for no apparent reason other than the fact that he is not Muslim. Insinuate that they could be on the chopping block next. Remember, Afzal will read this letter, so keep it short and polite,' said the king looking to Balaji in case he had any questions.

Balaji Awji was the king's personal secretary, and a die-hard supporter to the cause. The only difference was that his weapon was, the pen and inkwell. His father had been the personal secretary, of the Abyssinian *Siddi*, at the fort of Janjira Murud. The family was loyal, hard-working and well to do because of the father's high station. Balaji and his brother were learning the sciences, philosophy and languages, and by the age of four, Balaji was fluent in Sanskrit, and, of course, his native Marathi.

In a by-now familiar turn of events, the *Siddi* one day decided, that he could not rely on a Hindu secretary and a trumped-up charge was put up. All the property and belongings of the family were confiscated by the kingdom, and the man was sentenced to death, but in the unique fashion of that kingdom.

He was thoroughly beaten till both arms and legs were broken. Then he was placed in a large burlap sack which was then packed with lime powder and sewn closed. The sack was then thrown off the ramparts of the island fort into the sea. The soldiers loved making bets, as to what killed the man first, drowning or burning to death, as the lime reacted with the water.

Balaji's mother along with her two sons were then taken as slaves and sold to a slaver who put them up for auction at the slave market in Rajapur. The poor woman, in her early twenties was looking at a life of sex slavery while her children would be sold to work the mines in the region, or to rich Arabs who had a predilection for small boys.

Sometimes the divine does work in strange ways and her brother, who was a grain trader happened to be passing through Rajapur on the very day she was put up for auction. He put in an anonymous bid and bought back his own little sister and her boys and Balaji's life changed yet again.

'Sire, I will have a draft ready for your approval in the next ten minutes, and once you've approved, have the copies ready for your signature by evening,' said Balaji as he got to work.

*****

The Khan had risen in the world by sheer dint of capability and ruthlessness and he was busy inspecting the accounts of the campaign while three clerks stood nervously at attention to one side, ready to answer any inquiry he might have.

Suddenly, there was a commotion outside his tent and a guard came in and bowed low in salute.

'Some of the Hindu cavalry chieftains, wish an audience with you, lord' replied the man, gaze fixed firmly to the floor.

The Khan gazed shrewdly at the man. He was well aware of the rising tide of resentment, among the Hindu soldiers after Tuljapur and Pandharpur.

'Take their weapons away first, and then let the leaders in. Not more than four men,' he admonished the guard and waved him away.

He quickly reached for his turban and set it upon his shaved pate. He wanted to present a clear and dominating message to the men that he was indeed the manifestation of the absolute power and majesty of the Bijapur Sultanate. He schooled his features and awaited the coming of the men.

Presently, the flap of his tent opened, and four men trooped in. As expected, the old codger Pandhre was one of them.

Afzal inwardly sighed without letting even a flicker of emotion show. He decided that once he had taken care of this minor irritant, Shivaji, he would have to do something about Pandhre. He'd have to decide whether to have him poisoned or perhaps have him accused of intrigue and publicly executed. Yes! The latter. It was decided in his mind. It was always good to remind people of where the power lay.

However, none of this showed and with an expressionless face, he acknowledged the flurry of salutes and said, 'Naikji, how good of you to come. I could have come had you called. What ails you?' and the old rooster puffed up with pride.

'Lord, some of us have received letters from that Shivaji,' he said, proffering a rolled-up parchment to Afzal.

'Lord, none of us believe this of course, but he says, how do we know that we will not be next, if Bajaji is imprisoned for no other reason than that he is Hindu?' blurted out the man. The other three men were much younger and stood nervously fidgeting with their hands. The Khan had that effect on most men.

Afzal took his time reading the letter. This Shivaji was cannier than most. This is exactly what he himself would've done had the roles been reversed. He could not fault the logic.

He let the parchment spring back into a roll and he slapped the tube on the palm of his left hand as he thought through how to best navigate this situation. His kohl ringed eyes, swept back and forth across the men gauging where they were on the precipice. Would he have to plan for an open revolt, by the Hindus in his force?

'Come back in one hour' he commanded. 'I will have my decision ready by then' and he dismissed them with a wave of his hand, as the men flurried in salute backing out of the tent.

Next, he called a council of his Muslim commanders to assess the ground reality of the situation. Ankush as usual was all bravado while Musa was more thoughtful.

'There is resentment lord' he said. 'Men at Hindu campfires fall silent when one of us approaches. That is the first sign of impending trouble' he quietly remarked.

'Are you scared then?' blustered Ankush and Afzal saw the anger flare bright in Musa. Quickly heading off the impending argument, he held up a hand and said, 'Let us not bicker brothers. We need the support of these Hindus to take down Shivaji. Our Sultanates have showed us the way for centuries. We use the fault lines among these people and pit them against one another, fighting for scraps off our table. That means we have to walk a fine line in what we do.' And the men saw that he had made up his mind about what to do next.

***

Afzal's tent stood in solitary splendor on a small grassy hillock on the plain outside the town of Phaltan. The tents of his Muslim commanders ringed his in concentric order of tribalism, seniority and importance providing a natural ringed defense. The tents of the *kafirs* were on the periphery. Of course, they would also be the first to suffer if a raid came.

He stood outside his tent wearing his full regalia carrying *Jamdaad* by the scabbard in his left hand. He'd had his beard dyed with henna just that morning to hide the grey. Overall, he projected physical and political power as he stood there waiting for the men to gather, a respectful twenty feet away and slightly below him. All this was calculated theater, of course.

'All of you must wonder as to why I had Bajaji arrested,' he said in a deep voice that carried over the silent gathering. Several of the men nodded.

'I am your father. There are several things you do not know, and you must learn to trust me,' and he looked each man in the eye till their gaze dropped.

'But I am merciful and patient. I have heard some of your voices. Therefore, I have taken the decision out of the deep well of my compassion and wisdom to free him.

'And yes, before I forget! Out of the deep well of love and respect I have for the *kafir* religion, I have also endowed a small sum for the upkeep of the temple at Shinganapur,' in a slightly lower tone.

At this several men jerked in surprise, but he quickly countered, 'However, he will need to atone for his transgressions! He will need to pay a fine of one hundred thousand rupees and… and he will convert to Islam to be able to see the light of Allah!!' and a hubbub broke out as the men heard this startling news.

'Silence!!!' the Khan now thundered.

'This is not a debate! I have spoken. Now convey this to his family and be gone now, before I truly lose my temper!!' and he turned on his heel and strode back into his tent.

'Where now father, do we lay siege to Rajgad?' asked his son Fazal, when both men had changed out of their official robes and were being served refreshments in Afzal's tent.

A look of irritation crossed Afzal's face and he scowled at his son.'

'Dimwit! Do you not know that the *pargana* of Wai has been transferred to my name after Randulla Khan's death? His son Randulla Khan the Junior is only fifteen so, the Shah in his infinite wisdom decided to confer the honor on me.

I need to consolidate my position and take control of that area. When will you learn to think strategically?' he asked despairingly of his son.

Chapter 19

Wai July 1659 – Pantaji Gopinath Bokil

The mood on the fort was one of anger. Even the torrential rain and high winds at this altitude could not cool the simmering anger of the men. The king had traveled from Rajgad to Pratapgad, once word had reached that the Khan had set up camp at Wai. The monsoon had broken in all its fury. The jungles around Pratapgad and all the way up to Mahabaleshwar and then down to Wai were an explosion of greenery, representing every single shade of green. It rained for hours every single day and the rivers Venna, Krishna, Savitri and Koyna were in full flood. The normally clear waters were now a muddy torrent. In this season, all man could do was to shelter and wait for the passing.

By now, every single *Maavla* soldier knew of Afzal's provocations and was itching to exact vengeance. It was only the king's draconian discipline that stopped individual units from raiding and harassing the Khan's encampment at Wai.

Shivajiraje had made an entry into Pratapgad at the head of a contingent of the *deshmukh* chieftains with their armies. Kanhoji Jedhe had by example kept all the chieftains to the king's side, other than the powerful Khopde, who had gone over.

Hiroji had craned to see a glimpse of the king when the party rode in. Shivaji made a regal figure. He wore chain mail armor and a steel helmet on his head. On his left shoulder hung his bow, which he had named Sarang. His war mace, Kumudini, was sheathed in a holster by his saddle, and a beautiful sword, reputed to be made in Toledo, hung at his waist. He rode a beautiful white mare, and Hiroji was swept up in the majesty of the moment, when a thousand men flurried in the lowered bow of salute when he appeared. His eyes misted over. A Hindu king at last, one of our own! And he too bent low in salute.

Hiroji looked around for Ramaji and then remembered that his father had left the fort a few days ago.

'Your mother, may her soul find release, never asked me for anything,' Ramaji had said to his son.

'The only thing she asked the mother goddess was that she be taken before me. Though she never said as much, I know her dearest wish was that the beads of her *mangalsutra* the black necklace that all Hindu wives wear as a sign of matrimony, be scattered into the mother river Ganga,' and he pulled out the necklace of black beads that he had lovingly secreted away into a pouch at his waist.

'I wanted to bring you to safety, before I embark on my mission'.

Hiroji's throat had closed with emotion. Would he ever see his father again? Ramaji had instinctively understood and folded the boy into his arms as he was wont to when he was an infant. Ramaji stroked his son's back with a father's love while the boy wordlessly gripped his father tight.

Ramaji had set out early the next day, along with a small party carrying mail to Rajgad. From there he had decided to make his way north through Mughal-infested territory, avoiding Burhanpur and continuing in the direction of the Gangetic plain. Hiroji had watched from the ramparts as his father was lost to sight once he entered the expanse of the green forest cover.

***

And suddenly news arrived that a lawyer had arrived from the Khan's camp, thus forcing Shivaji's hand.

The king's style was to hear the thoughts of all the able men in any gathering, quietly taking in their points of view and listening to the men debate. He would then mull over all he had heard, and only then declare his decision. And once that was made it was final.

The meeting today was getting heated, despite the prime minister Shyamrajpant Ranzhekar's calming influence. The old warrior

Moropant was present, as were Raghunathpant Atre and Raghunath Ballal Korde, all three distinctive as *Chitpavans*. Today, they were not dressed for war, and wore the more scholarly robes of their calling.

The officers of Pratapgad fort were also present. Naropant, Sonopant, Ganoji Shetye, Veero Ram, and Krishnaji Babaji, the commandant of the fort. Many of the top administrators and warriors of the kingdom also came from this tiny warrior community of *Chandraseniya Kayasth Prabhus* kshatriyas.

'Let him come sire,' Krishnaji said quietly. 'This fort will never give up. Let the Pathans taste the spirit of the Marathi people.' In anyone else, this could've passed for a boast, but the man's quiet confidence and dedication to the cause was legend. He had been handpicked to the post by the king himself.

And then there was Yesaji Kank, stoic as always, and Tanaji Malusare, who managed to physically dominate any group he was in.

The group was evenly divided on the course of action. The common people in the kingdom were asking why their king was letting the desecration of their temples go unanswered. People were worried what Afzal might do to the holy temple of Mahabaleshwar, which was just thirty miles from Wai.

Half the group wanted to let Afzal dash his forces fruitlessly against the many hill forts, bleeding off his supplies and finances, while the others wanted to take the war to the Khan using their tried and tested hit and run tactics.

While this back and forth was going on, Bokil was announced, and the man swept in. Shivaji smiled at Pantaji, as the old brahmin entered, greeting him traditionally and bidding him to take a seat next to him. The men were gathered in the audience chamber in the upper fort. Though the windows were covered with rush mats, tied fast to keep out the rain, the high winds at this elevation and the attendant downpour, showered the group with a cold spray of rain when the wind turned.

'Our spies bring news each day about the Khan. He is wary sire,' replied Gopinath. 'He is no fool. He knows his position at Wai is impregnable,' and talk paused to hear the latest news.

'As an opening gambit, he sent Pandhre, Kharate, Ashraf Khan, Hilal Khan, and Kalyanji Jadhavrao, your cousin from Lady Jijabai's side, with seven thousand cavalry to take our stations at Pune, Shirwal, Supe, and Chakan. Our garrisons of around a hundred men each, fought but could not hold out' but even while relaying this, Pantaji saw that the king knew this already. Once again, he inwardly marveled at the importance the king placed on intelligence-gathering.

'He has arrayed his cannon to command all the passes that ascend up to Wai. He knows our penchant for cavalry raids, and spies tell me that our men would be cut down before they even got to the outer pickets. He has cleared the entire jungle around his camp creating a clear field of fire for his Pathan musketeers,' reported the lawyer glumly.

Suddenly a guard appeared and bowing low, announced that the Khan's lawyer had arrived and was waiting to be admitted.

'Let's hear him then. Have him searched for weapons, of course,' directed Shivaji schooling his features and preparing for whatever was to come.

As usual, the king was dressed casually, in a simple cotton tunic and leggings, with camel hide footwear. His long jet-black wavy hair, was neatly combed but unbound, cascading over his shoulders and his beard was neatly trimmed to a fine point. His forehead had the marks of sandalwood paste, attesting that he had already worshiped at the shrine of Kedareshwar early that morning.

The guard announced the Khan's lawyer. Krishnaji Bhaskar was ushered in, bowing low in salute to the king. Shivaji saw a young, good looking, slim man of average height and girth dressed in the traditional and conservative attire of a Brahmin. The group turned to listen to him in open curiosity.

'The great Khan-e-azam, Afzal Khan Mohammedshahi, has come to Wai from Bijapur with the sole purpose to meet you,' was his opening statement.

The Khan had not sent a gift as a sign of courtesy. This itself conveyed eloquently what the Khan thought of Shivaji.

'The Khan is an old friend of your father, the great warrior Shahaji Bhosle and there is great love and affection between them.'

This itself was a blatant lie given that Afzal had treacherously imprisoned Shahaji in the past, but Shivaji let the lie pass unchallenged.

'You are as a son to him. He requests you to meet with him. He will himself be your advocate with Adil Shah in getting him to bless your lands in the lower Konkan coastal area. He will let you keep all the forts you have taken as well. He will also honor any other wishes that lie dormant in your heart.

'All you need to do is come and meet the Khan personally at Wai,' saying which Krishnaji bowed low and offered the Khan's personal letter to the king.

Shivaji nodded to an attendant and the scroll was taken from the man.

For a few moments, there was only silence. The king looked grave as he regarded Krishnaji.

'I hold the great Khan with as much reverence as my own father. I, definitely look forward, to meeting with his illustrious personage. By ordering me to return the captured territories and sign a treaty, the great Khan has shown mercy on me. His power is legend. His prowess is like a flame. I know I have wronged the Sultanate and am prepared to correct my mistakes. I am nothing compared to the great Khan. I never expected that my minor actions in this region would warrant the attention of the great Sultanate. The Khan is indeed of large heart, to forgive my mistakes. I know he has no deceit in his heart'.

This speech was given with utmost sincerity and at several places the king's words faltered, as though overcome with emotion.

'I know the lord Khan, has ordered me to come to Wai, but I am terrified! I would beg the great Khan himself to come to the Jaavli to fetch me. That will increase my prestige as well. Normally I would not dare to meet his gaze, but now I am convinced that I can surrender my sword to him. I would only ask for an assurance of personal safety,' saying which the king looked down contritely at his hands.

The half-smile on his lips and the customary sparkle in his eyes was missing today and he looked just like a young man who had taken on more than he could chew.

'The great Khan is like my uncle, and I look forward to meeting him. Pantaji will accompany you back to Wai tomorrow. Kindly do make a humble request that the Khan provide a personal assurance of safety,' said the king indicating an end to the audience.

'But lord, you will be perfectly safe at Wai!!' protested Krishnaji paying heed to Afzal's specific instructions, but the king morosely shook his head from side to side indicating they were at an impasse.

Another nod to an attendant and a tray holding a silken robe was brought forth and Shivaji briefly touched it to indicate his blessing after which it was offered to the Khan's lawyer.

Once the man had left and was out of hearing, Shivaji nodded to Ranzhekar, who began reading the Khan's letter,

'Your irresponsible actions these days pierce Adil Shah's heart like an arrow. You have taken this mountainous region under your control along with some forts and therefore the *Siddis* of Janjira are exasperated with your actions as well.

You have forcibly taken the seat and kingdom of the Chandrarao More, our vassal, who rules for us in the region of the Maaval in the lower Konkan. The Muslims of Kalyan and Bhiwandi, also complain to my master, that you have destroyed many mosques and palaces of the nobility and are generally an impediment to the glorious spread of Islam. All these notables are seriously vexed by your actions.

In addition, you have also struck your own colors and title in the manner of an independent sovereign. And you refuse to answer to or comply with any of the Sultanate's norms. It is because of this that the great Shah has sent me here, with a six-pronged army, which exhorts me to do battle each day. I have in my army famed swordsmen like Musa Khan. Other notable warriors in my army press me each day to conquer the Maaval Jaavli region.

I order you forthwith to surrender all your forts and the regions you have taken over. Come to Wai, and meet with me, and we will decide on the next course of action'.

Ranzhekar closed the scroll and looked up. There was dead silence in the room. There had been no salutation, no flowery language, as was the norm of the day. The message was plain for all to see.

Interestingly, the contents of the letter were threatening, and completely at odds with the flowery assurances that the Khan's lawyer had verbally given.

'Lord, he means treachery!' blurted Yesaji and it was as if a dam had burst.

'Remember how he murdered Kasturirange Nayak sire!' exclaimed one. Afzal had laid siege to the fort of Sira a few years ago but despite months of concentrated attacks, the fort had held out. Afzal had finally invited the Nayak ruler Kasturirange to a meeting to parley peace terms. A personal passage of safety had been given to the Nayak endorsed with the handprint of Afzal himself. However, at the meeting site, Afzal had welcomed Kasturirange and then without warning stabbed him with his *katar* and in the ensuing panic taken over the fort. The Khan was not one to be taken at his word.

'Under no circumstances should you go there, sire!' blurted another.

Pingale had a more reasoned response. 'Remember their notion of *al-takiya*, sire. These Muslims do not consider us human, so, they do not feel bound to honor any word or treaty with us.'

Shivaji held up a hand calmly to quieten the gathering. 'Brothers, there is no question of my going to Wai. The question is what do we do next? Do we just wait, or do we press the issue?'

The hubbub started all over again. After hearing all the arguments and allowing each person there to speak his mind, Shivaji decided that a meeting should happen, but it should be held in Pratapgad, not Wai.

Then the question naturally arose as to who should represent the kingdom. Shivaji had thought long and hard about who had the necessary experience, wisdom and guile to deal with Afzal. Finally, the suggestion had come from Lady Jijabai herself. She had suggested Gopinath Bokil, a poor but brilliant lawyer, from the village of Hivre, who because of his mental prowess had been awarded the honorific title of 'Pantaji'. His authority and demeanor were such that he was hailed as 'uncle' by the king himself in a show of royal respect.

It was decided that Pantaji Gopinath would travel to Wai to convince the Khan to come to Pratapgad. Gopinath saw that this was not the abject, pathetic creature that Krishnaji had seen but the vital, forceful Shivaji that he knew.

The king signaled an end to the meeting and the men made their exits. Just as Gopinath was leaving, the king grabbed his arm and steered him to an alcove, bringing his lips close to the man's ear,

'Uncle Pantaji!!' he whispered.

'Try to find out what his real motive is in wanting to meet me. If possible, get him to commit publicly to providing his personal handprint in sandalwood as an assurance of my personal safety.'

'I need Afzal to come to the jungles of the Jaavli Maaval. Do whatever you have to do! Make whatever promises you need to make but bring him here!!' hissed Shivaji.

And Gopinath understanding immediately, nodded in acceptance.

***

Afzal Khan had been the *mukaasdaar* administrator of Wai, ten years ago and knew the area well. He knew full well how impenetrable the jungles of the Maaval lowlands to the west of him were. The forests of the Jaavli were best left to the men who had inhabited them since time began.

The army had settled onto the small hill station of Wai like a swarm of flies. By now the size of his force exceeded thirty-five thousand cavalry and infantry combined and a veritable sea of tents stretched out from the epicenter all along the undulating terrain.

The Khan had also repeated an idiosyncrasy of his, that had the Hindu contingent shaking their heads, in impotent rage. While touring the countryside around Wai he had chanced upon the village of Bavdhan, and in his infinite wisdom deigned to rename it Afzalnagar. He had immediately instructed his clerks to note the change in all official land registry records, despite the pleading of the village people who took great pride, in the ancient nomenclature of their village.

The affair of Bajaji had gone better than expected. He was told that the chieftain Naikji Pandhre had been approached by Bajaji's wife Savitribai. Pandhre had taken a loan, underwritten by the Nimbalkar clan from the banker brother duo of Babanbhai and Jaichandbhai, and paid the money to the Khan.

These banker brothers hailed from the Jain banking community that had ties all the way from Turkistan to Koryo. This secretive clan trusted only their own and moved money using the promissory note, or *hundi* system across thousands of miles of territory. Just based on a given word or a cryptic note.

Wai lay at about two thousand three hundred feet above sea level but on the landward side of the Sahyadri mountain range. The water-laden winds, coming off the *Sindhu sagar* sea, would break on the granite ridges of the Sahyadri, drenching the Konkan coast. Only what remained would make its way landward to the plateau of the *desh*. Also, Wai was itself at a slight elevation so the copious rainfall would drain away without causing any impediment to his settlement.

Despite all his goading there had not been a peep out of that dog Shivaji. The Khan grimly decided that it was now time to take the battle to him.

Krishnaji Bhaskar had been personally chosen by him to act as lawyer and emissary. The man was whip smart and endlessly ambitious. He had jumped at the opportunity to come into the employ of the Bijapur Sultanate already seeing a landholding in his future. Afzal's directions had been specific.

'Your job is to get Shivaji to come to Wai to meet me. I will do the rest!'

And word arrived that Krishnaji had returned from Pratapgad, along with Shivaji's own lawyer…

A special tent was set up to receive Shivaji's lawyer. Afzal wanted to impress the man with the number of chieftains he had brought into the field. The long tent was arrayed with his heavy carved chair at one end with room for all his chieftains to array on both sides of him. The man would have to approach him through a veritable tunnel of impressive warriors on either side.

And the man finally appeared. Afzal studied him curiously. He was a wizened old gnome. His dress, headgear and religious sandalwood paste marks on his forehead proclaimed him to be a devout Brahmin.

Afzal remained sitting, his bull head lowered, glaring at the approaching man out of kohl-rimmed eyes. The man's face was non-committal. If anything, he had a look of respectful attention as he fired off the mandatory low salutes and straightening up, adjusted the shawl across one shoulder and walked down the dual range of assembled chieftains.

The spies had already told him who was going to be present, but Gopinath mentally ticked off the men as he saw them. He spotted the

Pathan contingent first, easily identifiable by their dress. They wore long tunics, buttoned down the front, over baggy trousers and their long, oiled hair and beards were mostly dyed henna-orange. The men favored ringing their eyes with kohl, and the overall effect was menacing. There stood Fazal Khan, and the upstart Ankush Khan, and the famed swordsman Musa Khan.

Then there was the Abyssinian Muslim contingent, represented by Randullah Khan the younger, who had taken upon himself the glorious title *Rustum-e-zaman*. He was flanked by the tall, sinewy, dark members of his tribe. Lower down in importance came the Hindustani Muslims with Ambar Khan most prominent, and of course lowest in the hierarchy came the Hindus. Here were Rajaji Ghatge, Naikji Kharate, Naikji Pandhre, and most saddening, the king's own close relatives, Bajaji Naik Nimbalkar, or whatever his Muslim name now was, and Mambaji Bhosle himself, the king's uncle.

'Great Lord!' he began, 'Shivaji sends his deepest respectful wishes, along with these robes of honor. I, Gopinath Bokil have the honor of acting as the bridge between your esteemed self and my master if you would allow me to present this small gift to your most exalted person.'

Afzal like most men was not immune to flattery and he waved a hand expansively. Gopinath signaled to a man behind him, with a brass tray, covered with a fine embroidered silk cloth. He stepped forward, bowing low in front of the seated Khan and held out the tray. Afzal briefly touched the cover signaling his acceptance of the gift and an attendant took it away.

'If I have your permission, may I read out the letter that my master has addressed to your divine person?' asked the lawyer with utmost gravity and respect.

When Afzal nodded, the Brahmin unrolled a parchment and began reading.

'I, Shivaji Bhosle, son of Shahaji Bhosle, send greetings to the great Lord Afzal Khan. Your grace gives balance to the heavens and beauty to the earth. Your bravery is akin to a roaring flame. You hold the same place in my heart, as my revered father. I know I have wronged the Bijapur Sultanate and I am prepared to make full reparations.

I am deeply sorry for my actions. And I am prepared to give up all the forts and territories I have captured and accompany you to Bijapur to seek forgiveness from Adil Shah.

However, I am deeply scared. Please do not ask me to come to Wai. I cannot even imagine looking up and meeting your gaze. You would do me the utmost honor, if you would agree to accept my hospitality, at my humble lodgings at Pratapgad and come there to fetch me instead. I will surrender my sword to you and come with you to Bijapur.

I await your favorable reply to my humble request,' saying which he offered the document to Afzal, to see the sign and seal and the palm imprint in sandalwood paste to verify that Shivaji himself had addressed the letter.

'Nonsense!!' exploded Afzal and Gopinath took a step back in alarm.

'I will not go any further than Wai. I know first-hand how treacherous that terrain and jungle is. Tell him he has to come to Wai and prostrate himself before me. I will take him to the Shah, and he will have to bind his hands in the customary fashion of the court and stand in front of the Shah averting his gaze from the royal personage while the most gracious Shah decides his punishment' thundered the Khan with rage suffusing his face a deep pink.

'But Shivajiraje is terrified your Lord,' protested Gopinath.

'I beseech you, accept his invitation and grace us by your presence at Pratapgad.'

'Silence!!' hissed Afzal and Gopinath knew this was the time of maximum danger. The man might even have him decapitated on a whim to send back a message. He cast his eyes down and took a step back.

The Khan signaled to Krishnaji Bhaskar, who stood a half step behind Gopinath to provide his version of the meeting with Shivaji.

'Great lord,' the man began clearing his throat nervously.

'Shivaji is indeed terrified. I personally saw that his resolve is broken. He never imagined that the response would come in your esteemed personage and now wonders how to salvage the situation.'

'So why does he refuse to come to Wai?' asked the Khan looking alternatively between Krishnaji and Gopinath

'He fears treachery my lord..' began Krishnaji nervously and his voice tapered off.

Afzal gestured irritably for him to continue, and the man began again.

'I believe he means to come to Bijapur, but he is afraid of coming into this large encampment. He would much rather meet you, first in his territory, to get a sense of assurance and comfort. Remember, he has never met you. He knows you only through your wondrous exploits.'

The Khan's lawyer continued his analysis of the situation.

'I did not see any evidence of mobile cannon, elephants, or a large cavalry at his fort either, or preparations for war.'

'All you'd need to do is go and fetch him from Pratapgad,' said Krishnaji with increasing confidence.

The Khan ruminated on what he had heard, chewing his bottom lip in thought. He looked around at his chieftains. The reactions were typical. Ankush, Prataprao More and Khopde were champing at the bit, while Kharate, Hilaal and Musa were more circumspect.

Afzal raised an eyebrow in Musa's direction inviting him to speak. The tall Pathan straightened up and said, 'Lord, I sense malice here. We should not descend with our army into that crucible of the Maaval. I do not trust that dog Shivaji.'

As expected, the others started speaking up all at once saying the man's fears were unfounded and Afzal raised a hand for silence.

He pointed to Prataprao More, and the man brightened visibly at the importance shown him.

'Lord, I am a More. We have lived and ruled in the Maaval for centuries. It was only three years ago, that that infernal Shivaji, interfered in our affairs and killed my father Chandrarao taking over our seat. I know every path and turn in this forest. As long as my men and I accompany the army, you have nothing to fear,' saying which he stepped back beaming, running the back of his hand over his luxurious mustaches.

Afzal thought hard. If he did not force this visit, he could be looking at a prolonged campaign while Shivaji travelled from fort to fort. Laying sieges to some of these forts was nigh impossible and he would have nothing to show for his efforts. The land was not rich either to support the expense of his large army. Just his four hundred war elephants were eating through his budget at an alarming rate and at some point, he would be asked for a financial reckoning.

A thought suddenly flashed, and his green eyes snapped to Gopinath, who was waiting silently along with the rest of the gathering

'You! What did you say your name was?'

'Gopinath, lord' replied the man meekly.

'You wear that sacred thread across your body, do you not? So, you must be a Brahmin?' queried Afzal.

'Yes lord' answered Pantaji in puzzlement.

'Do you swear on your sacred thread, that there is no risk to me, if I were to meet Shivaji at Pratapgad?' said Afzal, moving his rook into position.

'Absolutely lord!!!! I swear by all that's holy to me that there is no risk to you all,' replied Gopinath with alacrity, castling his king.

'Hmm… all right then. I will let you have my answer tomorrow. Leave us now' he said waving for the meeting to end.

***

The interior of the tent was bathed with a rich yellow light from the many brass multi-wick stands placed at strategic points. The Khan sat on his usual chair deep in thought. Some of the chiefs lounged on thick mattresses strewn about the floor or leaned against embroidered bolsters.

'Lord, I have studied this man's movements. He is careful and calculated. He does not let emotion cloud his judgement. Look at how he has established his kingdom. He uses whatever approach succeeds, in getting him to his goal. In addition to open battle, he uses ambush, treaty, and even bribery to get what he wants. I would not, want to take his letter, at face value,' said Musa. This was almost a speech for the normally taciturn Pathan.

'Lord, I have been telling you this all along!' Kharate quickly interjected supporting Musa Khan's view.

'Nonsense!! The time to strike is now! The enemy is dispirited. Let's use this occasion to clean out this viper's nest once and for all!' shouted Ankush before Kharate had even finished speaking, and a lot of the others added their voice to his. A swell of noise ensued with men arguing back and forth.

Khan let the noise wash over him, as he sifted through the arguments, for and against. He considered himself a fine judge of character, and besides, these *kafirs* were predictable. He'd purposely put that old brahmin on the spot and the man hadn't even blinked.

The history books were rife with how the valiant Rajputs of the north of Hindustan had trusted the Delhi Sultanate's word and been double crossed time and time again. Yet they refused to learn. Yes, these people were destined for death cleaving to their quaint *dharmic* rules even when death stared them in the face.

Finally, his mind was made up. He held up his hand and all talk ceased as the men looked to him expectantly.

'I've decided. We go to meet him,' he said quietly in the silence.

'Lord, please reconsider!' blurted Musa over the triumphant yells of Ankush and Fazal.

'Enough!' the Khan's voice was steely now, and the men's gazes dropped.

'Do you take me for a fool? I killed my first man before you were swimming in your father's balls! I have thought through this matter very closely. As you say, Shivaji is no fool. Do you think he does not see the huge army arrayed in front of him? And what does he have? A handful of wretched hill farmers?' And Afzal spat into a spittoon at his side to reinforce his disgust.

'But I will not enter Pratapgad fort either. We will meet somewhere in the middle. Meanwhile, keep a strong garrison at Wai in case this is a feint. Keep our heavy cannon and elephants here, but move the majority of the cavalry and infantry to the village of Paar which lies midway near the fort on the winding *Ambenali* trail that descends from Mahableshwar to the coast.'

'Take the light cannon and mortars. Yoke them to the bullocks.'

And suddenly a thought occurred to him. 'Take my Pathan musketeers as well. That corps itself will stop anybody getting any wrong ideas,' he said smirking into his beard.

***

Pantanji meanwhile had an agenda of his own. There seemed to be no check on his movements in the camp at Wai.

He visited the Pathan quarters first. The smell of roasting mutton made his nose crinkle in disgust. It was rumored these Pathans used no spice in their cooking.

He visited Ashraf and Ankush, carrying presents for each. He saw that the mood was one of jubilation. They had all ratcheted down the threat level a few notches after realizing that Shivaji was going to capitulate. Ankush was openly talking about how to carve the kingdom among the Bijapuri nobles.

The Siddi and Hindu contingents were no different. His theory about why the Hindus were up in arms against their co-religionist was ratified. Shivaji had realized the evils of the landholding *watandari* system. The foreigner Sultans were doling out parcels of land that were not theirs to give anyway. Many times, the recipients had to capture the territory first from the neighboring Sultan and then 'accept' the gift. The irony was lost on most.

Most *watandaar* nobles proceeded to misrule and terrorize the inhabitants of their landholding. As long as the Sultan got his share, nobody cared about the plight of the common citizen.

Shivaji had put a stop to all that. He had created a central treasury, and everybody was paid a salary, including him. This naturally made the erstwhile chieftains look askance at this new arrangement. And this was the reason why the Nimbalkar, Mohite, Khopde, Ghorpade and other powerful clans were arrayed with the Khan. Economics had trumped self-respect.

Gopinath Bokil did a thorough circuit of the settlement of Wai, noting exact corps strengths, levels of preparedness, levels of laxity and stocks of material and munitions.

The camp was almost a mini city, complete with streets and quarters for traders, musicians, dancing girls, and other creature comforts. The primarily meat-eating Muslims had bought up all livestock within a fifty-mile radius, and the meat market was doing brisk business.

At the end of his visits, and reading between the lines, Pantaji Gopinath was convinced that this was not a straightforward mission to subdue Shivaji. The Khan meant ill-will to the king's person.

Walking along with his shawl held to his nose to ward off the odious smells, Gopinath stumbled across a strange discovery. There was even a jeweler's quarter. The famed gold fields of Kolar and the diamond mines of Golconda were among the richest veins in the world, and the quarter was abuzz with merchants anticipating the fall of Pratapgad. The soldiers would be flush with loot and they could do brisk business. Given the value of their wares, they had attached themselves like limpets to the juggernaut that was Afzal Khan's army.

Pantaji approached the merchants and respectfully asked if they would be interested in selling their wares to Shivajiraje on Pratapgad. The merchants inwardly smirked. 'How silly was this fellow?' They'd sell their goods once on Pratapgad and buy them back at a fraction of the price from the marauding Sultanate troops, only to sell them back a second time to the nobles in the same army. They effusively accepted his invitation to parade their wares at Pratapgad.

Chapter 20

Pratapgad September 1659

The rains had eased and the month of *Shraavan* was underway. The fort was a hive of activity as weapons were forged, repaired, or sharpened and plans were laid out. Discussions each day lasted well into the night.

And then terrible news came.

Queen Sai, the king's principal consort and mother of Prince Sambhaji, passed away. She'd been fighting tuberculosis for the last two years and the disease had finally won. Sai was the daughter of the Nimbalkar clan, and his first love. They had been married as children and grown up together sharing the joys and sorrows of the awakening kingdom. All the king's later marriages were for the sake of political alliances, but this one had been for love.

When the news arrived, the king was dining in the great hall in the lower bastion along with as many men as could fit. He ate with the men and the troops vied with each other for the honor of spending time with their king. The meal was always simple. Green *moong* khichdi which was a thick gruel of rice and lentil providing both strength and energy. The king ate only once a day and mostly shunned meat. Alcohol was completely forbidden on any of his forts and the punishment for any soul who transgressed was fifty lashes.

An aide brought the news to the king and a shadow passed over his face. He quickly regained his composure for the sake of the men, but everyone could see something was off.

One man, mistaking the cause for the king's upset blurted, 'Do not worry sire, my life is yours. We will prevail over the Khan!'

Hiroji, who had had the luck to squeeze into this lunch banquet was astounded when every single man there immediately shouted, 'I am yours to the death great king! This life is yours!!'

The king smiled then, a ghost of a smile 'Brothers!! Do I not know this? It is on your strength that this *Swarajya* independence is founded! *Jagdamb! Jagdamb!*' as he invoked the name of the mother-goddess.

And the hall erupted with cries of '*Jai Bhavani!! Jagdamb!! Har har Mahadev!!*'

The king had been astounded when Pantaji Gopinath had announced that he had brought along all the jewelers from Afzal's camp. Here they were locked in an existential struggle and what was the man thinking buying jewelry they could scarcely afford?

However, the king's confusion cleared when Pantaji explained his logic.

'Sire, where do you think the wealth of Bijapur comes from? They squeeze our people dry. Let's worry about how to pay back these merchants and at what price after the meet,' and the king immediately accepted the logic of the argument.

The jewelry merchants from Bijapur had been relieved of all their wares after a careful searching of their persons so that no jewel could go missing. All the jewels were inventoried and added to the state treasury and a vague promise was made, that the king would decide the price once his mind was free of the preparations of the impending meet.

The Khan's army meanwhile had begun the trek from Wai up to Mahabaleshwar. Mahabaleshwar lay at an elevation of above four thousand feet to the west of Wai. From Mahabaleshwar, several routes descended to the coastal lands of Konkan to the west. The most challenging was the precipitous switchback descent down to sea level via the *Ambenali* trail. Spies brought reports daily back to Pratapgad as the Khan's army made the tortuous journey down into the forests of the Jaavli. The Khan had decided to make camp at the village of Paar which lay adjacent to fort Pratapgad but at a distance of several miles through thick forest.

The Marathi troops had strict instructions to not harry the army as it made the descent. While the men lamented the loss of easy pickings, the iron discipline meant they could only observe from afar the overfed and disoriented troops, as they made the trek down from the heights of Mahabaleshwar. Slowly, Paar transformed from a sleepy, dusty village into another mini city as over twenty thousand troops descended upon it.

***

The Khan meanwhile made several attempts to convince Shivaji to meet with him in his, the Khan's camp. He suggested that Shivaji come to his camp at Paar, or then meet at the foot of Pratapgad with both sets of armies in tow, but the king refused to budge. Both lawyers sent letters back and forth with proposals and counter proposals till finally an agreement was hammered out.

The terms of the meeting were finalized. The meeting would take place at a location that was half a mile from the main gate of Pratapgad, on a small meadow located on a tongue of land slightly above the surrounding forest called *Jani's temb*.

Both principals would come fully armed and would be accompanied only by their respective lawyers. Each would have ten personal bodyguards, but they would be stationed, at a distance of one bow shot from the meeting venue.

The king ordered a tent to be put up at the meeting place. The task was entrusted to the young, enthusiastic architect Anaji Malkere.

'Anaji' ordered the king, 'leave no stone unturned. Give your creativity full flow. I want the Khan to be dazzled when he enters the tent. I want him distracted and thrown off balance. Requisition silks, satins, pearls, and anything else you need from the treasury. Spare no expense!'

A portion of the jewels recently liberated were catalogued and handed over to Anaji to weave into the decorations and slowly the tent took shape.

'The meeting place lies south- west of the fort. I want the door of the tent to face due west. When I approach the tent in the late afternoon, I want the Khan to be staring into the setting sun,' instructed the king and once again Anaji was impressed with how much attention to detail his king gave to every aspect of the war theatre.

It was agreed that the meeting would take place three days after the Khan reached the village of Paar and both lawyers would work out the finer details in the days to come.

***

The king held meetings with individual chieftains and gave each their marching orders. Whatever be the outcome of the meeting, the king stressed that these men were to concentrate only on the task that they'd been given.

Sunset had passed and still the discussions were in full flow.

'Sire, my apologies for speaking my mind, but your orders to send out cavalry in the cardinal directions right now to prepare for future battle has reduced my strength,' said Mankoji Dahatonde, the grizzled, but still vital commander of the cavalry, with some hesitation.

'Mankoji, this fight is going to happen, but think beyond that. Whatever be the result of my meeting with the Khan, can you imagine how much confusion will reign in the days following? We must, we must sow the seeds of disinformation and spread this fight in all four directions,' said the king, patiently explaining the grand strategy that had been evolving in his mind.

'Also, we must not forget the Mughal. The only reason we've had peace for the last four years is because that sinner Aurangzeb has finally managed to capture the throne at Delhi. Not only did he imprison his own father but he allied with his brother Muradbaksh by swearing a treaty on the Koran to jointly attack the forces of the eldest brother Dara.'

'What is the latest from Bahirji?' inquired the king of a quiet man in the gathering, who nobody had even noticed.

'What is your name?' enquired Moropant, surprised that he had not registered the presence of this man at all.

'My name is unimportant lord,' said the stranger quietly, deferring to Moropant's rank.

'I work for Bahirji, and the news from Delhi is bad,' he said with a sober face.

'We all hoped that Dara would win the fratricidal struggle. Maybe he could have healed the open wound that divides the Mohammedans and the rest of Hindustanis today. Alas, that was not in Mahadev's plans,' he said with his face registering disappointment.

'It was as you predicted sire. Mirzaraja Jai Singh, who was earlier allied with Dara switched sides. God alone knows why, and with the force of the Rajputs behind Aurangya, Dara's army was scattered to the wind.

Not that Aurangya ever wielded a weapon himself, staying true to the rest of his cowardly lineage, but Dara was taken prisoner alive. Aurangya then had his slave behead Dara with a dagger, and the head of his own brother was then presented to him.

Our spies in Delhi tell us that the head was presented to Aurangzeb as he was sitting in the garden, in the evening and it was only then that he effected a few cuts on the head with his dagger – and such a creature sits on the throne of Delhi,' and the man's face twisted with revulsion.

The gathering meanwhile was listening spellbound to the tale. 'What happened to Murad?' someone in the group asked.

'What do you expect?' snorted the man. 'All that nonsense about swearing on the Koran was just that. The minute the battle with Dara was won, Aurangya had Murad imprisoned and killed as well, and then there was nobody to stand in his way as he took the throne for himself.'

'A man who kills his own brothers by treachery, even going to the extent of breaking an oath,. sworn on their holy book; how do you think he will treat us brothers?' asked Shivaji to a quiet room. Each man was thinking of the enormity of treachery, greed and duplicity that must reside in a man who now headed one of the most powerful kingdoms in the world.'

Tanaji blurted out, 'A war is coming sire, and it will be to the death.'

'Exactly!' said Shivaji. 'And we are beset by enemies. We need to tame the southern Sultanates now. Mark my words. Aurangzeb fancies himself a holy warrior. He has already desecrated the temples of Kashi and Mathura and demolished hundreds of other temples converting them into mosques. He cannot afford to let us live. This idea of a Hindu resurgence that we have begun is like poison to the soul of Islam, and he will move heaven and earth to extinguish this flame.'

'It is worse than that sire,' the spy quietly remarked, and all eyes turned to him.

'There is not a single Hindu temple, left standing, within a hundred-mile radius of Delhi, and he has embarked upon a mass conversion of Hindus by force. The entire district of Azamgad, which was populated with Hindu weavers, was forcibly converted to Islam last year.'

'But yet the Rajputs continue to serve him' remarked Shivaji. 'Sometimes I feel we are cursed to continually fight among ourselves while the invaders watch in amazement at our short-sightedness,' said the king bitterly.

'But one problem at a time, brothers,' said Shivaji shortly, bringing each man's attention back to the matter at hand.

'I want Doroji to take eight hundred cavalry and station himself outside the port of Dabhol. Afzal Khan is very wisely planning for the eventuality of the war spreading down to the coastal Konkan region--- has stationed three cargo ships laden with war material in the port. Ask him to keep watch, and the minute the news reaches the port about the results of the meeting, confusion will ensue. He should strike and strike hard. Strike all the Turks first and cut them down to a man,' said the king looking at Mankoji, who nodded his head in acceptance of the order.

'What is the size of the encampment at Paar now?' Shivaji asked of no one in particular.

'Around ten thousand of their heavy cavalry and an equal number of infantry sire,' said the spy quietly.

'But they continue to transfer men and materials to Paar each day, sire. I fear he plans to lay siege to Pratapgad.'

'I have no doubt that is his plan,' said the king, smiling into his beard.

'Three hundred of the small cannon and mortars have been moved to Paar, and the Pathan musketeers are all there already. The elephants and camels have been kept at Wai though. The army at Paar is going through ten bullocks a day, the same creatures that faithfully carried their cannon and provisions down the *Ambenali* trail,' said the spy with the last part twisting his face in distaste.

'Let me know when the movement of soldiers from Wai to Paar stops' ordered the king to the spy. 'Now leave. Your work is God's work, and remember we are relying on you for the most accurate and up to date information,' and Shivaji waved the man away.

'So, men, the bulk of Afzal's army and materials will be stationed at Paar, which is about ten miles from Pratapgad, while I will be meeting with him correct?' asked the king, looking round the room, and the men nodded in confirmation, not understanding the intent.

'Kanhoji, you have the heaviest and most critical role here,' said the king turning to Kanhoji and the man immediately leaned forward, a look of rapt attention on his face.

'Whatever happens at the meet, once the cannons from fort Pratapgad thunder, I want you along with the men from the Bandal and Maral *deshmukh* chieftains, to fall upon the camp at Paar. The Khan feels he has already won. They have not bothered to even clear a field of fire around Paar. Spirit your men among the forest all around Paar.

'Fall upon Paar from all sides. I want the first charge to be with spears, and then go to swords and daggers immediately. I want all the

Pathan musketeers cut down. This is not a hit and run. There will be total confusion in the camp and I want you to start the killing from the outside and work your way in till our troops meet each other in the center.'

'But in that mayhem, surely some troops will escape outwards,' reflected Yesaji.

'And where will they go?' asked the king turning to him.

'They have only four routes to escape the slaughter. Descend to the Konkan via the Paar trail, ascend to Mahabaleshwar via the *Ambenali* trail, escape via the *Bochedholi* trail, or then disperse into the forest,' said Shivaji and the men knew this had been brewing in his mind for a long time.

'Moropant, you will block the access to the *Paar* trail, so that the Bijapuris have either to return to the killing field of Paar, or then surrender,' and the old man nodded curtly.

'Netoji!' the king called to his up- and coming cavalry commander. 'I did not see you here?'

'Here, sire,' said Netoji as a young, sinewy, dusky man bowed low 'I was late coming to the meeting, my apologies.'

'You have a critical role. When the Jedhes and Bandals attack the camp at Paar, there will undoubtedly be some leakage. Some men may escape the dragnet and find the road up to Mahabaleshwar, and on to Wai. I want you to station a thousand men where the *Ambenali* trail starts. Let the panicked men come to that step, and then cut them down ruthlessly. Not a single man should escape,' and Netoji bowed low to accept the order.

'But your work doesn't stop there Netoji!' continued the king.

'Once you see that the camp at Paar has been decimated, I want you to keep a hundred man watch for stragglers and make your way with your force immediately to Wai. I want you there no later than one day. There will be total confusion at that camp by then, and I want you to wreak havoc there. Destroy as many men as you can and take possession of all the material that the Khan has brought with him.

The men were by now all looking at the king in stupefaction, but he was not done yet.

'And you Shilimkar, I have kept for the last, but not the least. You will take five hundred men and guard the entrance to the *Bochedholi* trail, which is the other obscure trail that could be used by the Khan's men to escape our assault. I have seen your men, they are sons of the sword, and I don't want a single man to escape there alive,' and Shilimkar *deshmukh*, the chieftain of his clan bowed his head to acknowledge the rare honor and responsibility that had been reposed in him by his king.

Ranzhekar, being the prime minister, and one of the oldest men there broke the silence.

'It appears you have thought all this through sire. But... but what if the unthinkable happens?'

'I still say, let us sue for peace and give up a few forts and kick this problem down the road. Even the Khan knows that it is almost impossible to lay siege to Pratapgad. Why expose yourself to risk in meeting with the treacherous man' asked the man, looking around the room for support.

Several men nodded in agreement and a chorus of voices arose. It was evident that the men were not convinced that the king should put himself directly in danger in meeting with the Khan.

'Yes sire! Let us sue for peace and deflect this danger. This is our territory. We can always win back the few forts we have to give up,' said a chorus of voices and Shivaji had to hold up a hand for silence.

'Brothers, I have decided. We need to settle this here and now. I have thought long and hard about this problem. This is the only course of action that makes sense. It is late now brothers. Sleep. Rest. We will need all our strength on the morrow,' saying which the king bid farewell to the group.

***

Barely an hour had passed since the king had dismissed the meeting. The moon had barely begun its stately journey across the night sky than an attendant ran to the barracks where the men were sequestered. There was no special treatment based on rank for any person.

'Hurry, hurry, the king has called you to the audience chamber immediately!!' cried the man as he went from door to door waking the men and recalling them back to the upper fort.

It was a few minutes by the time the men had rubbed the sleep from their eyes and stumbled to the great hall. Several carried swords not sure whether an attack had taken place. Tunics were unbuttoned and turbans were absent as the men had scrambled to obey the royal order.

The same crew, looking somewhat shambled, scrambled and assembled quickly in the audience chamber. The room had been freshly lit by twenty brass lamps. The king sat before them bare-chested, with his hair loose, his sword held in his left hand, and fire in his eyes.

The men had never seen their king so animated.

'Brothers!!' the king cried when most of the men had made their way blearily to the hall.

'I had a dream! The mother goddess Jagdamba herself appeared in my dream,' said the king, and it was as though an otherworldly voice emanated from his throat. Several men folded their hands in religious awe and prayer.

'Her forehead was smeared with vermilion, and she was aflame with battle-lust! Nine of her hands held war weapons and the tenth was extended to me in blessing!

'Child, she said. Do not fret. I will work through you to achieve your goal. The Brahman godhead is the final decider of things, but I will work through that cosmic energy to grant you victory.

'Take your normal precautions but understand that I am now your sword, and I will give you victory!!'

And as she finished saying this, there was a bolt of lightning and the goddess herself descended into my sword!!' and he held up his sword for all the men to see.

For a moment, there was awestruck silence, and suddenly the dam broke.

'*Jai Bhavani*!!' one man chorused and other took up the cry. '*Jagdamb, jagdamb..*' the king muttered with his eyes closed reverently, and the group of men, who just moments earlier were half-asleep were suddenly enthused with awe and reverence.

'Yes, now victory is assured! The goddess is with us! She resides in your sword! Hail to the Bhavani sword, oh great king!!' and most of the men folded their hands in reverence.

All doubts were now set at rest. The goddess herself had ratified the course of action!

Chapter 21

Paar camp early Nov 1659

Afzal Khan was feeling good about the situation. The last six months had been tiring, but it looked like his trials were coming to an end. He was now with the bulk of his army in the Jaavli valley, which also comprised part of his *vatan* landholding of Wai. Best of all, Shivaji had been subjugated. The man was clearly terrified. Taking a few random forts here and there on the outskirts of the Sultanate was one thing, but when faced with the might of the Bijapur army the man's morale had crumbled. A sneer crossed Afzal's face.

Once he had dealt with Shivaji, he'd need to transform Paar into a proper military encampment and maintain a standing force there. That was the only way to keep these Maaval *deshmukh* chieftains in check.

'Summon Krishnaji,' said the Khan suddenly, startling the clerks who were bent over their desks recording the inventory of men and material that had been transferred from Wai to Paar.

Presently, Krishnaji arrived bowing low and firing off a salute to the Khan.

'Lord?' he queried respectfully.

'Where are we with the negotiations? What has been decided with that dog's lawyer?' asked Afzal with a hint of amusement.

'When do I get to meet him finally?'

'Lord, the meeting has been set for the tenth of this month. The king's lawyer…'

'Don't call him that! He is no king, just a petty bandit,' thundered the Khan.

'Begging your pardon lord, Shivaji's lawyer Pantaji Gopinath Bokil will arrive at our camp to escort you to the meeting, which has been set for noon,' said Krishnaji shakily, recovering quickly.

'Each party may come armed. Only the principals and their lawyers will parley in the tent. Each party may have ten armed bodyguards, but they will be stationed at a distance of one bow shot away from the tent,' completed Krishnaji.

'Is there any other condition that you'd like added lord?' asked the lawyer hesitantly.

Afzal chewed his lower lip in thought. He had to tread a fine line here. Any show of force on his part would spook Shivaji and he'd just disappear into his fort. While laying siege was possible, it was not foolproof, and the man could easily escape to the other handful of forts he held. Following him from fort to fort would be time-consuming, expensive. and eventually fruitless.

'No, this will have to do,' said the Khan making up his mind. 'The tenth of the month then, and we will remove this minor nuisance from the board,' and saying that he waved his hand indicating the audience had ended, already moving on to other things.

'Abdul!' he called to his man servant and the man promptly appeared.

'Send for Musa and Pandhre. I want them here in the next ten minutes,' and Abdul hurried away to pass his master's order to the guards outside.

Musa and Pandhare arrived, bowing low in salute to find the Khan deep in thought. He brushed aside their greetings and said, 'Come in! you must've heard about the conditions of the meeting by now. Each person may bring ten bodyguards, and I'm considering whom to take. Any suggestions?' asked the Khan quirking a brow.

'I'd be honored to come lord,' said Musa without a moment's pause.

'No, I need you here to start knocking this camp into shape. Remember the meeting is just a formality. I want to send a few messages to Shivaji' he said ticking them off on his fingers.

'I've already mentioned you in my first letter. Now I want to dazzle him with the depth of our soldiery. I want to impress that there was no need to get the great Musa along because we have so many great warriors underneath him' and Musa bowed his head in thanks for the fulsome praise.

'Second, I want some of his relatives present, to show that other than these peasant *deshmukhs* living hardscrabble lives in the Sahyadris, his own relatives and co-religionists are against him.'

'And third, I want to show him the range of all the warriors that have flocked to our banner from all the Islamic nations in this world,' said the Khan forcefully ticking off the points as he spoke.

'I know one person you have to take along,' said Musa without a moment's hesitation.

'Pehelwan Khan,' and Afzal nodded immediately. The man was a beast, almost as huge as he himself. In the wrestling ring he had allegedly killed an opponent by breaking his back.

'Abdul Sayyad and Shamsher Khan for sure,' said Musa. 'Those Pathans are fearsome fighters.'

Realizing that he was being left out, Naikji Pandhre ventured a potential candidate. 'What about Bajaji Nimbalkar.'

'Not him,' said the Khan shaking his head. 'Maybe he harbors some ill will in his mind. I cannot have even a modicum of doubt in any of my men.'

'Then Pilaji and Shankraji Mohite!' said Pandhre as inspiration hit him. 'They are brothers-in-law to Shivaji from his other marriage. What better way to throw his own family in his face?'

'Yes, they'd be perfect. Not only are they sworn to us, but I also know how jealous they are of Shivaji,' agreed the Khan.

'And give me a few *habshis* to showcase the spread of our Islamic empire. What do you think of Rahim Khan?' asked the Khan and both men immediately agreed.

'I know these hill people set store by their *danpatta* warriors, lord. And truly it is a fearsome weapon in the right hands,' said Musa thoughtfully.

'There is one man I noticed during weapons practice at Wai. His name is Sayyad as well. I have rarely seen such skill with the *danpatta*. He is also a devout Muslim and fiercely loyal to the Adil Shahi Sultanate. I think he should be first among equals among your bodyguards,' said Musa looking to the Khan for his reaction.

'Excellent idea!' enthused Afzal. 'We show these peasants that we have the best warrior in the use of their own weapon!'

'Musa, I'll leave you to fill out the rest of the list. Leave me now. I need to write a detailed report back to the Shah' saying which he acknowledged their salutes as they left the tent.

***

The same scene was being repeated at Pratapgad fort. The king was seated at the head of the audience chamber and a knot of men stood in front listening intently. The spies had already provided an inventory of the ten men who were to accompany the Khan.

'Remember men, each of you has been chosen to take on a specific opponent based on what our spies report from Paar,' said the king and the light dawned suddenly on the faces of some of the men, who were common troopers, a little in awe at having been summoned to the audience chamber.

'Your job is not to focus on the tent and what is happening there. These people believe we have already lost. At worst they believe Afzal will emerge with me as a prisoner, at best they believe he will kill me in that tent. They're going to assume you are all beaten men. The minute you hear an uproar, you take out your opponent in the shortest possible time. No warning, no quarter.'

'Sambhaji' the king turned to the ox of a man who had been his erstwhile wrestling opponent, and the man straightened up smartly.

'You are to take on and dominate Pehelwan Khan. When he falls, it will break the morale of the rest. He's considered some sort of champion there,' said the king with a twinkle in his eye.

'Yesaji, you and Kondaji Farzand take on Abdul Sayyad and the men attached to him.'

'Ibrahim Khan, you take on the *Siddis*, and Kathaji Ingle, and Visaji Murumbak will back you.' Ibrahim Khan was a Berber from the north of the African continent and there was a long-standing feud between the Berbers and the Abyssinian Muslims in their own country. This was the reason he had joined the Marathi forces to fight the habshis. As a rule, Shivajiraje did not enlist Muslims in his army and had given the same advice to his half-brother Vyankoji, who ruled in Thanjavur. Ibrahim was the sole exception because he hated the habshis even more than the Marathis did.

'Krishnaji, you and Soorji Katke will take on Shankraji and Pilaji Mohite,' said the king grimly.

'Sire, they are your relatives…' blurted out Soorji.

'Not anymore. Not since the day they turned traitor to a Hindu *Swarajya* and decided to take up arms against me,' said the king stonily. 'Just remember that Pilaji is left-handed. Don't let him take you by surprise. Adjust your move accordingly.'

'And finally, the man who focuses entirely on me is you Jiva,' said the king, and the man's chest pulled tight with the immense honor shown him. Jiva Mahala Sankpal was a barber by profession from a village near Wai but his exploits with a *danpatta* were legion.

'You zero in on Sayyad, their *patta* champion. The minute you hear an uproar from the tent, you neutralize him.'

'And once you're done there, all of you fall back on me, if I am alive that is, and we retreat to the fort,' said the king with a grim smile.

'Any questions?' But there were none. Each man there knew the importance of the task allotted to him.

'Very well. Go meet your families and prepare for the meeting two days away. Brothers, the storm is about to break.'

Chapter 22

Jani temb, 10 November 1659

4:00 am

Hiroji came awake when the twittering of the birds in the thick forest cover came alive as though a signal had been thrown. The sky was still dark and blazed with stars. He could make out the *saptarishi* or group of seven sages who appeared as stars perennially in the skies above.

Wild roosters, called the *kokitre* in these parts came alive first, A chorus of calls started, joined soon after by the chittering of doves, wild pigeons and other birds. These wild roosters reach an adult height of over three feet with iridescent plumages of teal, brown and black. The hens are all a mouse brown and it was an amazing sight to watch a *kokitra* rooster strut through a highland meadow with a harem of hens in tow. Hiroji remembered that they made fabulous eating as well and his stomach rumbled in protest. For the last two days, no fires had been lit and the men had subsisted on cold *bhakri* flatbread, salt, and dry roasted beans. The moment was peaceful, idyllic and Hiroji savored it for he knew the day would progress in a very different fashion.

His squad had been sequestered deep in the forest around the Paar encampment of the Bijapur army. He was part of a platoon of ten infantry, and the havaldar heading his unit was a lad only a few years older than him. He was extremely experienced though as he had been in constant battle, other than the planting season and the monsoon for the last five years. Advancement in Shivaji's army was strictly based on merit.

'Gather up men!' called Ramaji, which was the name of this young *havaldar* or platoon leader. The ten men under his command gathered to him, rubbing the sleep out of their eyes and stifling yawns.

'Today is the big day' he said soberly, looking at each in turn.

'We are not a normal platoon though. We have been honored to provide cover for the great Godaji Jagtap' and the men looked in awe at the eleventh man who was sitting with his back against the bole of a wild mango tree. He was calmly and methodically passing a whetstone over the blade of his *danpatta*.

'I know I'm repeating myself, but the aim of this platoon is to spear through the Paar camp and locate Musa. Our spy is already working as a cook in the camp, and he has provided rough directions and a description, but he will stay near Musa to point him out to us when we penetrate the camp,' said Ramaji making doubly sure his words were understood.

'The platoons that attack before us will destroy the lookouts and the first ring of enemy troops. Do not stay and engage!! We stay in formation watching out for the man next to us and make for Musa's tent. Once there, do not engage him! We let Godaji handle him and we cover his back. We help him as needed. This is not supposed to be a fair fight,' he warned again.

'The camp is celebrating. Many will have drunk themselves to sleep last night and will be hung over. Some might be asleep, others eating. Cut them down as you find them. If they cannot reach their weapons, so much the better. Remember, they would do the same to you, and worse, and to your women and children if you let them live.'

'Now get ready, eat sparingly and stay alert for the sound of the cannons. The entire corps will now be moving as close to the encampment as possible as the hour nears noon. I want you to be no more than a few trees inside the tree line and ten long strides from the first tent.'

Having made his speech, Ramaji returned to the tree trunk he'd marked for himself and busied himself with a last check of his weapons. He unwound and wound the cloth padding around the handle of his *dhop* sword tightly knowing that a sweat slicked palm could sometimes jar the sword from the hand, especially when impacting something solid like a shin bone or spear staff.

'Have you fought in tight formation before Hiroji?' asked Godaji and Hiroji had to shake his head in the negative.

'The difference is that you have to trust the man to either side of you and to your back implicitly. We move forward like the tip of a spear. Ramaji is the tip and he will crack open the opposition. Once he does that, we slice in cutting down men on either side moving relentlessly forward,' said Godaji slicing the air with his palm to reinforce the point. You must concentrate your attack only in a forty-five-degree segment, letting the men on either side overlap slightly with you.

'Once I've taken care of Musa Khan, we slow the pace but keep moving forward, killing as many as we can, till we meet our troops coming from the opposite side. Mark my words, I've seen these Jedhe and Bandal men fight. If all works well, we will tear into them from three sides and shred them and those that try to escape out of the pincer will encounter Moropant's force if they try to descend to the coast, and Shilimkar if they try to ascend to Wai via Mahabaleshwar' he remarked to the metronomic strokes of the whetting stone on his *patta* blade.

Hiroji saw that an immense calm had descended on Godaji Jagtap. It was almost as though he was wired differently from most men. His heart rate slowed, and vision sharpened when it came time for combat.

***

Shivaji arose as usual at the crack of dawn and finished his ablutions. With his hair still wet from his bath, he walked bare-chested in a simple cotton *dhotar* to the small temple of Kedareshwar in the upper fort.

Prabhakarbhat Rajyopadhay was the priest officiating at all important ceremonies for the Bhosle clan and he had already prepared everything needed for the king's *puja* ceremony.

The king sat in front of the idol of Kedareshwar and the priest began the ceremony. By now a crowd had begun to form in the courtyard of the temple. Most sat in poses of meditation with their eyes closed listening to the grave, baritone voice of the priest chant the ancient Sanskrit invocations.

'*Keshav*, I pray to thee, *Vaman*, I pray to thee, *Govind*, I pray to thee, *Achyut*, I pray to thee, and finally *Madhav*, I pray to thee' intoned the king invoking the various facets of Lord Krishna while pouring water from a brass tumbler onto the palm of his cupped right palm and ritualistically bringing it to his lips in the *aachman* opening, as a prelude to the *puja* ceremony.

The east painted with the false dawn and slowly shapes began to materialize out of the dark. The smell of incense played hide and seek as currents of air swirled at this high altitude.

The men in the courtyard shivered with each breeze, but the king sat motionless, hands folded in prayer, eyes closed as the priest continued the ceremony.

Presently the ceremony finished and the king opened his eyes whispering '*Jagdamb, Jagdamb*' paying obeisance to the mother-goddess Tuljabhavani. He stood up, betraying not a hint of stiffness at having sat immobile in the same position for over an hour in the cold morning air and exited from the shrine to the courtyard greeting the crowd assembled there to a flurry of *muzra* salutes.

He signaled to an attendant and a cow and calf were led into the courtyard. He gave the pair in alms to the delighted Prabhakarbhat, and then in full view of the crowd, got down on his knees and placed his head on the feet of Prabharbhat. This homage was to the authority, invested in the man in his role of priest to the entire Bhosle clan.

'*Yashasvi bhava!* May you be victorious!' intoned Prabhakarbhat, placing his right palm in blessing over the king's head.

Day had broken and the sun was beginning to burn off the cotton wool strands of mist that lay over the forest that surrounded the fort two thousand feet below. The king's calm gaze swept over that expanse in a silent blessing of his own to his men who were dispersed like phantoms in its depths waiting for the day to come.

As he walked from the temple to his quarters, people stopped to bow and salute, but it wasn't just a homage paid, to a central authority. The king made a majestic figure. A young man not yet thirty in the prime of life. Handsome, learned, intelligent, virtuous and personally courageous. Several saw him as the embodiment of Narasingha, the half man half lion mythical figure, who had killed the demon Hiranyakashapu. Others saw in him the great sage Parshuram, who had been of mixed priest-warrior parentage and who brought the best qualities of both to the fore. Of him it was written in the ancient texts,

'Steeped in Rig, Atharva, Yajur and Sama
His trademark axe and a bow on his arm
When needed warrior, when needed scholar
With knowledge or weapon, able to do harm'

Shivaji's attendant hurried to the king when he entered his personal chambers to throw a shawl across his shoulders to ward off the chill

He dressed simply, and as was his custom, went to the large hall in the lower fort to eat with the men. The ministers gathered around him, worry writ large on their faces and entreated him to eat a little, to not go to the meeting on an empty stomach.

The king let none of the apprehension that lay in the pit of his stomach, show on his face and calmly ate what was put in front of him, though he'd have been hard pressed to even identify what he ate, given his state of mind. He drank a little water aware that he was the cynosure of all eyes, and then stood up, politely making his excuses.

'Brothers, it's going to be a long day today. I still need to finish some correspondence before I leave for the meeting,' he said making his way back to his quarters accompanied by the four members of his personal guard.

***

9:00 am – camp at Paar

The Khan and his brother chieftains had celebrated the night before. Several oxen had been butchered for the occasion. A troupe of dancing girls led by the noted Turki courtesan Fatme had come from Surat the day before, and their numbers had been augmented by a few local women his marauding parties had managed to lay hands on. They'd kept only the youngest and prettiest of course. They'd be let go this morning having been enjoyed by multiple men and the Khan well knew that their families would never take them back. It was a death sentence. The only way out for these women was suicide or prostitution, for they would never be accepted back into their families or society despite no fault of theirs.

It had been this way for hundreds of years and it'd be the same for hundreds more, and the Khan shrugged mentally and forgot all about it.

That old fool Gopinath had arrived at six that morning and had been waiting ever since to greet the Khan and escort him to the meeting place.

'Let him wait,' muttered Afzal to his manservant while he went about getting dressed.

The Khan wore cotton leggings and tunic and a fine silken embroidered overcoat with a crimson sash. He dabbed perfume on his earlobes and wiped his fingers to get the excess off on his robes. He ringed his eyes with kohl and inspected that Abdul had done a good job of shaving his upper lip. In Pathan fashion, he grew his beard while shaving off his mustache. He chose a simple double stranded pearl necklace for adornment and tucked a spray of pearls into his turban along with the ruby. Finally, he tucked his eight-inch-long triangular *katar* dagger into his sash and arranged himself to receive the lawyer.

'Great lord' began Pantaji Gopinath bowing low in tribute to the man not showing any hint of the irritation for being made to wait three hours.

'I came early in case you had any last-minute instructions for me.'

'Quite the opposite. I was wondering whether your master sent you early to let me know he was too terrified to even meet me!' chortled the Khan.

'Not at all great Khan. My master is eager to meet you and hand over all responsibility to you,' said Pantaji soberly.

'He is relieved that things have come to an end here and is anxious to seek favor from the Shah. I will wait for you outside and we can leave whenever you are ready. It will a few hours to make our way to the meeting place' saying which he bowed again and backed away from the Khan's presence.

A little after nine the Khan exited his tent. He made an impressive figure. Over six feet of solid man-flesh in ruddy middle age adorned with all the panoply of the Bijapur Sultanate. He held his trademark sword *Jamdaad* by the scabbard in his right hand. Even that broad bladed thick sword looked tiny in his massive hands.

He took a minute to look over the camp, which had by now come to life. His palanquin lay in position outside his tent. It was in intricately carved mahogany. Given his size and weight, the carrying poles on either side had been specially lengthened and four men each, fore and aft were needed to transport him.

He stepped into the palanquin and held onto the large woolen bob attached to the horizontal bar that ran across the top for balance as the eight men picked up the contraption with a synchronized grunt of effort.

His ten bodyguards fell into step behind him while Pantaji and his own lawyer Krishnaji walked beside the palanquin keeping pace with it. As they exited the camp, each person stopped whatever they were doing and bent low at the waist in salute to the Khan. The mood was relaxed and cheerful. Their leader was off to vanquish yet another rival.

While outwardly calm and sanguine, Gopinath was tuned for any change in the camp that could affect the outcome of the meeting. Any recent change in the quantity or quality of the troops or level of preparedness if missed by their spies would need to be reported immediately somehow back to Pratapgad.

However, things looked pretty much the same and Gopinath relaxed a bit.

And then something out of the ordinary happened!

They had barely gone half a mile outside the camp and the gawping stragglers had begun to fade when Gopinath realized that a line of Pathan musketeers continued to follow the palanquin!

'Lord' blurted Gopinath to the Khan in alarm and the man looked surprised back at him as the porters stopped.

'Lord, why are these Pathan musketeers following us? That was not the agreement! Lord' entreated Gopinath.

'Enough! I have made up my mind. These are my special men, and they will accompany us to the meet. I'm not sure I trust your master enough to leave them behind.'

'Carry on you fools!' he shouted to the porters and the plod continued.

Gopinath saw that a verbal battle was going to be useless so the tried a different tack.

'If that is what you want Lord, but I fear your trip is going to be wasted,' muttered Gopinath with downcast eyes

'What do you mean?' said the Khan, his face starting to flush pink and at his tone, the porters stopped again.

'You know Shivaji is terrified. If he sees these thousand men, he will just not come to the meet, and your effort will be completely wasted. There is nothing I can do. He has men posted on the ramparts and he will get word immediately.'

The Khan peered at Gopinath in irritation, his face puckered in disgust.

'Is your master, man or mouse? Can a grown man, and that too who struts about calling himself a king be such a coward?' sneered the Khan. He thought for a moment and then called out.

'Sayyad!' and the man trotted the ten steps to the palanquin

'Tell the musketeers to turn back and return to the camp. Move on!' he instructed the porters and the caravan slowly started on its way again. The instructions reached the file of Pathans who turned back for Paar.

It was a cool, pleasant day and the path ascended gradually as it winded its way through the thick woods towards Pratapgad. The scouts that Pantaji had brought with him led the men confidently through the maze and inexorably towards the fort that could be glimpsed whenever the tree cover thinned.

The sun had burned off all the mist when the party arrived at *Jani's temb* and the porters gratefully let down the palanquin carefully in front of the door of the tent. The Khan stood up unaided and gazed up at the fort towering over him. 'It'll soon be mine' he thought to himself but said nothing.

'Welcome lord,' said Pantaji Gopinath respectfully folding his hands in the traditional welcome given to a guest in Hindustan.

'Wait!' barked Krishnaji Bhaskar and quickly entered the tent himself first to ensure it was empty and that no assassins lurked within its interior. Having satisfied himself, he bowed low to the Khan and invited him in.

Barely had Afzal taken two steps in that he exploded in anger 'Where did your master get all this wealth?? Even the Shah himself does not possess jewels such as this!!' as he gazed at the splendor in front of him.

The tent panels had been overlaid with panels of *Paithani* fabric, produced by the weavers of Pratishthan, once the capital of the Yadav dynasty. The cloth was woven with a warp of fine wires of pure gold and a woof of silk and it changed color depending on the direction the panel was viewed. Pearls had been stitched onto that shimmering elegance in patterns tracing Hindu religious symbols in the shapes of clusters of mango leaves, lotuses and *kalash* symbols. Rich shawls had been twined around the tent supports and diamonds, rubies and emeralds were studded into the fabric. The panels that gathered in clusters to the pointed roof shimmered like gold, and the saffron-colored swallow-tailed Marathi *zaripatka* flag flew proudly from the top of the tent.

Afzal wandered about the tent touching the panels muttering in anger to himself.

'Do not fret lord. All this finery will return whence it came from,' said Pantaji Gopinath calmly, to placate the man.

A platform of unfinished granite blocks thirty-three feet by forty had been prepared on which to erect the tent. The floor was then overlaid with rich woolen rugs. A raised padded seating area with bolsters had been provided for the Khan's comfort.

'Seat yourself my lord, and avail of the refreshments placed there for your pleasure' invited Gopinath and finally the Khan settled against the bolsters. Sayyad had come into the tent, the gauntleted *patta* in his right hand. He planted his feet apart and settled stoically to wait, gazing fixedly at a point in front of his nose.

'Um… begging your pardon my lord, but what is this man doing here?' asked Gopinath.

'The terms of the agreement were very clear. Only the principals and their lawyers will stay in the tent, all the bodyguards are to stay one bow shot away. Your other men have already arrayed themselves at that distance,' said the lawyer in some haste

'A pox on your agreement!' growled the Khan. 'Sayyad stays right here with me. I want no further talk from you about this!'

Pantaji Gopinath saw the man's jaw was set in determination. Now he was caught in a bind. He could not leave the tent, but how was he to warn his king that danger lurked within the tent??

As the minutes went by, Pantaji paced the tent trying to figure out how to warn his king…

***

1:00 pm

Shivaji started to get dressed for the meeting. He wore cotton leggings and a cotton shift. On top of that the attendant lowered a coat of fine chainmail. Over that went a long-sleeved cotton quilted overcoat which had been sprayed with a splash of saffron water. A saffron sash was tied around his waist and the attendant eased stout leather sandals onto his feet.

On his head we wore a steel skull cap. Finally, his trademark headgear in spiraled white silk was placed on the rim of the steel cap. A spray of pearls adorned his headgear. His beard and mustaches had been carefully combed and trimmed. His earlobes were pierced in the Hindu tradition, and he had a tiny gold ring with a pearl adorning each ear. His forehead was adorned in the thumbprint of the priest in vertical vermilion from his earlier worship.

'Sire, I have never known you to be late for a meeting, yet it is now one-hour past…' said the attendant hesitantly.

The king smiled calmly and replied 'I want him to wait. I want him angry and unsettled. Come now fetch me my weapons.'

First came a set of tiger-claws. The king passed the index and small finger of his left hand through the two rings that sat upon an iron bar with four three-inch curved iron talons attached to the bar. The talons curved inward and when the fist was closed, the talons were hidden within the fist and all that was seen were the rings on the index and small finger.

The way to operate the weapon was to slap an opponent's abdomen with the open palm driving in the talons and then sweep the palm transversely across, tearing the stomach open. It was a vicious, close combat weapon.

Next the king chose a *bichwa* or scorpion dagger. The dagger was northern Hindustani in origin. It was smaller than the *katar* and easier to conceal. The five-inch blade was double edged and razor sharp and tapered to a needle point. Shivaji tucked the dagger into the inside of his left sleeve, making sure the bone handle while concealed by the fabric was still easily accessible.

Looking over the tray of weapons in his chambers, the king next chose a small sword called a *kripani* which he tucked into his sash instead of the standard *katar* dagger. The *kripani* was longer and more versatile.

Finally, the attendant handed him his fine Toledo steel sword. People had started calling the sword '*Bhavani*' after the time the king had narrated his dream to his subjects. They now believed the mother-goddess herself resided in the blade.

One final prayer in front of the small shrine in his quarters and Shivaji stepped out of his quarters beginning the long walk down to the meeting place. His personal guard stepped smartly behind him. Jiva had already threaded his hand into his *danpatta* and fell in behind the guard.

Knots of men were gathered all along the route, worry writ large on their faces. The king's face was calm and collected and he acknowledged the *muzra* salutes thrown his way with a half-smile and slight inclination of the head.

As he descended to the lower fort, the number of soldiers stationed at the bastions all hurried to catch a look at their king, and suddenly it was as though the iron discipline that held the men silent, crumbled!

Several men ran to him and fell at his feet. 'There is danger there, sire! The Khan is treacherous! Take us with you! Please sire!!' Going forward was impossible with the crush of men entreating him to not take this risk.

'Brothers!!! Naik!!!' said the king grasping the brawny arms of a bare-chested man raising him to his feet.

'Hear my last words! The mother-goddess will of course give us victory, but if something untoward were to befall me, do not cease our struggle. Crown the princeling Sambhaji and continue to fight under the leadership of war commanders like Netoji, Yesaji, Moropant and the others!'

'Never, ever give up the struggle my brothers!!' and as the knot of men parted, the king made his way down to the main gate.

The sally port in the main gate opened, and the king stepped out with his ten chosen bodyguards leaving his personal guard behind.

It was nearing two in the afternoon and as the path wound downwards in the south westerly direction, the winter sun was directly behind the group of men descending from the fort.

Three men were stationed periodically, at a distance that a clap could be heard. This human chain ran from the main gate to the clearing where the tent stood.

The king walked leisurely but the bodyguards briskly broke off and descending quickly walked to where the Khan's bodyguards stood, each man taking up position opposite their allocated foe. There was no talk between the groups. For the moment weapons were sheathed but Shivaji's men were on a hair-trigger waiting for the signal from their king.

Shivaji and Jiva had descended half the distance when Shivaji suddenly stopped. The opening in the tent had purposely been made tall and wide, and such that it faced the direction of the fort. He had glimpsed four men inside, when by all accounts, there should have been only three!

The men inside the tent, as well as the Khan's bodyguards were all looking up as the king descended the path. Even from this distance, they could see the man in front was extremely fair and well-built though not excessively muscular, while the man behind was lithe and wiry. The long blade of the *patta* in the bodyguard's hand flexed with each step and the sun sparkled off the naked blade. Each man was eager to see this Shivaji who had merited such a drastic response from the Adilshahi Sultanate.

While the Bijapuri bodyguards were relaxed, Shivaji's men had their attention locked on their adversaries alive to any slight movement out of the ordinary.

Seeing Shivaji stopped, Afzal retorted 'What's happened? Why does he halt?' and Pantaji Gopinath, waiting for just this excuse quickly replied, 'I will check lord!' and left the tent walking rapidly up to the king

'Who is that with the Khan?' Shivaji enquired

'It is Sayyad, the *patta* master' replied Gopinath. 'I insisted, but he refuses to let him go'

'Well then, tell him I am returning to the fort' replied Shivaji grimly. 'I will wait till I see you return and then perhaps a minute more'

Pantaji Gopinath hurried back to the tent and relayed the king's message to the Khan watching his expression change from irritation to amazement to finally, mirth.

'And you call this man your king?' chortled the Khan with a belly-shaking laugh; but he signaled to Sayyad to leave the tent and go join the rest of the bodyguards at a distance from the tent

Only when Shivaji saw that Sayyad was safely away did he resume his walk but now his pace became more determined.

As the pair neared the tent, Jiva split away and trotted to the two lines of men facing each other, coming to a halt directly opposite Sayyad. Both men, blades in hand looked levelly at each other in deadpan gazes with about ten feet separating them

When Shivaji was within thirty feet of the tent, he saw the huge figure lolling against the bolster straighten up and come to his feet and a warning bell went off in his brain. Afzal was the victor and senior. If that were not enough, he was also the Musalman, and no individual of that religion ever showed respect to any non-believer. He should expect

Shivaji to stand and only after a suitable period had passed would he himself then come to his feet.

This was unexpected. And unexpected was dangerous

Shivaji entered the tent and both Afzal and he looked questioningly at their respective lawyers. Both lawyers affirmed that each was truly who they purported to be and only then did both men size each other up

Afzal had expected a sniveling, scared pup, but what he saw was a vital young man, confident and calm who met his eyes with his own piercing gaze.

Shivaji was the first to break the silence.

'If I must choose to fear someone, it'd be Lord Rama, why would I fear you?' he said with a sneer, and a twist on his lips.

Afzal did not know quite what to make of that remark. Choosing to ignore it, he showily handed *Jamdaad* to his lawyer Krishnaji, and said in his gravelly baritone, 'Shivaji, you heed no one, not even the great Adil Shah. You wreak havoc on our subjects and act like you have no master, no overlord

Change your ways. Come to heel. Come, embrace me so that I may forgive all your sins!' saying which he held out his arms to greet Shivaji in the traditional welcome.

Shivaji too had handed his sword *Bhavani* to Pantaji Gopinath to mirror Afzal's action to show that he too had no treachery in his heart. He tucked his chin into his chest and moved forward the three steps to enter the Khan's embrace.

The top of Shivaji's head barely came to Afzal's clavicle and the men embraced in the traditional triple-embrace with Shivaji's head going first to Afzal's right, before switching to Afzal's left.

Just as the second embrace set in, Shivaji sensed a sudden coiling of Afzal's core and before he could react, Afzal's arm whipped with the speed of an adder's strike over and across his head. Before he could counter, his head was pushed down by the massive bicep and held immobile in the man's left armpit! At the same instant, Afzal whipped out his *katar* and struck down vertically at Shivaji's left side. Had he not worn the chain mail, the eight-inch blade would have pierced his left lung, and exited at his hipbone, slicing him open from armpit to waist. However, all that happened was that the padded overcoat tore as the blade of the fearsome dagger skittered harmlessly across the chain mail.

Realizing his mistake Afzal raised the dagger again aiming this time for the joint where the man's neck met his shoulder. Shivaji's head was caught in a vise and all he could see was downwards because of the hold, which was also starving his brain of blood.

No sooner had the first blow landed than Shivaji reflexively brought his left hand which had been wrapped behind the Khan's waist in the embrace and slapped the open palm against the Khan's right side. The blow punched the talons of his tiger-claw weapon firmly through the layers of skin, fat and muscle that covered the man's stomach reaching into his intestines. In the same moment, he raked his palm hard from left to right punctuated by an explosive grunt of effort pushing back the man in the same move.

A fountain of blood erupted as the talons dug deep and opened four channels in the Khan's belly finally exiting out near his navel.

Afzal reared back in shock and his dagger dropped from his hand as he slapped his right palm against the ruby lips of the terrible wound. The explosive exhalation that erupted from his throat saw his insides starting to bulge out from the transversal cuts.

Shivaji took a half-step back and reached for his *kripani* half sword with his right hand. The stars in front of his eyes were fast clearing. Using every ounce of determination and pent-up hate, he stabbed the point of the demi-sword into the soft flesh above the man's left hipbone underneath the clutched palms till the entire blade went in and then viciously yanked the blade from right to left. The blade easily penetrated through to the viscera on Afzal's left side, and then tore through the

Khan's intestines before exiting out the man's right side bringing out a trail of intestines in its wake.

Breathing heavily with both the explosive exertion as well as adrenaline and dizzy with the choke hold, Shivaji stepped back to survey what he had wrought.

The Khan's face had gone ashen and as blood and gore erupted from his body, the man was trying desperately to stop his intestines from tumbling out of his torn abdomen.

'Blood!! Blood!! Treachery!! This dog has killed me!!' erupted from deep within the Khan's throat and he bellowed like an animal being slaughtered.

To his credit though, the Khan seeing Shivaji was armed only with the short sword took one big faltering step towards Krishnaji and grabbed *Jamdaad*. Before Shivaji could comprehend how this ruin of a man could still fight on, the sword circled with all the man's strength and descended on Shivaji's head. There was a dull *thud* as the blade clanged against the steel helmet under Shivaji's headgear, but the force of the blow drove him to his knees and the world blackened and swam in front of him, as he dropped to his hands and knees in front of the Khan.

Afzal thought his blow had struck home, and with horrific wounds and the attendant blood loss, he swayed and dropped his sword and tumbled back grabbing a tent pillar for support. The great ox of a man slowly tottered to the ground, mewling sounds and strings of drool issuing from his rictus of a mouth. The floor of the tent resembled an animal slaughterhouse with blood and gore soaking into the rich carpets.

'Blood!! Blood!!' As the panicked baritone issued from the direction of the tent, the attention of all the Khan's men jerked as though pulled by an unseen puppeteer. The Marathi soldiers were focused, and this was exactly the moment they were waiting for. Several things happened as one.

Sayyad spun on his heel and sprinted for the tent closely followed by Jiva.

All nine of Shivaji's men used the moment of confusion and in one instant delivered death blows to their opponents. All the planning had come down to this moment and in a matter of ten seconds, all nine of the Khan's bodyguards lay on the field, some missing heads, others limbs, as they sat glassy-eyed and watched their life blood flow away.

Sambhaji Kavji decapitated Pahalwan Khan with the same stroke that started with unsheathing his sword and ended with removing the surprised man's head. Inflamed with bloodlust he bellowed like a bull elephant in *musth*, '*Har har Mahadev*' and all nine men ran in the direction of the tent, bloodied swords held at the ready and teeth bared in the thrill of combat.

Sayyad ran through the door of the tent and pulled up short, his feet squishing on the blood-soaked carpets. What he saw sent a chill of anger and hate down his spine. His lord was sitting down with legs spread out, his torn intestines yellow-brown pooled like ropes into his lap with the blood still pulsing out of his stomach. His pants came through tortured lips as saliva drooled out of his open mouth. His eyes were dazed with shock and pain and he barely kept his upper body erect with the aid of the tent pillar.

'Kill this dog...' he panted as his eyes entreated Sayyad to action.

Sayyad's eyes followed Afzal's and he saw Shivaji reeling on his hands and knees with his head dropped in front of him. His headgear had been severed and the steel cup helmet had fallen off as well. His robe had opened in a massive tear on his left side and the cotton in the quilting had tumbled out falling like white flowers on a red lake. Shivaji's tunic was blood-soaked as well, though he couldn't tell with whose blood, but he could see blood dripping from Shivaji's chin.

Sayyad took all this in in a fraction of a second and with an explosive '*Allahu Akbar*!!' his *patta* cycled overhead to come down neatly on the exposed neck of the man at his feet.

Jiva, meanwhile burst through the opening of the tent a half second behind and he had even less time to take this all in. All he saw was the blade begin its downward descent and instinct and training took over. Without conscious thought, his own *patta* came up while the other's was descending and the combined upward and downward forces took off Sayyad's arm at the bicep. The man's blade attached to his right forearm cartwheeled in the air falling to the side as a fountain of blood erupted from the severed limb. Sayyad had barely an instant to register surprise before Jiva's blade described its own reverse circle and took off Sayyad's head neatly off his shoulders.

Having done what he'd been tasked to do, Jiva immediately hurried to his king and helped him to his feet. Shivaji's face was a mask of blood. The massive blow had dented the metal cap and caused a dent above Shivaji's left eyebrow from which blood flowed copiously.

'Are you okay sire??' asked Jiva worriedly.

'Surface wounds bleed more than hurt! You should know that!' whispered Shivaji with a shaky smile with blood staining his teeth red.

'Go out and see how the others are doing. Make sure our flank is protected' and Shivaji pushed Jiva away, pointing him back out.

'Sire…' began Pantaji, his face ashen white. Diplomacy was his world, not this raw carnage. He offered up the B*havani* sword to Shivaji and that mere touch seemed to give the man strength. With huge relief, Pantaji saw the cobwebs clear and focus come back into his king's eyes.

Krishnaji, the Khan's lawyer had been watching the proceedings with his mouth open in disbelief. Now he suddenly came to life.

'What have you done??' he shrieked and at the same instant picked up the Khan's fallen sword

With that he suddenly advanced on the king and attempted a mighty but completely untutored swipe. Had it landed, it would've cut Shivaji in half, but Shivaji parried it effortlessly and stepped back lowering his sword.

'Go back! The lord Mahadev will laugh at me if I take the life of a brahmin' he replied evenly.

This seemed to infuriate Krishnaji even more and he attacked like a crazed man again. This time however, Shivaji swept off the strike and with the return slashed across his front opening him up from sternum to hip and the man fell back with a keening cry.

The Khan meanwhile was watching all this with through blood-red eyes, his breath panting through an open mouth as he regarded Shivaji balefully.

Sambhaji Kavji had meanwhile entered the tent and Shivaji quickly turned to him.

'What news of his ten?'

'All gone my lord!!' leered Sambhaji with his crazed grin, holding up his bloodied blade for emphasis.

'Good,' muttered Shivaji and his teeth flashed whitely for a moment. He walked the couple of steps to the Khan who watched him come with numb, hate-filled eyes.

Without another word, the B*havani* sword flashed left to right again and sliced through Afzal's neck, crunching through the vertebra before, thunking into the tent pillar. As the Khan's head tumbled onto the mess of purplish entrails in his own lap, Shivaji wrenched the sword out of the post and turned to leave the tent.

The instant he was outside he sheathed the sword and clapped twice, and like magic, those two claps were taken up in a daisy chain up to the rampart of the fort, and within five seconds, the *naubat* war drums started up with their booming war message accompanied by the wail of the *tutaari* war horn. Another second and three cannons thundered adding their own voice to the war trumpets and drums

Shivaji had already started walking back towards the fort now enveloped by his bodyguards. Blood dripped from the naked blades and the men shepherded their king back to safety alert for any ambush or mishap.

Back at the tent, one porter looked in and hurriedly called to his fellows. They all piled through the open doorway and while seven carried the Khan's body out to his palanquin, the eighth reverentially picked up his head and placed it beside the body. All eight picked up the palanquin and began to run back to Paar.

Sambhaji had started to follow the king, back to the fort, when he saw the palanquin begin to be taken away and he whirled back immediately.

'*Har har Mahadev!!*' grunted out of his barrel chest as he ran after the palanquin.

'Stop!! Stop!!' but there was no stopping the terrified men.

With a curse, Sambhaji reached the procession and with one mighty hack cut off the legs of the two porters at the end. The men shrieked in terror and the palanquin dropped with the six remaining men running helter-skelter for their lives.

Sambhaji ran to the palanquin and looked inside and with an evil grin, picked up the head of Afzal and started back for the fort

Hearing the cries of the men, Shivaji and the bodyguards had halted and were looking back. They were treated to the macabre sight of a whooping and hollering Sambhaji running towards them, bloodied blade in his right hand and Afzal's head held by his beard in his left fist.

'To show Jijau saheb sire!' panted Sambhaji.

'She did tell you to repay what was owed this pig!!' and the king smiled grimly, resuming the climb back to the fort.

***

2:00 pm – camp at Paar

The camp was peaceful. The men looked forward to returning home. The guard pickets outside the camp were resentful of this continued vigilance. That dog Shivaji had been brought to heel finally. What was the point in standing out here? The rest of the camp was preparing for lunch, and the smells of meat gravies and grilling offal made the lookouts stomach rumble. Just their luck to pick this rotation.

Suddenly, three cannons boomed, almost like one rumble, and men who were going about their menial tasks, stopped mid-stride in surprise. Men who were eating, paused with morsels of food suspended in mid-air, as they looked at each other in puzzlement.

Barely had the booms faded away, than the jungle erupted on all side with cries of '*Har har* Mahadev!!'

The lookouts were cut down by archers from the cover of the forest and the tree line suddenly birthed masses of crazed Marathi warriors bearing down with spear and sword.

Hiroji barreled forward in the tight formation headed by Ramaji. Every second man held a spear in his right hand, and they vectored past the fallen lookouts and within twenty lunges were at the periphery of the camp.

They caught men in all manner of unpreparedness. Many were dining at communal fires and were cut down almost immediately. Several did not have the time to reach their weapons at all.

Hiroji's group passed several areas of stacked spears which the enemy had not even had the time to reach.

As they passed through the Afghan musketeer's tents, the group slowed a little to kill as many of the Pathans as they could. Several tried putting up a fight, but the muskets were not loaded, and they were caught enmassed and were cut down quickly.

The blood ran like molten lava in Hiroji as he gave himself up to the pleasure of killing. This was life at its most basic. His *patta* flicked out like a lover's caress, slicing through a neck here, puncturing an abdomen there, or severing a spine if the man was turned away.

They could hear the cries of the Bandal and Jedhe men, as they shredded the enemy to either side, all of them converging on the center of the camp.

Hiroji was panting in his excitement and he looked to his left to see how Godaji was doing. The man was like a killing machine. There was no emotion on his face. He could've been harvesting sugar cane but for the fact that his *patta* dripped blood, and his face and clothes were streaked in gore. Hiroji looked down at himself and realized that his clothes too were caked with blood from the destruction they were wreaking.

They were finally at the cooking fire and Baji looked for their spy to point out Musa. Hiroji casually took off a man's left leg below the knee with his return cut after blocking the man's strike and moved on

And suddenly there was Musa! He was trying to muster resistance by infusing spine into the few troops around him. A defense was also starting to form around him when Baji's platoon cannoned into the half-formed corps of men.

Two men armed with swords and daggers were cut down immediately as they turned to face the new threat.

Musa whirled with a feral cry to address this new threat but just then the man next to him buckled, his throat pierced by a Jedhe man from the other side. Musa shifted yet again to close the gap in his ranks without missing a beat. Had there been time, Hiroji would have stopped to admire his footwork and swordplay.

Godaji however did not let the opportunity pass. For the first time he stepped out of formation and struck like a cobra, taking advantage of Musa's distraction. His blade descended from above, like *Indra's* weapon, *vajra* and fell transversely on the crook of Musa's neck, while he was half-turned away. The blow was so artful that it sheared the man vertically slicing through the ribs on his left side and destroying his lung till the blade's momentum was stopped by the spine. With cool precision, Godaji retracted his blade, using his left foot to push off Musa's carcass and bring his blade free. There was an explosion of blood and gore, and seeing Musa fall in this fashion, finally broke the nerve of the men around him. They dropped their swords in terror but there was no mercy to be had here. The months of desecrating temples and defiling women had built up and the Marathi warriors paid no heed, paying no attention to screams for mercy.

It was finally four in the afternoon, before the blood lust was brought under control, by the arrival of the senior commanders in the Marathi army.

The Shilimkars and Moropant's force had reaped a bloody harvest, as well blocking all the available escape routes, out of the Paar squeeze. The unbelievable news that Afzal had been slain reached Wai early the next morning and the camp erupted in disarray. The cavalry chief, Netoji, rode hard for Wai arriving slightly after the news broke and demolished the demoralized and leaderless enemy there.

His force rested for a day before striking for the capital of the Sultanate Bijapur itself as planned by the king.

The king meanwhile set out that evening, on the road to the major town of Kolhapur, to take the massive fort of Panhalgad. This was the veritable jewel in the crown of the Sultanate. Some enemy troops were allowed to escape to spread the panic that spread like wildfire through the region!

Randulla Khan, the son and Fazal Khan did manage to escape. When the attack started, they had got hold of the More chieftain and begged him, to spirit them away using obscure trails through the forest. The More had grown up in the forest, and he was able to spirit away a handful of men to safety after a week of travel. These men arrived back in Bijapur, half-crazed with hunger, thirst, and fear to relate to a shocked court what had transpired here.

For all intents and purposes the rout was complete. All the provisions, brought into the theater of war, by the Sultanate fell into the Marathi treasury.

A new chapter began in the history of Hindustan. The small, guttering flame of independence, crossed over to the next wick and suddenly grew in volume and intensity, paving the way to finally break the stranglehold of the Islamic invaders of the last five hundred years.

'Har har Mahadev!'

'In the name of Shiva the Destroyer*!'*